What the critics are saying...

Cupid Plot Factor 5, Cupid Pleasure Factor 5 "*Secret Thirst* is a powerful tale leading you in a treacherous and dangerous world where only your hidden secrets, blind trust and unconditional love may be the key to survival... *Secret Thirst* is nothing less than a powerhouse of a book that just should not be missed!" ~ *Frauke @ Cupid's Library Reviews*

Rating: 5 Stars "A very well done journey into the world that opens after dark descends; *Secret Thirst* was one spine tingling thrill after another... Step into her world and allow *Ms. Anderson* to dazzle you with the dark side and lure you with a sensual feast! ~ *Keely Skillman, EcataRomance Reviews*

Rating: 5 Stars Heat level: O "Lauren and Kris are fabulous characters with complex personalities... *Secret Thirst* is most definitely a keeper!" ~ *Susan White Just Erotic Romance Reviews*

"*Secret Thirst* by *Evangeline Anderson* is one thrilling and erotic story! Lauren is a very strong-willed heroine who is secretly a submissive by heart. While Kris, the hero, is an equally strong-minded vampire who holds the key to disengaging Lauren most erotic desires... Amazingly deep and erotically exciting, *Ms. Anderson* has created a winner with *Secret Thirst*. I would recommend this novel to anyone who craves a scorching hot story jam-packed with D/s erotica." ~ *Contessa Scion Just Erotic Romance Reviews*

SECRET
Thirst

Evangeline Anderson

ELLORA'S CAVE
ROMANTICA PUBLISHING

An Ellora's Cave Romantica Publication

www.ellorascave.com

Secret Thirst

ISBN # 141995279X
ALL RIGHTS RESERVED.
Secret Thirst Copyright© 2005 Evangeline Anderson
Edited by: Pamela Campbell
Cover art by: Syneca

Electronic book Publication: April, 2005
Trade paperback Publication: October, 2005

Warning:

The following material contains graphic sexual content meant for mature readers. *Secret Thirst* has been rated *E-rotic* by a minimum of three independent reviewers.

Ellora's Cave Publishing offers three levels of Romantica™ reading entertainment: S (S-ensuous), E (E-rotic), and X (X-treme).

S-*ensuous* love scenes are explicit and leave nothing to the imagination.

E-*rotic* love scenes are explicit, leave nothing to the imagination, and are high in volume per the overall word count. In addition, some E-rated titles might contain fantasy material that some readers find objectionable, such as bondage, submission, same sex encounters, forced seductions, etc. E-rated titles are the most graphic titles we carry; it is common, for instance, for an author to use words such as "fucking", "cock", "pussy", etc., within their work of literature.

X-*treme* titles differ from E-rated titles only in plot premise and storyline execution. Unlike E-rated titles, stories designated with the letter X tend to contain controversial subject matter not for the faint of heart.

Secret Thirst

Dedication

Dedicated to my good friend Douglas Rodriguez MD. Not a hematologist but still a hottie. Thanks for your support and for being so great to work with.

Trademarks Acknowledgement

The author acknowledges the trademarked status and trademark owners of the following wordmarks mentioned in this work of fiction:

Mac: Apple Computer, Inc.

Atkins: Atkins Nutritionals, Inc.

Jaguar: Jaguar Cars Limited

Ho Hos: Interstate Bakeries

Jello: Kraft Foods Holdings, Inc.

Rolex: Rolex Watch U.S.A., Inc.

GQ: Advance Magazine Publishers Inc.

Rolling Stone: Rolling Stone, L.L.C.

The Gap: Gap (Apparel) Inc.

Old Navy: Old Navy (Apparel) Inc.

Cadillac: General Motors

Disney World: Walt Disney Company

Campbell's: CSC Brands LP General partner Campbell Finance 2 Corp

Chapter One

He's not a gentleman. He takes without asking. Dr. Lauren Wright typed rapidly, her long fingers flying over the keyboard of her sexy, super-slim Mac laptop. It was, she sometimes reflected, the slimmest thing about her since she herself was a curvy size fourteen. Not that she had a man in her life to care. She paused a minute to think, chewing the inside of her full bottom lip, and pushed a wisp of honey-blonde hair behind one ear before she resumed typing.

~ ~ ~ ~ ~

He comes in while I'm busy at the counter at home. Maybe doing research, maybe cooking—doesn't matter. I'm standing there and he comes up behind me. I feel his breath on the back of my neck. It's warm, almost hot, and it sends a cool shiver of need through me, tracing the length of my spine like a wandering finger.

"What do you want? I'm busy," I say, knowing he won't be refused even as I speak the words.

"Not too busy for this," he says, and I feel his hands, large and capable, cup my breasts. He massages me through my thin, silk blouse and lacy, half-cup bra. I love to wear a half cup under silk. The soft material feels so good rubbing against my nipples. He knows what I like. He pinches them, twisting in just that way he knows makes me breathless. Still I resist.

"Stop it. I told you not to bother me," I say, hearing the little catch in my voice even as I speak. He is kissing and biting my neck, sharp little nips that make me quiver and press my thighs together tightly. His hands reach inside the silk blouse and touch my bare breasts, molding to them. His fingers are warm. Then one hand is tracing a path over the curve of my ass and down the back of my thigh.

"Spread your legs," he says. His tone is low and commanding, it makes me terribly wet when he talks like this and he knows it. I try to resist but it's useless. His hands spread my thighs and he raises my skirt, baring me, shaming me, making me unspeakably hot.

"No! Stop!" I say, but the words come out in a moan as his warm fingers reach under my skirt brushing against the innocent, white cotton panties I am wearing, now damp with my desire for him.

~ ~ ~ ~ ~

Lauren stopped typing to picture this image. Under the table she was sitting at, she was squeezing her thighs together tightly, deep into the fantasy that unspooled inside her head and played out under her fingers. She bit her lip a little harder and concentrated on the laptop screen.

~ ~ ~ ~ ~

"You don't want me to stop," he says, his voice low and sure of himself. Sure of me. "If you want me to stop, why are you so wet?" His fingers pull aside the crotch of my panties, parting the slippery folds of my aching sex and then he is caressing me lightly, teasingly, brushing blunt fingertips along one side of my swollen clit. It makes me moan and arch my back, eager for his touch even though I won't admit it to him or myself.

"I can't wait to be inside you," he says and proceeds to tell me how he'll fuck me—hard and slow until I come all over the place, all over his cock. He had me pinned to the counter with the weight of his body and I hear a low purring sound behind me as his zipper comes down. Then, the sensuous brush of flesh on flesh as the head of his shaft rubs against my inner thighs, seeking entrance. He finds what he's looking for and at last I feel him pressing up and into me.

"Don't..." I whisper but it's too late. He is spreading me, filling me, fucking me...

~ ~ ~ ~ ~

"And this is Dr. Lauren Wright, one of our top researchers." The loud but cultured voice floating down the hallway was dangerously close. Lauren saved quickly, and closed the laptop with a snap, just in time. Into her lab walked Dr. Henry Sloan, the head of her department. Behind him was a short, monkey-faced man in a blue-and yellow-striped power tie and an expensive-looking gray suit, which did nothing to enhance his simian features.

"Hello, Henry," she said, nodding at him as casually as she could. It was lucky for her that he had a voice that could wake the dead or she would have been toast.

"Ah, Lauren," Henry said fondly, beaming genially in her direction and nodding his round, brilliantly bald head. He had been educated at Cambridge and still had the accent and mannerisms to prove it. "Still hard at work on the research I see." He looked pointedly at the laptop and Lauren tried not to blush.

"Yes, have to keep a lid on it though," she said, caressing her Mac protectively. "Highly confidential material. It goes everywhere I go." There was no need for him to know that most of her research was kept encrypted in her computers at home and work respectively. The cherished Mac was full of nothing but years' worth of naughty fantasies. She pushed the closed laptop to the far end of the desk behind her back and hopefully out of the line of vision. "Who's your friend, Henry?"

"Ah, yes of course, introductions are in order. Lauren, meet Mr. Charles Presco. He's a representative from Berlex Pharmaceuticals and he's quite interested in your little project." He gestured to the monkey-faced man who held out a small, damp palm for Lauren to shake, which she did, trying to keep the distaste from showing on her face. Henry could have warned her he was going to start bringing in pharmaceutical reps instead of just springing them on her.

"Pleased to meet you," she murmured neutrally.

"And as I was saying, Mr. Presco, Dr. Wright is heading our research in artificial blood. She holds degrees in Hematology and Oncology respectively, and the formula we're working on was her conception in the first place. Quite the little genius, our girl." He grinned proudly, as though he was Lauren's father instead of her supervisor, and she nodded politely while Henry went on.

"She says this formula will revolutionize the entire medical field and we believe her because..." He paused dramatically and Lauren had to stop herself from groaning—*please* let him not make that stupid old pun on her name again. "We believe her because Lauren can't be wrong. She's always right. Lauren Wright." He laughed loudly at his own joke, causing the pharmaceutical rep to join in politely. Lauren could only manage a weak smile.

"Well." The rep's voice was thin and reedy. "All I can say is that you must have graduated medical school when you were twelve, Dr. Wright." Ah, he was trying to be charming. Just great.

"Close," Lauren said. "I was thirteen and a half." There was no need to disclose her true age of thirty-something to this man her boss had dragged in. The monkey-faced rep frowned a little. "I assume you're here to get a sneak peek at our little project, Mr. Presco," she said, all business suddenly. It seemed to put the rep off-guard.

"Well...yes." he said slowly. "I'm just wondering what makes your oxygen carrier so much better than anyone else's. The market's becoming saturated with such products, what makes yours different?"

"What makes it different is that NuBlood isn't just an O_2 carrier," Lauren responded briskly. "It also has a clotting factor and artificial leukocytes, thrombocytes and erythrocytes that act exactly like the real thing yet it's compatible with any blood type. In fact, it's virtually indistinguishable from real donor blood. It even looks and smells like it and I guarantee if you tasted it, you'd think you had a mouthful of O negative. Not that you'd want to, of course." She smiled confidently and reached into a small refrigerator located beside her desk. "Here." She handed the rep a small plastic bag filled with crimson liquid that sloshed gently when he shook it.

"Really..." He looked interested. "There's not a product on the market today that can mimic all the functions of real blood." Reluctantly he handed the bag back after studying it closely.

"I know," Lauren said simply. "The pharmaceutical company that gets our formula is going to have a corner on the biggest market in the world. Think what it will mean for patients with anemia, thrombocytopenia, leukemia, hemophilia and any number of other coagulopathic diseases. Think of the effect on surgical procedures..."

"Think of the effect on the whole world for that matter—no more blood shortages, *ever*," Henry jumped in enthusiastically, much to Lauren's annoyance. She thought she had been selling the formula quite well, not that it really needed much selling.

"Of course, it still has to go through more extensive testing before the FDA approves it for use," she said, reaching down to slip the small plastic bag back into the refrigerator at her feet. "But when it does..." She let the sentence hang, monkey-face could certainly fill in the blanks for himself.

"Well, I have to say this is certainly most exciting. I'm sure Berlex will be very interested." The rep smiled broadly, looking, Lauren thought, like a chimpanzee who had found a particularly plump banana.

"Well, we've taken enough of Dr. Wright's time." Henry smiled and took the excited rep by the arm of his expensive suit. "We must let her finish her work, it's getting quite late you know. Gets dark so early this time of year." He gave a meaningful nod out the window where the gray January day had faded into a pale, unlovely twilight. The yellow sodium lights of Century Research Center's parking lot were already on, casting a wan glow on the few cars still parked there.

Henry steered the rep back to the hall and began talking about other projects but Lauren knew he had done what he wanted to do. Berlex would be hooked the minute their rep explained what was going on down at Century Labs. Soon the bidding to back the more extensive research needed to get NuBlood off the ground and into hospitals around the world would be on.

In the meantime, it was later than she had realized, and way past time to get home. Lauren rose from her chair stiffly, yawned and stretched luxuriously. Seeing Henry and the monkey-faced pharmaceutical rep had put a damper on her erotic mood. She would go home and maybe finish the fantasy she had been working on later, before she went to bed.

She gathered her jacket and purse and then reached for her laptop absently. But as her fingers brushed across the paper-strewn surface of her desk, they encountered only empty air.

The Mac was gone.

Chapter Two

Nicolas Kris, formerly Nickoli Kristov, grinned as he sank soundlessly into the black leather couch, the only piece of furniture in the living area of his penthouse apartment. He lived alone and didn't believe in having more furniture and household items than were absolutely necessary. He'd had enough of that in his First Life and preferred to keep his Second Life uncluttered.

The room was done in a stark black and white motif with a few touches of color like the original Georgia O'Keefe over the completely unnecessary fireplace. The view of the Houston skyline was breathtaking from the floor to ceiling windows which dominated this part of the apartment. Although, Kris never got to enjoy the view except at night. It was just as well, he reflected, you couldn't see the smog at night, nothing to detract from the beauty of the scene.

The moon was only a week from being full and he felt its pull through the smoky glass. His equinox was fast approaching—the century anniversary of his entry into the Second Life. If only he could find the one who had ushered him in to this bleak existence, this would be the time to thank him in style.

He had other things than the view to think of right now. The anonymous tip he had received had been correct—Dr. Wright actually *had* perfected the formula for artificial blood and he had it in his grasp.

Eagerly, he fired up the laptop, waiting impatiently for it to run through its warm-up sequence. The Mac hadn't been easy to get, it seemed that the little human kept it within her line of vision every waking moment and he hadn't been able to tell where she hid it at night. It had been a risky proposition, taking it this evening as she spoke to the two men in her lab, but he was running out of time. The Gathering was barely a week away. Being Unseen at such close quarters was a delicate and tiring task and Kris knew he would have to feed sooner because of the energy he'd expended tonight. For once though, he didn't care. Ah, here it was at last...

He clicked on documents and looked at the list. He had half-expected to see some kind of encryption and he was more than prepared to break whatever insignificant barriers stood between him and the prize. There was nothing like that, just an ordinary-looking list of documents. Well, maybe not *quite* so ordinary. Kris frowned as he looked down the list. *Bathtub Sequence* read one. Another said *Crowded Theater*, and another, *Forced to Perform*. Why would she put her research about artificial blood under such headings? He looked further, the list, which was apparently arranged by date, only got stranger further down. He read titles like *Slave Girl*, *Slow and Dirty*, and *Love Bonds*. It didn't seem to make any sense. Kris opened a document entitled *Naughty Girl* and read.

~ ~ ~ ~ ~

He comes home early, and I know I'm in trouble just by the look in his eyes. They are cool and stern and just seeing the way he stares at me, so level and cold, makes me want to cross my legs in fear and desire.

"What have you been doing today?" he demands abruptly, coming towards me. I have to fight the urge to back up. Running from him when he is in this mood never does any good, it only makes the punishment worse. I shrug instead.

"Nothing, Master," I say, my voice quavering. I have on a short plaid skirt and white knee socks, just the kind I used to wear in Catholic school when I was twelve and first began to understand the needs of my own body. The crisp white uniform shirt does nothing to hide the fact that I'm not wearing a bra and my nipples are already erect, pressing against the scratchy cotton.

"Why aren't you wearing a bra?" he says in an ominous tone that makes me shiver. He comes closer, to stand over me and look down my blouse at the swells of my breasts. Really, it is much too tight and the skirt is much too short. I hope he won't find out I don't have on panties either and yet, in a way, I want him to. I spread my legs. Under the short skirt I can feel the cool tickle of air between my thighs, caressing my naked, freshly shaved sex...

~ ~ ~ ~ ~

Kris stopped reading and shook his head. Was it some kind of code? Some kind of secret language that she had made up for her research? He scanned lower—it didn't seem to be anything of the sort. In fact, it appeared to be very cut and dried. Well, maybe she stored some personal things in her Mac as well as her research. He clicked on another document at random and read.

~ ~ ~ ~ ~

The restraints are made of black satin and he binds me gently, almost lovingly to the bedposts.

"Please," I gasp, tugging uselessly at the ties, my arms and legs spread wide to accommodate him. "Please, Master..." I can't think of anything else to say. The need has driven every other word out of my head and even now I don't know if I am begging to be released or begging to be ravaged.

"Hush, my darling," he says tenderly, stroking my face while he places the blindfold, also made of a heavy length of black satin. "Struggling only makes it harder."

I know he is right, but I can't help pulling once more against the satin ties around my wrists. Suddenly I feel his breath, hot and featherlight as he moves down my body.

"What—" I begin to ask, but he silences me again, this time with his mouth on my body. His hands spread my thighs even wider and I can't stop my back from arching as I feel his tongue enter me...

~ ~ ~ ~ ~

Kris stopped reading again, feeling frustrated in more ways than one. He shifted positions on the couch to ease the sudden tightness in his pants. Was she serious? Surely there must be more than this on the Mac. There were over a hundred documents—some of them had to have something to do with her research. He clicked on another document—and another—and another…

~ ~ ~ ~ ~

…his hands on me…rough, and yet exactly what I need… "Spread your legs for me, Lauren. Good girl, let me in," he says…

…the way he kisses, as though he wants to posses me entirely…

…inside me, thick and hot, filling me completely, while I brace myself against the headboard, unable to muffle my cries and moans as he thrusts into me again and again…

~ ~ ~ ~ ~

It was all the same. Well, not quite, but every document he clicked on seemed to be about the same subject and that subject *wasn't* artificial blood. It was incredibly frustrating and amazingly arousing at the same time. Kris didn't know whether to throw the Mac out the fifty-seventh-floor window or take care of himself.

The little human wrote about sex the way a starving man might write about a banquet and it made him goddamn hungry, though not for food. It was hard to tell under the shapeless white lab coat she wore, but she looked tasty enough and her face was beautiful. Her slanted green eyes reminded him of a cat, and her soft blonde hair reminded him…well, it was better not to think of those memories. But she was beautiful. Why had she not found a human male to take care of these needs?

He sighed and ran one large hand through his fall of dark brown hair. Well, it was definitely a setback, and The Brotherhood of Truth would be none too pleased to hear about it, but it wasn't the end of the matter—far from it. He needed the formula for NuBlood and he needed it soon. There was more than one way to get it. He hadn't wanted to take the Mac in the first place, preferring to approach her directly, but he had been overruled. Now he had no choice but to do things his way. So the little human doctor had a fantasy world that she liked to keep private? He would see about that.

Kris clicked on the first document entitled, appropriately enough, "The First Time" and started to read.

It was time for Plan B.

Chapter Three

He's reading them, Lauren wrote in her new journal. She hadn't been able to make herself buy another laptop although she certainly had the money. *He's reading them — I can feel it.* She paused and stared at the words scrawled in her own spiky, unlovely script and then slammed the small leather-bound book shut. It wasn't the same — it would never be the same.

She turned over in her queen-sized bed and buried her face in the softness of the goose down pillow she had inherited from her grandmother. She wished Gram was alive now to give her some advice, though there was no one, living or dead, that Lauren felt she could trust enough to tell the exact contents of her Mac. And now, some stranger was picking apart her private fantasies, probably laughing at her, or else thinking what a pervert she was. She hadn't pulled any punches in what she wrote since the fantasies were strictly for her own personal fulfillment and some of them were a little...well...extreme.

"They're *kinky*, Lauren. Why don't you just admit it?" she muttered to herself angrily. The Mac was filled with her most secret desires. Filled with fantasies of being tied down and dominated in ways no modern woman, especially a successful professional like herself, should crave.

She sat up in bed and looked at the mirror across from her bed. It showed bloodshot green eyes and tousled blonde hair — another sleepless night. Her Nordic heritage showed in her high cheekbones, her slightly tilted eyes and her full mouth that was sensuous when she felt relaxed. Right now her lips were thinned down to a narrow line of impotent anger.

She lay back on the bed, turned over again and punched the pillow beside her. It gave an unsatisfying *whoosh* as it flattened under her fist. What she really wanted to be punching was the face of whoever had stolen her laptop. How they had done it was beyond her. She would have sworn on a stack of Bibles, as Gram used to say, that no one besides herself, Henry and the monkey-faced rep had been in the lab at all that day. She had turned her back for a moment and the laptop filled with all her private fantasies of delicious submission to a stern, but loving Master, had disappeared.

It didn't really matter to Lauren whether whoever had stolen the Mac had been after the formula for NuBlood or whether they just saw the expensive laptop and thought it would be great to have. Either way, the result was the same – the Mac was gone and Lauren felt...

"Violated..." she whispered into the pillow. It didn't do any good to keep running the matter over and over in her head. Another of Gram's sayings came to mind – "You can't saw sawdust." In other words, what's done is done, get over it.

Tomorrow, after work, she might even go looking for a new laptop. This time she'd chain it to her wrist.

* * * * *

"Lauren, we have another visitor." Henry's foghorn voice preceded him down the hall and Lauren sighed and pushed away the pile of paperwork she'd been fighting with for most of the afternoon. Another rep no doubt. She would really have to speak to Henry about this little trend. He ought to warn her before he brought someone back to the lab.

Lauren noticed that the sky outside the windows was already mostly dark. Why did he always have to bring people just when she was about to go home? In the morning, when she was fresh, would definitely be better. Still, the rep was here now... Lauren pasted her most professional "I am a serious scientist" look on her face and prepared to meet him.

"Dr. Lauren Wright is one of our top researchers..." Henry went through the whole song and dance again but Lauren didn't hear him this time, she was too busy looking at the man standing behind him.

He was tall, maybe six two or three. Hmm, nice—she liked tall men. He had pale skin, a thick fall of hair the color of expensive dark chocolate which was pushed back from a high forehead, and longish sideburns that looked like something either a younger or a much older man would wear. He looked to be in his mid-thirties and from what she could tell, his conservative dark suit was covering a very powerfully built body. Broad shoulders strained the suit's fabric and tapered to a narrow waist and strong thighs. Nicely developed, but not over-muscled in a veins-popping-out-all-over-spends-too-much-time-at-the-gym kind of way was Lauren's assessment.

What really caught and held her attention though, were the man's eyes. They were the palest blue Lauren had ever seen and they were utterly cold. Words like *icy* and *glacial* popped immediately to mind. Lauren had only seen eyes like that once, on a husky at a dog show her friend Clair had dragged her to. There was something about this man's eyes that bothered her, she thought, they were…strange somehow. Animalistic? No— she couldn't quite pinpoint it…

"I am most pleased to make your acquaintance," the man was saying and Lauren blinked. She realized that she'd been staring at him for a full minute while Henry rattled on, no doubt including the stupid pun on her name, and she hadn't heard a thing.

"Nice to meet you as well, Mr…" Lauren reached for the offered hand which was large and cool without being damp. His grip was firm and he wasn't afraid to use a little strength. Again, nice—she hated men who acted like your hand was made of glass and might shatter inside theirs.

"Kris, Mr. Kris but please, call me Nick. All of my friends do and I hope to get to know you and your esteemed colleagues quite well," the man said. He smiled genially and Lauren noticed how very white his teeth were. He could've done a toothpaste commercial with that smile—except that it never quite reached those cool blue eyes.

His accent was strange too, the consonants all had sharp edges but the vowels sounded almost guttural and he seemed to have a slight tendency to pronounce his Ws as Vs. It was nothing like Henry's Cambridge-educated English or the usual Texan drawl that Lauren was used to from living in Houston for so long. She filed this information away to think of later, right now the man was staring at her expectantly, as though he thought he was the only show in town.

"We're glad to hear about your interest in our product, Mr. Kris," she said firmly. "But I'm afraid we've barely started taking offers from pharmaceutical companies. In fact, you're only the second rep I've met with."

"Mr. Kris represents a small, privately owned company that has taken an interest in our product, Lauren. He's not your typical rep." Henry smiled at Mr. Kris, who smiled back with his mouth if not his eyes.

"Well, it's nice you've taken an interest, but I'm afraid the FDA has yet to approve…"

"We don't care about the FDA," Mr. Kris said smoothly.

"But how—"

"In fact," he said, interrupting her, "I'd like to take you to dinner tonight and discuss our interest in your formula and its immediate application in an area of dire need." He smiled charmingly. "Shall I pick you up at eight o'clock? Or perhaps eight-thirty would be better. That would give you time to go home and change if you like."

"I have a previous commitment, but I'm sure Lauren would love to go and represent Century Labs," Henry said at once, an idiotic smile fixed firmly on his face.

"Henry, can I see you for just a moment, in private?" Lauren said through gritted teeth. Mr. Kris nodded deeply, a move that was almost a bow, and stepped out of the lab shutting the door behind him. Lauren turned to her boss at once.

"Henry, what are you doing?" she demanded. "You have no idea who this man is or where he comes from, and yet you volunteer me to go to dinner with him and discuss a possible offer?"

"He seems very trustworthy." Henry's mild brown eyes had a glazed look that Lauren didn't like at all. What was going on here?

"Trustworthy? Henry, you heard what he said, they're not concerned about the FDA. How legitimate can his corporation be if they aren't willing to go through proper channels?"

"Oh, legitimate, very legitimate." Henry spoke slowly but firmly, as though repeating something very important—some unimpeachable truth which he believed in absolutely.

"Well, you can go to dinner with this guy if you want but count me *out*," Lauren said angrily. She wasn't sure what had gotten into Henry but she wanted no part of it. Not concerned about the FDA indeed!

"No—you'll be going to dinner with Mr. Kris, I insist on it." His voice was flat and final.

"You can't...you wouldn't..." Lauren sputtered, so angry she was at a loss for words. What in the world had gotten into Henry? He had never been a controlling type of boss, yet now he was ordering her around like some petty dictator.

"You *will* go, Lauren, and hear everything Mr. Kris has to say," Henry repeated—he still had that glazed look in his eyes. Lauren furiously thought that he looked like a sheep.

"Like hell I will!" she said forcefully, completely losing her carefully cultivated professionalism entirely. "You know damn good and well you can't tell me how to spend my off hours. I can't even believe..."

"Pardon me." It was Kris again, his sharply handsome features creased into an apologetic expression as he spoke from the doorway. "I couldn't help overhearing your little disagreement, Dr. Sloan, Dr. Wright. I hate to be the cause of any unpleasantness. I understand my dinner invitation is somewhat inconvenient but forgive me for not withdrawing it. Timing is critical to my company at this juncture. Dr. Wright, if I may appeal to you to accompany me. I promise I won't take more than an hour of your valuable leisure time and it would give me immense pleasure to take such a beautiful woman to dinner." He was utterly charming but Lauren didn't give a damn.

"I'm sorry, Mr. Kris, but I'm afraid that's impossible." She glared daggers at those cool blue eyes. It was a matter of pride now. No amount of flattery could induce her to go with this arrogant son of a bitch to buy a pack of gum, let alone subject herself to his company for a whole evening.

"But our dinner need not be all business, Lauren, may I call you Lauren?"

She opened her mouth to say he most certainly could not, but he continued smoothly in that slightly foreign accent.

"Perhaps we might even find a few personal matters to discuss, no?" A small leather briefcase that Lauren would have sworn wasn't there a moment ago suddenly appeared in his hands. He opened it for a split second but it was long enough for Lauren to see a flat, dull silver shape nestled within the bag. Her heart stuttered — the Mac!

"Why you—" she began.

"Yes?" Kris inquired politely. He nodded meaningfully at Henry who was still standing there with a blank look on his billiard ball face. Lauren took his point at once. She couldn't accuse Kris of being a thief in front of her boss for the same reason she hadn't been able to report the laptop stolen in the first place. There was too much private information she didn't want falling into the wrong hands in there. And it wasn't exactly the delicate research material Henry thought it was.

Kris was positively beaming at her with that blindingly white smile he obviously knew he had her between a rock and a hard place. Lauren had a decidedly uncivilized urge to knock those white teeth down his throat. Instead she gave him the frostiest look she could.

"When and where?" she said at last, her hands clenching at her sides in helpless fury. Obviously, she would have to meet this man for dinner or lose the chance to get back the Mac but she was damned if she'd go anywhere alone with him in his car.

"Le Jardin. Be there promptly at eight-thirty please. I'll be waiting." His cool, blue gaze might have held a hint of triumph but it was so fleeting Lauren couldn't be sure.

"Fine. I'll be there," she said shortly. Kris nodded again, that nod that was almost a bow, and walked briskly down the hall, the black leather briefcase held firmly under one arm.

"Well, I'm so glad we got that all settled." Henry was blinking owlishly, seeming more animated now that the mysterious Mr. Kris had disappeared. "I do hope you two will have a nice—"

"Oh shut up, Henry!" Lauren snapped. Grabbing her purse she left to get ready for dinner.

Chapter Four

Her mirror showed a very disgruntled woman, dressed completely in black. Lauren's first impulse had been to dress down, way down, to show this strange man exactly what she thought of his blackmail dinner. But Le Jardin was extremely upscale.

An intimate little bistro that had only six tables and was booked months in advance, the restaurant served dinners that cost as much as her monthly mortgage payment. Lauren had only been there once, with her ex-fiancé, Michael, and she wondered how Kris had managed to get a table on such short notice. Or had he been planning this whole thing for months? Now *there* was an ominous thought.

The black skirt was on the short side and the fitted, long-sleeved blouse hugged her curves and showed off a little more cleavage than she liked but everything else that was nice enough to wear to Le Jardin was at the cleaners. She freshened her makeup, flipped her honey-blonde hair over her shoulder, and added a necklace set with garnets and matching garnet earrings that had been a gift from her father. She surveyed herself again. Not bad if you liked your women queen-sized, she thought, though she didn't really care what Kris thought in that particular department.

She was shaped like an hourglass, double D on top and plentiful hips to balance down below. Michael had called her body voluptuous and inviting. That had been before they realized that med school was all they really had in common and had called it quits. The last time she had seen him he was with his new wife—a size six on her worst day, Lauren was sure. So much for voluptuous and inviting. It seemed Michael had decided to try bony and angular.

Currently she was doing Atkins, though not as strictly as she should, but it would still be a cold day in hell before Lauren ever saw a six. A ten would have made her deliriously happy — even a twelve would have been acceptable, but so far no luck.

The voice of her Gram spoke up inside her head. "Some people just aren't meant to be skinny, honey," she had told Lauren, time and again when her granddaughter had complained that she would never be as small as the girls in her high school. "All our family come from Norwegian and Danish stock — we're big-boned people. You're a beautiful girl with those big green eyes and high cheekbones, make the most of what you got."

Lauren sighed and let the memory go. After her Mom had died, her Gram had practically raised her even though she lived with her father, a kind, but distant man. She wished again that her Gram was here to give her advice. She was probably crazy, agreeing to meet this strange man for dinner, but she *had* to get back the Mac. She didn't even want to think about the fact that he had probably read her fantasies, just the idea made her flush crimson with embarrassment.

She glanced at her watch — time to go. Eight-thirty sharp, he had said. Arrogant bastard. Grabbing her favorite black leather jacket with the faux-fur collar, Lauren left.

* * * * *

She was only five minutes late, Kris noted with satisfaction, as Lauren threaded her way through the small tables to the back of the dimly lit bistro where he sat. He didn't care so much about the time but they had a lot to get through and he wanted to feed before dawn. He had been forced to forgo his usual early-evening snack in order to catch Lauren and her boss before they left for the day.

Kris frowned a little at the memory. The man, Sloan, had been ridiculously easy to Cloud but Lauren had been absolutely impossible. When he had shaken her hand and expressed his desire that they become good friends, the suggestion should have taken root in her mind as a certainty. Instead, she had fought him and he had been forced to show her the laptop in order to coerce her to meet him, which wasn't the way he had planned things at all. It was becoming increasingly clear that the only way he would be able to enter her mind in any way was with her permission and cooperation. Kris wasn't used to having to ask for either.

Now, as she reached the table, the scowl on her lovely face showed she wasn't happy about the situation. Without the shapeless white lab coat she looked absolutely luscious, Kris observed, like a ripe fruit just waiting to be plucked. Her slightly slanted green eyes flashed at him and the angry flush on her high cheekbones and the tops of her breasts made him think of the salty-sweet blood pumping just under the surface of her creamy skin. Her hair was loose around her face, a honey-colored cloud, and Nick could smell her shampoo—something light and floral. Suddenly, he felt ravenous.

He could hear her heart pounding hard as he rose to pull out her chair. Lauren waved him away, apparently unmoved by such courtesies, and sat across from him at the small round table.

"Where is it?" she asked, getting straight to the point.

"In a safe place," Kris said coolly, admiring the way the light from the small candle on the table cast a rosy glow over her oval face. "First we will discuss business."

"Fine. Shoot," she said directly, obviously meaning that he should state his case. She had a slight southern accent, he noted, though it wasn't nearly as thick as it might have once been. It was almost as though she had tried to get rid of it, mute it somehow. Was she ashamed of her background or did she downplay her accent to sound more professional?

"Where are you from?" he asked, looking at her intently.

"What do you care?" she shot back, her brows pulled down in irritation.

"I like to know my business partners," Kris said mildly. Just then the waiter, a bored college student with a fake French accent, came by and asked for their orders.

"Would you like to pick a wine or shall I?" Kris asked her. She shrugged noncommittally. He chose an old red, something he hoped would loosen her up a little since she was all prickles and thorns at the moment. The waiter left them menus and he pretended to peruse his as he talked.

"Where did you say you were from?"

"I didn't." She sighed heavily. "All right, I may as well tell you. I'm from a little town in Virginia—Staunton—in the heart of the Shenandoah Valley. Their main claim to fame is that Staunton is the birthplace of Woodrow Wilson. Now you know. Happy?"

"Ecstatic," Kris said. "As I recall Wilson was a particularly good President. Your little town has a right to be proud."

"As you recall? Are you a history buff or something?" Lauren frowned.

"Or something," he said and left it at that. Lauren opened her mouth and closed it again, apparently changing her mind. "I was just interested to know where your charming accent came from," Kris continued, still pretending to be lost in the menu which she hadn't even glanced at.

"You're one to talk about accents," she remarked.

Kris looked up sharply. Was her mind really so completely Unclouded? He ought to sound completely American and ordinary to her. If she could pick up his accent...

"I mean, what are you, Yugoslavian...Hungarian...?" She let the sentence hang. Kris shook his head. This was worse than he'd thought—he would have to redouble his efforts.

"Russian, originally," he said. "Although, I have been living in this country for so long, I thought my accent quite undetectable. My name was Nickoli Kristov but I changed it when I came here. I am now Nicolas Kris." He wondered why he was telling her so much. Maybe because he felt he knew her in some way already, at least as well as one *could* know a human. It was impossible to read all her most intimate fantasies as he had done and not feel so.

Just then the waiter brought the wine which he approved. Without asking, he poured her a glass and one for himself as well. When she tasted it and he politely brought the rim of the crystal goblet to his lips and pretended to do the same, Lauren spoke again.

"We're wasting time. What do you want from me? I hope you don't think I'll trade the formula for NuBlood to get back my laptop." She blushed as she said it and Kris knew she was wondering if he had read what was stored in the Mac.

"Naturally not. But I prefer to discuss my proposal with you during dinner. In the meantime, I would simply like to enjoy your company and get to know you a little, Lauren." The longer she spent with him the better chance he had of Clouding her.

"I never said you could call me by my first name." Her voice was icy.

"Fine, Dr. Wright, then. You haven't even looked at the menu. I'm told the lamb is particularly good here." He looked at her briefly and then down at the menu in his hands again. Lauren muttered something he knew he wasn't meant to hear but Kris answered anyway.

"I can be sadistic on occasion but I assure you that tonight I simply want the pleasure of your company. Let's cut to the chase," he said abruptly. "You're angry because I took your laptop and you're wondering if I read its contents." He reached across the table and took her hand, holding it firmly in one of his, and caressing her palm with his thumb. "I read *everything*," he said looking at her, holding her eyes with his own. "Why should I deny it? It doesn't really bother you, does it?"

"Hell, *yes*, it bothers me!" Lauren yanked her hand out of his, to Kris' surprise. It was the strongest Clouding he had ever tried and it hadn't even fazed her. There was something different about her, not one human in a thousand could have thrown off his charm so easily. "How could it not?" she continued angrily. "I suppose when you took it you thought you were getting the formula for NuBlood."

Kris nodded silently, there was no reason to dissemble now. Evidently he would need her cooperation in order for any of the deeper vampiric tricks to work as she threw the lighter ones off with no trouble whatsoever.

"What a disappointment for you," Lauren said sarcastically.

"On the contrary, it was the most interesting reading I've done in a while." Kris smiled at her and she blushed furiously. It pleased him to tease the little human—to make her blush and press her thighs together under the table as he knew she was doing. He could smell the scent of her lust in the air—her need, stretching between them like a slender thread of honey.

Just then the waiter came back to take their orders.

"Lamb," Lauren snapped. "Rare. No sides, no sauce. I'm on a low-carb, high-protein diet," she explained, seeing the waiter's look of incomprehension. He shrugged and turned to Kris.

"Nothing for me, thank you," Kris said politely. "I am also on a special diet." Lauren looked at him sharply and he shrugged and smiled. "I prefer to talk to you right now. There will be ample opportunity for me to satisfy my appetite later."

* * * * *

Lauren couldn't figure him out. First he invited her to one of the most exclusive restaurants in town and then declined to eat anything when he was so pale it was obvious he was hungry. He kept saying things that were mysterious and insulting and vaguely intriguing all at the same time and he seemed surprised that she had noticed his accent, as though it wasn't perfectly obvious.

He admitted to taking the Mac and reading her fantasies with no remorse whatsoever, and the way he had looked at her when he said it... Well, she refused to think about the strange shiver that had gone through her when he'd pinned her with those pale blue eyes and admitted that he'd liked what he'd read. That look had made her shiver, had caused an unexplainable heat and wetness to grow between her thighs.

The lamb came and it was so rare she almost sent it back. However, that would only prolong the dinner, which was the last thing she wanted. Taking a tiny bite, she stared at Kris expectantly. He leaned across the table and Lauren had the feeling he was finally ready to get down to business.

"I represent a group of people desperately in need of your NuBlood right now. We cannot wait for the bureaucracy of the FDA to approve it and we already have the means to manufacture it in large quantities. All I need from you is the formula. For this you will be handsomely paid and you can keep the patents yourself. We don't care about generating any wealth from your discovery as a typical pharmaceutical company would—only in using NuBlood for the immediate benefit of our community."

Lauren took a moment to swallow another tiny bite of bloody lamb before answering. "I...that's the strangest offer I've ever heard. What people do you represent anyway, Mr. Kris, a community of severe anemics?"

"You may call me Nick," he replied. "And you could say that we are terminally anemic—you see, we're vampires."

It took a moment for what he had said to sink in, but when it did...great, just great. He was crazy.

"Okay, that's it." Lauren threw her napkin down and began getting up. "I knew there was something strange about you, Mr. Kris. I'm leaving now and if you try to follow me I'll call the police."

He let her get all the way out of her chair before saying quietly, "Look at your hand."

"What?" Lauren looked down at her hands, what was he talking about? It was hard to tell in the dim lighting of the restaurant, but there appeared to be something strange happening to the back of her left hand. She sank back into her seat and examined it closely.

One of the veins there was growing, twitching and writhing like an obscene earthworm beneath her skin as it pulsed and filled with more and more blood. She had a sudden, sick memory of going fishing with her father when she was six and not wanting to put the fat pink worms on the hook. Nightcrawlers, her daddy had called them. They had given Lauren nightmares for a month.

She stared at her hand in fascination and horror as the vein grew larger, beginning to look more like a snake than a worm.

"It is a talent we all have," Kris explained quietly.

"Huh?" she said stupidly, looking up. He had a look of intense concentration on his face, like a man trying to work out a difficult math problem inside his head and he was staring fixedly at the back of her left hand.

"Calling the Blood—that is what we name it," he said. "Without this skill, no vampire would last long. Finding a good vein to drink from is not nearly as easy as the ridiculous movies they make about us would have you believe. Would you like me to stop?"

"Yes…I…yes," Lauren said faintly. To her relief, the vein in her hand immediately began to shrink much faster than it had grown until it was the normal size again.

"We use it only on humans, of course. Our powers are largely ineffective on each other or there would be considerably fewer of us." He grinned, white teeth gleaming.

"How…how…" But she couldn't get anything else out. Kris answered anyway.

"Enchantment of course—dark sorcery. At least that is what my people believed for generations. Then, with the advent of new sciences we began studying ourselves more closely, looking for more rational explanations for what we are, at least some of us did." He frowned. "The current thinking is that we can exert a narrowly focused magnetic field that pulls the blood to the surface because of its iron content."

"But I didn't think you could focus a magnetic field like that." Lauren was trying to remember her rotation through the MRI department of St. Luke's back in med school.

Kris shrugged. "Have it your way then—black magic it is. But by whatever means, I can achieve it, and I am not alone. There is a community of others like me and we desperately need your formula. Are you willing to speak of this now?"

He was asking if he had convinced her and Lauren realized that he nearly had. There was just one more thing.

"If…" She cleared her throat nervously. "If you're a vampire where are your fangs?"

"Do you really wish to see?" Kris raised one dark eyebrow at her.

No words would come out so she had to settle for nodding decisively.

"Very well. Watch my upper teeth," he instructed. Opening his mouth, he leaned forward and raised his chin a little so she could have a clear view.

Lauren had expected to see two of his existing teeth, most probably the canines, elongate and sharpen. Instead, two entirely new teeth began to appear, thrusting through the pale flesh of his barely pink top gums in a way that looked extremely painful. She wasn't sure if the other teeth in his mouth were moving out of the way or if the new teeth were coming in by main force.

Teeth, she thought again and shivered. Fangs. They really were fangs. Long, curving and horribly sharp. It was like his mouth had sprouted a pain of sixteen gage needles. As she watched, Lauren noticed a drop of pale blue liquid clinging to the tip of one glistening point. Was it venom of some kind? Perhaps to paralyze the victim so they couldn't protest…couldn't struggle?

"Have you seen enough?" Kris asked. She realized, abruptly, that she'd been staring for a while. He was probably tired of sitting there with his mouth open. He shouldn't have been able to talk normally with that mouthful of pearly white razorblades, but his speech patterns remained completely unchanged. Perhaps he'd had decades to learn how to talk with fangs. Perhaps centuries?

Hesitantly, she nodded.

"Have you any further questions about what I am?" His tone wasn't impatient, just inquiring.

Lauren opened her mouth, uncertain of what would come out. The scientist in her would have liked to ask a number of questions about anatomy and physiology. How did his mouth accommodate the two extra teeth? Were they hollow like a cobra's? What exactly was the blue liquid that she'd seen? Instead of any of that though, she heard herself asking, "Do you ever bite your tongue?"

The fangs shrank away abruptly, much faster than they had elongated into sight, and his other teeth moved back to their original positions smoothly. The whole exercise had been completely bloodless. Kris gave her a smile that almost reached his ice blue eyes. "Hardly ever," he said. "And now, are you convinced at last?"

Lauren nodded. There was no way to fake what he had just shown her. "All right, I've never seen a display like that before." She took a deep breath and straightened her shoulders. Pushing the plate of bloody lamb to one side, she leaned across the table and looked at him. "It's obvious you're more than capable of...getting what you need to survive. So why do you need NuBlood?"

He blinked. "It has become...inconvenient to hide in the dark corners and edges of the human world any longer. We wish to come out to the world and be legitimate members of society, at least some of us do." Kris looked annoyed. "We are tired of skulking in the shadows, hiding what we are and pretending to be only figments of your imagination—the boogeyman in your closet so to speak. We have legitimate business concerns that would be much easier to conduct as recognized members of the world community. We wish to declare ourselves."

Lauren sucked in a deep breath and blew it out slowly. "And if you have the formula for NuBlood…"

"We can show the world that we can be trusted. That we are more than mindless predators as many of your books and movies portray us." He laughed bitterly and Lauren realized that he found pop culture's take on vampires amusing and slightly offensive, like an off-color ethnic joke.

"So you can say, 'Look, we don't need to feed on you. We have another food source that sustains us.' Right?" she asked, catching on to what he wanted. "You do feed on humans, on us, I mean." She hoped her voice wasn't shaking.

"Oh yes, Lauren." His blue gaze blazed fiercely at her, making her shiver as she realized why he had declined to order supper. She hoped he wasn't thinking of saving her for dessert. Then he smiled that white, charming smile, which looked almost harmless now that she realized what it *could* look like if he extended his fangs, and relaxed back into his chair. "But with the advent of NuBlood there will be no need for such feedings anymore."

"But how do you know it will sustain you?" Lauren was still first and foremost a scientist and therefore skeptical.

"You, yourself said that it was virtually identical to donor blood. Like having a mouthful of O negative, I believe you said."

"You were there!" Lauren's eyes widened. "But how…? I never saw you."

"Because I didn't want you to." He smiled and suddenly disappeared into thin air only to reappear a moment later. Despite his earlier demonstration of Calling the Blood and the sight of his fangs, Lauren still wasn't prepared to see him suddenly become invisible. She looked around the room to see if anyone else had noticed, luckily everyone else in the dim room seemed to be concentrating on their food.

"That's amazing," she said frankly. "But how do you explain it? Scientifically, I mean?"

Kris shrugged lazily. "We haven't gotten around to explaining that particular ability yet. It's called being Unseen. Not everyone can do it, as it is tiring in the extreme and requires a lot of stamina."

Lauren wondered what he was trying to tell her and decided not to comment on his last statement.

"So you want my formula for NuBlood to come out to the world in a peaceful manner. But what's the big rush? The world's not going anywhere. Why not wait for the FDA to approve it?"

"Because there is a conference next week—the Gathering, we call it—that meets only once a century. It is there that our decision to be known to the world will be voted on and ratified by our ruling Council, the Council of Ten. Without the formula for your NuBlood, the Brotherhood of Truth, the organization I work for, will have no chance of convincing the Council. If we miss this opportunity we will be waiting another hundred years. This must not be." A grim look of pure determination passed over his face.

Well, well, Lauren thought, an impatient vampire. Kris must have a personal stake in this somehow—pun definitely intended. She smothered a smile.

"I don't know what to say. This requires a lot of thought," she said at last. "I mean, it's like some surreal dream. I'm expecting to wake up at any moment."

"I can give you tonight and tomorrow to think about it, but I am afraid if The Brotherhood sends another representative he or she will not be as civilized as I have been."

Lauren felt her temper rise and her cheeks flush. "Are you threatening me?" she demanded. "What would your 'Brotherhood of Truth' do, turn me into a vampire too?"

Kris frowned. "Hardly. It is more probable they would simply kill you and take what they wanted. Many of them are older than I and do not feel the need for social niceties such as payment for goods and services rendered."

Lauren sucked in a breath at his casual tone and tried to keep her face from betraying her. "That seems...a bit harsh, Mr. Kris. It seems like turning me into one of them—one of you—would be more practical. That way I would have a personal interest in your cause. Not that I *want* to be...what you are," she finished lamely.

"My dear Dr. Wright," he said, reverting to her last name, his tone decidedly sarcastic. "If it were that easy, the entire planet would be peopled with vampires and we would keep humans as our cattle. Fortunately for you, the conversion process is not so simple. In all probability, you could not be turned into a vampire whether The Brotherhood deemed it necessary or not."

"Why not?" she demanded, stung at his sarcastic tone.

"What is your blood type?" he asked, answering her question with one of his own.

Lauren wondered briefly if this inquiry might be something like a human man asking her bra size but decided to answer anyway. "I have a rare type," she said. "Very rare—it's not even classified as A, B or O. My mother had it as well and she died from a faulty blood transfusion. It's the main reason I went into Hematology research."

Kris narrowed his ice blue gaze and stared at her for a moment. "A rare blood type? Mmm—that would explain many things. But as your type is not classified by the usual nomenclature you will shortly see my point. If I, or any other of the Second Life tried to make you a vampire, you would, in all probability, begin to experience most distressing symptoms."

"What symptoms?" Lauren asked, fascinated despite herself.

"They start off mildly enough—chills, fever, sometimes a dull ache in the lower back. This progresses to itching, shortness of breath, severe head and chest pain. I see by your lovely face that you understand what I am talking about."

"Transfusion error," Lauren whispered. The memory of her mother, sweating and shaking in the hospital bed, barely able to breathe, surfaced despite her will to hold it back. Lauren had only been twelve when her mother had died and it had made a deep and lasting impression on her. "You're talking about transfusion error—giving someone the wrong type of blood. The two incompatible types clump together and the red cells crack, leaking toxic hemoglobin into the recipient's bloodstream."

Kris nodded, unsmiling. "Indeed. In fact, hardly anyone who is not of the correct blood type, which is AB positive, can hope to survive the process."

"The universal receiver, of course...that *would* make sense," Lauren muttered. "Otherwise you would go into shock and die if you tried to feed off a person who wasn't compatible with your own blood type."

She felt as if a whole new branch of Hematology had suddenly been unveiled before her eyes and she was the first person to be permitted inside the new mystery. It was mind-boggling...fascinating. "The scientific implications of a study into nonhuman blood...the papers I could write..." Lauren stopped herself. That had sounded entirely too eager.

"Your reactions lead me to believe you are interested in my kind, in our physiology. Perhaps you wish to study us? This could be easily achieved if we were legal residents of your society." Kris' tone was silky-smooth and his teeth were very white when he grinned charmingly at her.

"Throwing me a bone, Mr. Kris?" she asked sarcastically, flipping a strand of hair out of her eyes. "Trying to bribe the formula out of me now that you can tell I don't scare easily?" Privately she thought the offer he was making her was almost worth the formula for NuBlood, but she had no intention of letting him know that.

Kris leaned forward, capturing her gaze across the table with his own. It burned with blue fire now, a smoldering intensity that was frightening and seductive at once.

"I am offering you anything you want. Money is no object, we are wealthy beyond your wildest imaginings. Or perhaps…" His voice grew lower, seductive. "You wish to be paid in a different coin?" The Mac was suddenly in his large hands and he caressed the dull silver cover with an infinite patience that sent a sharp shiver down Lauren's spine. "Any of it…all of it…everything you have written I can make come true," he whispered, holding her eyes with his. "And it would be my pleasure to do so, Lauren."

"I asked you not to call me by my first name, Mr. Kris," she said through numb lips. "That…" She struggled to regain control of herself, to behave the way she had been brought up. "That is the most insulting offer anyone's ever made me," she finally managed.

"And yet the scent of your desire hangs heavy in the air between us." He leaned forward, his pale skin glowing with some inner fire. "You are full of unfulfilled needs, Lauren, let me meet them." His hand brushed hers, the touch full of sensual promise. "I would tie you if that is what you wished. Tie you to the bed and make you beg…" The room seemed to grow smaller, to narrow down to just the two of them, his hand on hers and his eyes seemed to burn in the darkness, the pupils eaten entirely by the pale blue fire.

"I…" Her mouth was dry and she felt a sort of hysterical laughter bubbling up inside that she ruthlessly suppressed. It's not every day that a genuine vampire offers to make all your kinkiest sexual fantasies a reality. Unable to find the words, she mutely shook her head.

"But why? I am offering you something you crave greatly. Do you not find me attractive?" Kris frowned slightly.

"No…I mean—I'm sure you're aware that you're quite attractive. But I can't just… I'm not like that. I'm not into casual, um, relationships." All the same the offer was tempting, though she would never admit it out loud. The look on Kris' pale, chiseled features made her think he already knew how she felt without her saying a thing. She could feel herself blushing harder and harder as he looked at her silently. The silence grew uncomfortable.

"Would you prefer a different fantasy, perhaps?" he asked at last. "There were so many to choose from in your laptop, it was difficult to know which one you favored the most. Although, bondage and discipline appear to be featured in most of them…"

Okay, this conversation had gone far enough. Lauren gathered her purse and jacket and rose. "Thank you for dinner, Mr. Kris, but I really have to go now." She used her frostiest tone. "I'll be happy to consider your…offer and get back to you later. If you'd be good enough to hand me my laptop?"

"Wait…" His hand on her arm made her pulse beat faster. Lauren stared down at him, wanting to tell him to let go and get the hell away from her, but the words wouldn't come out of her mouth somehow. Instead, she found herself sinking back down at the table. Her purse fell to her side from suddenly nerveless fingers.

"What…is it you want?" she asked, fighting to get the words out past the pounding of her heart.

"To give you a taste of what I am offering—you rejected my offer out of hand. Do I not deserve a chance to convince you?" He cupped her fingers with his own and his thumb rubbed a slow, sensuous rhythm over the palm of her hand.

Lauren wanted to pull away but somehow she couldn't. "Look, if you think for one minute I'm going to go into the ladies' room and have hot, torrid sex with you so you can prove your point you're sadly mistaken." Her lips felt numb, but at least they seemed to be saying the right thing.

But Kris only grinned at her, showing just a hint of needle-sharp fang that made her heart beat faster. What would it feel like to have those bright white teeth piercing the tender flesh of her throat? She refused to think about it.

"There is no need for us to go anywhere, Lauren," he said, using her first name again to her intense annoyance. "I believe, with just a little cooperation from you, I can demonstrate my abilities without the two of us ever leaving the table—metaphysically speaking."

"What are you talking about?" she demanded, a little breathlessly. She pulled at her hand but he wouldn't release her. "Let me go!"

"Unfortunately, I cannot. I need to be in physical contact with you and have your complete cooperation to make this work."

"Well, you don't have either one, now let me go before I call the waiter." She felt halfway to panicking now. His touch on her arm was doing something to her, was melting her from the inside out. Was it another one of his "tricks" like Calling the Blood or being Unseen? Or was it just the attraction between them, the electric crackle in the air, making her breath come short and her heart feel like it was trying to batter its way out of her ribs?

"Hush." Kris' voice was firm but gentle. "I will not harm you, I promise you that. If you will only give me a moment of your time, I promise I will let you go. Will you trust me enough to sit a while longer and let me try to make my point?"

There was something in that deep tone that spoke to her, something that made her relax and stop yanking to get away. Could it be that she did in fact, somehow trust him? That was a stupid thought but Lauren nodded her head. "All right—but I want it understood that I'm not going anywhere with you."

Kris nodded, as though this was a fair statement. "We will never leave the restaurant, or even this table," he promised. He entwined their fingers and leaned forward across the table, fixing his eyes to hers. "Look at me, Lauren," he commanded. "Really *look* at me and see what I see."

"I don't understand…" Lauren started to say, but the words died on her lips. As she watched, the pupils of Kris' extraordinary eyes grew until the black had entirely eaten the pale, wintry blue of his irises. She found she was looking into the obsidian depths of his inhuman eyes and it was like falling into a bottomless pit.

"Look deeply," she heard Kris' voice command and indeed, she found herself unable to tear her gaze away from what she saw. Was he hypnotizing her somehow? Lauren found it difficult to believe. She'd gone to a hypnotist for a while, trying to lose weight, but it had been a total failure because she was completely immune to the hypnosis.

"I don't know what you're trying to do, but I'm immune to…" she began. But that was when everything changed.

Chapter Five

"Where are we?" Lauren looked around in bewilderment. The room she found herself in was dimly lit but exotically furnished. Swathes of deeply colored silks hung from the ceiling, dividing it into mysterious compartments, and there were large piles of satin pillows strewn carelessly across the marble floor. Banks of candles around the large space offered the only light, casting a gentle glow over the whole scene. It was oddly familiar somehow but she couldn't quite put her finger on why.

"I said where—?" She turned to look at Kris, meaning to demand an answer, and was surprised to find him dressed much differently than he had been only a moment before in Le Jardin. Gone was the severe black business suit with the pale blue tie that had set off his eyes so well. In its place, he wore only a pair of tight, black jeans that hugged his muscular ass and thighs lovingly. The dark color of the jeans seemed to emphasize his pale skin and the candlelight played over his muscular chest and broad shoulders like a caressing hand.

"Why are you dressed like that?" Lauren finally managed to ask, trying not to stare at the way his biceps bulged and rippled when he crossed his arms over his chest.

He shrugged. "For the same reason you are dressed as you are right now—because this is how you imagined us, Lauren."

"What are you talking abo—?" She looked down at herself and the words died on her lips. The black shirt and skirt she'd been wearing were gone, replaced by a gauzy confection of see-through scarlet silk that looked like something out of the Arabian Nights storybook she'd used to read when she was a little girl.

"Oh my God!" Lauren gasped, recognizing the place they were standing in at last. It was a place she'd visited often enough, in her dreams and fantasies, at least.

"I see by your face that you begin to understand where we are." Kris smiled at her, showing more than a little fang this time and Lauren felt a nervous shiver in the pit of her belly. Somehow, he'd transported them to the inside of one of her own fantasies, specifically, into the one called *Slave Girl*.

"H-how did you do this?" she demanded in a shaking voice. Looking down at herself, she was shocked to see that her nipples, hardened by fear, were plainly visible through the gauzy collection of scarves. She tried to cover herself and saw that on both wrists she had thick gold bands. Each band had a ring of metal extending from it. Lauren remembered the purpose of those and shivered all over again. She tried to take the bands off but couldn't. It was like they had been welded to her arms. She looked up at him, angry and frightened and aroused at the same time.

"Kris, I demand—"

"No." He strode over to her and took her by the wrists, pinning them together behind her back easily. "In this place it is I who will make the demands." He leaned down to kiss the side of her neck softly, making her gasp. "After all, isn't that the way you like it, Lauren?"

"No," she whispered, knowing it was a lie. Apparently, Kris knew it too. Suddenly his mouth on the side of her neck grew rough and demanding. She felt the sharp edges of his fangs skating dangerously down the side of her throat, tracing the thumping pulse she felt beating under her skin.

"In this place there are penalties for lies," he whispered softly into her ear. "While we are here you will obey me completely or pay the consequences. Do you understand?"

"I...yes." Lauren nodded breathlessly. "But I still don't understand how you're doing this...or why."

"Have you ever heard the expression, 'It's all in your mind'?" Kris' voice was soft and dangerous in her ear. Lauren nodded, knowing he would feel the gesture. "Well, we are," he breathed. "Inside your mind, inside one of your most forbidden fantasies. In actuality, we are sitting back at the table in Le Jardin, staring into each other's eyes while I hold your hand. Quite a romantic picture, is it not?"

"I..." Lauren gasped when he nuzzled her neck warningly. "I suppose, but why? Why are you doing this?"

"I told you, I am offering you a taste of the delights in store for you if you will only be reasonable and strike a deal with me. In this way, you can satiate your lustful curiosity without compromising your so-important chastity. Do you begin to understand?"

"Yes..." Lauren half moaned when his hot mouth traveled lower, molding to the rigid peak of one nipple through the gauzy material that barely covered her breasts. "I understand, but y-you're wrong if you think I'll agree t-to do anything with you, even if it is all in my mind. I mean...I just met you."

"You would try to set time limits on lust?" Kris laughed low and mockingly in her ear, making her shiver. "I wanted you from the first moment I saw you, Lauren. I stood Unseen against the wall of your laboratory, watching your shapely ass and luscious breasts beneath that shapeless, white coat you wore, wondering what it would be like to do this..." Keeping her hands pinned behind her back easily with just one of his own, Kris palmed one ripe breast and then trailed his fingers down the curve of her side until he was cupping the soft mound of her sex.

"No..." Lauren gasped, but it was too late. She could feel those long, strong fingers rubbing against her, parting her folds through the gauzy silk and pressing the slippery material against her throbbing clit in a maddening rhythm.

"Will you try to deny that you find this arousing?" he demanded, pressing deeper into her with those long, insistent fingers. "Will you try to lie to me again, tell me you don't want this, don't want to feel me filling you up, taking you long and hard and deep?"

"Oh, God!" The words were torn from her as he reached the end of her channel, still pressing hard into her wet heat. She bucked her hips sharply, not wanting the orgasm she could feel building inside herself and yet, needing it so damn badly…

Kris' fingers left her abruptly, just as she was nearing the brink and he had her by the wrist, pulling her farther into the silken darkness. "Come," he said.

"W-where are we going?" She was amazed she could walk at all. Her legs felt like they were made of some kind of jelly and the tender vee between her legs still throbbed and burned with need.

"Deeper into your fantasy, Lauren." The answer floated back to her, sending a shiver down her spine. It had been a while since she wrote this particular fantasy…how exactly did it go?

When she saw the wooden frame looming in the dim, candlelit room she suddenly remembered. "No…oh, no!" She tried to back away, but Kris had her firmly by the wrist and wouldn't allow so much as one backwards step.

"Come, Lauren," he said sternly, pulling her inexorably closer. "Do not force me to whip you to make you obey. That is a whole different fantasy and I prefer not to mix them."

Knowing what came next, Lauren still tried to struggle away but his grip on her was too secure. He pulled her forward, to stand in front of the wooden frame. It was a simple structure, two sturdy oak beams with one cross piece that joined them at the top. Like a doorway, Lauren thought. A doorway to a whole different world…and the chains dangling from the dark, well-seasoned wood, which gleamed mellowly in the candlelight, were there to make sure that once you entered that world, you couldn't leave.

"Now, Lauren." Kris took her chin firmly and forced her to look at him. "Tell me which you prefer, to be chained lower or higher. There are two parts to this intriguing little scenario of yours but we have time for only one. So choose."

Lauren looked despairingly at the two sets of chains that were bolted into the wooden frame. One set descended from each side, ensuring that she would be on her knees if he put her there. The second set hung from the crosspiece above. If he chained her to that set she would be stretched helplessly, her wrists above her head, unable to hide or defend herself from anything he might choose to do to her.

"Make your choice." Kris' voice had grown more demanding. He turned her chin again so that she was staring into his pale blue eyes. Those eyes were filled with lust, with a hunger she knew he would satiate very soon. But there was no pity in them, no mercy at all. "Do you want my cock in your mouth or in your cunt?" Kris growled, still looking her in the eyes. "Decide *now*."

Unable to put it into words, Lauren raised her eyes to the crosspiece of the frame again, looking helplessly at the dull metal chains dangling there.

"I see." Kris dropped his hand and for a moment she was free. She had a sudden impulse to run...but to run where? There was no place she could hide, here inside her own fantasy. Instead, she walked silently to the tall wooden frame and stretched her arms above her head.

Kris came to her, and fastened the chains through the metal rings in her golden wristbands. "Now, Lauren," he whispered softly in her ear, trailing one gentle finger along the sensitive underside of her arm. "Tell me how you want to be fucked." His hand slid lower as he spoke, teasing over the tight peak of one nipple and finding its way across her stomach to the wet mound of her sex once more.

"I..." Lauren couldn't speak to answer the question. Her heart was pounding so hard she couldn't get a deep enough breath to form the necessary words. Kris didn't seem to mind.

He was parting the silky material that covered her now, making her completely bare for him, and stroking over her damp curls with gentle fingers. "Do you want me to take you softly?" he whispered, parting the lips of her sex, now swollen and hot with desire, with one teasing fingertip. He traced her throbbing clit slowly, lightly, until Lauren had to bite her lip to keep from screaming. Kris leaned closer, burying his face in her neck and breathed in her ear, "Or do you want me to ride you hard?" The teasing finger suddenly turned deliciously rough, pressing demandingly against the sensitive bundle of nerves so that Lauren lost the battle not to cry out.

"I don't care… I don't care, just *do it! Fuck me!*" she gasped, not believing that she was shouting such words at the top of her lungs. Dimly, in some forgotten corner of her brain, she remembered that this was all taking place inside her head. That she and this mysterious, fascinating man were simply sitting across from each other and holding hands at the most expensive French restaurant in downtown Houston. But none of that seemed to matter now. Every sensation, every touch on her skin, every breath against her neck and prick of his fangs against her throat felt so *real…*

"I think I know what you need and it has nothing to do with gentleness," Kris breathed in her ear. She felt him spreading her legs and then the moist, blunt probe of his cock was pressing between her inner thighs. It hit her then, he was really going to do it. He was really going to fuck her. Inside her head or not, it was a terrifying thought. She tried to struggle away, knowing she shouldn't want this to happen, but she was held firmly in place by the chains at her wrists and his hands on her body.

"No, Lauren, there is no going back now," she heard him breathe. He reached down with one large hand and lifted one of her thighs, opening her for his assault. She gasped as she felt the head of his cock nudge her, spreading the soft lips of her cunt to rest directly over the wet entrance to her drenched sex. "You're so wet for me, my darling," he breathed in her ear, rubbing against her, deliberately stroking the broad head of his cock over her throbbing clit. "So wet and ready and open…"

Lauren gasped as she felt the wide head and thick shaft breach her entrance, pushing hard and deep, reaching for the end of her channel to bottom out against the mouth of her womb.

"This is what you need," she heard Kris whisper, while his large hands lifted her, supporting and spreading her at once for his cock. "To be taken, to be open and helpless for me while I fuck you. While I fuck your sweet…wet…*cunt*." On the last word he pulled out suddenly and slammed back in, pressing hard and fast into her, setting up a rhythm that had her moaning helplessly from the start.

Lauren gasped breathlessly. Holding tightly to the chains above her head, she wrapped her legs around his waist, feeling the bunch and play of his tight abdominals as he pressed his cock inside her, so damn deep, as though he was reaching for her heart with every thrust. She shouldn't be enjoying this, she lectured herself. Shouldn't be spreading her thighs even wider for him, or moaning, or begging him to take her harder…faster… And yet her need was undeniable and the feel of his cock in her body, filling her up, kissing the mouth of her womb with every brutal lunge, felt so good…so utterly right…

"Come for me, Lauren," Kris was breathing in her ear, his voice rougher but still in control. "I want to feel you coming all over my cock…want to feel your sweet cunt squeeze me until I have to let go and fill you up. Come for me and take me with you."

"Yes! Oh, God…" Eyes squeezed tightly shut, she felt herself tilting over the edge, felt herself losing control exactly as he had commanded. Kris' fingers dug into her thighs as he pressed deeply into her, filling her with his heat, filling her with his cum…

* * * * *

"Yes! Oh...oh, don't stop!" Lauren opened her eyes abruptly to find that she was sitting back at the small round table in Le Jardin. A quick look around told her that all of her fellow diners, as well as the waiters and one busboy, who had apparently come in from the kitchen, were staring at her with wide eyes and open mouths.

"Oh, my God," she whispered in mortification. She realized she was still holding Kris' hand and dropped it hurriedly. He was smirking at her, pale blue eyes returned to normal, and just a hint of fang showing beneath his upper lip.

"Well, that was most enlightening...wouldn't you say?" he asked. "And to think, during our whole...encounter, if you will...I touched only your hand. Just imagine, Lauren, how much more fulfilling it would be, were you to yield to me in reality."

He reached for her hand again but Lauren snatched it back. "I've had quite enough of your graphic demonstrations for one night, thank you very much," she said through gritted teeth. "I have never been so embarrassed in my entire life. Now if you'll excuse me, I'll be going." Grabbing her purse and jacket she rose from the table on shaky legs that didn't want to support her.

"My laptop," she demanded.

Without comment, he signed the check and rose as well, handing her the Mac, which he had slipped back in the small leather briefcase. "Keep it," he said when she tried to hand back the case. "Let me walk you out to your car." He stepped around the table and put one large hand on her elbow. The touch made her shiver, she hoped not noticeably.

"If you don't mind I'd rather just go alone."

"As you wish." He nodded at her, all business now, as though the X-rated encounter they'd just been through inside her head hadn't happened at all. "I will come to you tomorrow night and we will speak some more."

He wasn't asking her, Lauren realized, he was telling her that he was going to show up on her doorstep tomorrow night, presumably after it got dark. Well, she had promised to speak to him later, though she had never invited him to her house. Apparently he was inviting himself. Not quite sure how to uninvite him, Lauren settled for nodding stiffly.

"It has been a pleasure." He held out his hand and Lauren reluctantly offered hers as well, assuming he wanted to shake. Instead, he brought her hand to his lips and pressed a soft, cool kiss in the center of her palm, drawing a little unwilling gasp from her. She looked up and found herself momentarily lost in a sea of palest blue before she pulled her hand away.

"Good night," she said. Her heart was galloping in her chest and she wondered if he could hear it. All eyes in the restaurant were still on them and she tried to keep her chin high and not meet any of her fellow diners' eyes.

"Be careful going home," he said. As she turned and walked out of the bistro on wobbly legs, Lauren thought she heard him say, "I eagerly await our next meeting."

Chapter Six

Stepping out into the cool darkness behind the restaurant, she was so preoccupied with her thoughts that she nearly stumbled over the homeless man who was sitting on the curb by the parking area.

"Oh, excuse me," Lauren muttered. "I'm sorry, I didn't see you there."

The man looked up at her and she waited for him to ask for a handout, in fact, she was already fumbling in her purse when she looked at him, really *looked* at him for the first time. He was wearing a shapeless brown coat and a mop of thinning, greasy gray hair covered his balding scalp. So far, nothing unusual. But when he turned his face up to hers in the pale light of the streetlamp, she could see that something was terribly wrong with him.

She noticed his pupils were contracted to pinpoints despite the low lighting. When he turned his head a little, she could see that he had some kind of open wound on the side of his throat. There was a jagged, gaping hole that actually showed the sickly white tendons of his neck when he moved and it was clotted with dried blood.

It looked as though some kind of wild animal had been gnawing on him. Lauren thought it was a miracle that whatever had done the damage—probably a dog—had left his jugular and carotid artery intact. She was a doctor before anything else, so she couldn't help bending down to get a closer look at the poor man who sat like a zombie at her feet.

"Sir, are you all right? How did this happen?" she asked, as gently as she could. She wanted to examine him but she had no latex gloves, and who knew what diseases and infections he was carrying? Looking closer she saw that the wound was worse than she had at first thought.

Angry green streaks radiated out from the ragged hole in his neck, climbing up towards the side of his face and down his collar. Wait a minute…*green* streaks? Red streaks would mean blood poisoning but what the hell was green? Did he have some new disease process she'd never heard of before?

Forgetting her lack of gloves, Lauren transferred her Mac to the other hand and reached out to turn the man's chin so she could get a better look. He needed immediate medical attention. "Look, buddy, this wound on your neck looks serious. I think we'd better call an ambula—" was as far as she got because it was at that moment that the homeless man came to life as suddenly as a toy that has been switched from off to on.

Grabbing the arm in front of his face he brought it to his mouth, jaws stretched wide. Lauren had just enough time to see that the jagged, broken brown stumps of his teeth were much sharper and longer than they had any right to be before he sank what felt like a mouthful of needles into the vulnerable underside of her forearm and bit down hard.

She screamed, a high, breathless sound that was more shock than pain at first. *Infected!* her mind insisted. *I don't know what he's got but he's giving it to me!* She tried to pull back but he had latched onto her arm and was gnawing like he thought it was an ear of corn. *I think I'm going to faint…* The Mac dropped with a dull, unimportant clatter to the uneven pavement beside her.

Lauren fell awkwardly, still trying to get away but instead of connecting with the sidewalk, she felt a hard, warm chest against her cheek. Then someone was shouting in a vaguely Slavic-sounding language, and she was jolted to the side as whoever was holding her made a convulsive movement of some kind.

She saw an expensive, Italian leather loafer connect solidly with the chest of the homeless creature who still had her arm clamped between those jagged brown needles. There was a ripping, bright red agony along her arm as the thing's teeth came free of her flesh and then everything went dark.

* * * * *

Kris' second kick connected just right with the revenant's jaw and its head snapped back in a spray of filthy gray hair. He felt, rather than heard, the brittle crackle of its rotten spine shattering and then it lay twitching on the ground by the side of the parking area like a broken toy whose batteries had wound down suddenly.

Kris stared at it in contempt. It was an old revi, almost at the end of its lifespan. If The Dark Eye thought no more of him than this, then they were badly underestimating the threat he posed to their organization.

They had long represented all that was twisted and wrong among those of the Second Life who chose to claim membership. They still committed ritual sacrifice on All Hallows Eve and some even believed they were minions of Satan himself, which was, of course, ridiculous. They were reluctant to come into the present day but Kris had never found them to be so careless before. It was an insult he would have to address later.

He scooped up the Mac in its leather case and lifted the woman in his arms, then bent to get one last look at the revi's markings before he took her home. That was when he noticed the greenish streaks climbing up the mottled skin on the side of its jaw.

Kris swore low and fervently in his native tongue. So they hadn't underestimated him after all. The revi was Tainted. He took a closer look at the unconscious human in his arms. The greenish streaks were already starting around the ragged bite-mark in her forearm. Damn it, now he would have to get her to a safe house for treatment within the next hour or she was as good as dead. Someplace that had the equipment to make the necessary anti-Taint serum. He swore again.

The nearest safe house was The House of Pain in Montrose, the notoriously "wild" side of Houston, and it was owned by

Simon Travain. If he had been given the choice of anyplace he would rather *not* take the one human that held the secret to artificial blood, The House of Pain would be at the top of the list, second only to the stronghold of The Dark Eye itself. He grew more powerful as his equinox approached, but to enter that house with no one to back him up and survive Simon's intense scrutiny was a feat even the strongest might not survive.

Still, if he didn't take her and quickly, she would die and he didn't want that. It wasn't just that she held the key to the Brotherhood's greatest ambition or his own heart's desire, either. He had to admit he was beginning to like this little human, almost against his will. She reminded him of a time long past, before his Second Life.

She had an absolutely luscious exterior—those full breasts and curvy hips—and of course that was part of it but he liked what was inside as well. Liked the way she stood up to him when she felt threatened and the way she had blushed when he offered to fulfill her sexual desires. She was obviously a woman who was very much in control of herself, which amused and intrigued him, especially in light of her deeply submissive fantasies.

He especially liked the way she had lost that all-important control when they had entered her fantasy. The way she had yielded to him, giving herself completely to the pleasure that consumed her. He could only imagine what a true submission outside the metaphysical realm of her mind would be like.

Kris usually found human women boring. They were necessary, of course, both for food and for sex, but they were so easy to Cloud they presented no challenge at all. Taming Lauren Wright would prove a considerable challenge, of that he had no doubt.

It was a challenge he would have to undertake immediately if they were to stay at The House of Pain. If Simon Travain had any inkling at all who Lauren was, or the nature of the secret she possessed, she would be enslaved or dead faster than if he left her without treatment.

Kris walked to his car, a silver Jaguar which he found useful for conveying the image of wealth and power when he moved visibly in the human world, and slid Lauren carefully into the passenger side seat. She was still limp and he had some difficulty fastening her in place with the seatbelt but he managed at last. He examined her arm again as he settled her and frowned at what he saw. The green streaks were advancing at an alarming rate. If the Taint reached her heart before he got her to Simon's club no treatment in the world could save her.

Kris shrugged. Well, he had drunk Tainted blood before although not by choice and he could certainly metabolize the poison more easily than a human. It was distasteful but he could manage to overlook that. It helped that he was very hungry from not having hunted that night.

Taking a quick look around the dim parking lot to be certain he was not observed, he lifted her arm to his mouth, feeling the familiar sharp pleasure-pain as his fangs extended. He was aware of the slight tingle in the back of his neck as his body began producing essence, as it always did when he was about to feed. Then he called a pulsing vein, green with the venomous Taint to the surface of her lacerated skin and clamped onto the ragged wound.

One quick pull and he understood that Lauren Wright was special in more ways than one. Even with the Taint flavoring it, her blood was the most intoxicatingly delicious thing that had ever passed his lips. A rare blood type, she had said. To Kris it was like a rare vintage of wine with a subtle and delicate flavor.

Though she was unconscious, her body reacted to the essence injected by his fangs as he fed. A low, needful moan parted her sweet pink lips and Kris could see her nipples hardening beneath the tight black top. The air was suddenly full of the wild, feminine scent of her arousal and he felt his cock hardening as one appetite was satiated and another was awakened. It had been a long time since he desired a woman so much. Well, there would be time enough for that later.

Kris sucked more slowly, savoring her unique taste and made himself stop long before he wanted to. Even one of the Second Life could only ingest so much of the Taint at one time before it made them ill.

He licked gently at the last drops of blood, knowing the healing agent in his essence would cause the wound to stop bleeding quickly when his fangs were withdrawn from her flesh and frowned. Here was another secret to keep. If Simon tasted Lauren's blood he would do anything in his power to keep her — any rival vampire would. Kris would have to deny a Host Tasting and watch her every minute. He sighed. Things were becoming more and more complicated.

Lauren stirred slightly and moaned in her sleep, her cheeks already flushed a hectic red with the Taint-induced fever. Kris shook his head as he pulled into traffic. He was about to introduce the little human doctor to his world and he was afraid it would be a rude awakening for her. Very rude indeed.

Chapter Seven

~ ~ ~ ~ ~

"Hush my darling, don't struggle so." He tightens the knots just a little, forcing my arms over my head, causing my naked breasts to jut forward, the nipples helplessly hard.

"Don't," I whisper even as my traitorous thighs spread for him, welcoming him into the tender vee between my legs.

"But all this must go, you know that." He runs long, teasing fingers through the silky blonde curls on the mound of my sex, making me tingle and gasp for breath. He leans forward, his full mouth so close to my ear I can feel his warm breath against the side of my neck.

"Please, no," I beg, but my plea has no effect on him.

"I want you naked," he breathes in my ear. "Completely naked for me. I want to see the tender lips of your cunt utterly bare. I want to taste your sweet submission on my tongue when I lick you, when I eat your sweet, ripe pussy…"

"But…I'm frightened," I plead.

"There is no need to fear me as long as you obey," he whispers soft and low, making me shiver helplessly. "Can you prove to me that you can do that, Lauren? Prove your obedience by trusting me now."

I feel his hand on my sex, gentle and utterly relentless. He is lathering me down there, getting ready to take away the soft curls that are the only thing left between us. I feel the cool moisture of the lather he uses and the wet, shameful heat building between my legs. Why does this helplessness, this shame and submission make my breath come short and my legs spread wide for him? Why does being tied while he takes me make me come so hard?

I close my eyes, unable to watch as he wields the razor, denuding me tenderly, baring me completely to his gaze. His fingers are long and certain as he holds me steady for the razor's stroke, stripping away my last defense.

At last, he is done and I feel the warm wet cloth between my legs, washing away the last traces of lather. And then, inevitably, one gentle finger is tracing the length of my slit, testing my wetness, my readiness to take him.

"So beautiful, my darling," he whispers, spreading the lips of my sex to examine me further. I turn my head away, unable to watch, feeling the hot blush rise in my cheeks. I am so ashamed that he should see how wet and hot he made me, just by forcing me to submit.

"No, look at me, Lauren," he commands, still stroking me softly. His fingertips play over my tender clit, swollen with desire and I gasp and force myself to meet his gaze.

"Look at me while I touch you," he says and two long, strong fingers are suddenly entering my sex, stroking up into me, filling me as he watches the play of emotions over my face, the parade of feelings behind my eyes.

"Please…" I beg, loving the feel of his fingers but needing more…so much more…

"Please what? What is it you need, Lauren?"

I writhe with mingled shame and desire as I realize he's going to make me say it out loud. I shouldn't want this…shouldn't want him to treat me like this. And yet I can't seem to help myself. "Please," I beg him in a low voice. "Please…make me come."

"That's good, my darling, I love to hear you beg in that sweet voice." His fingers thrust deeper into me, making me gasp and bite my lip to keep from crying out.

"Don't hold back, Lauren," he instructs me softly, and now the long fingers are joined by his thumb, rubbing firmly over my tender clit. "Come for me, darling. I want to see the look on your face, feel your hot, wet cunt clamp down on my fingers while I fuck you this way."

His words, coupled with the intense sensations between my legs are too much. Gasping, I feel myself tilting over the edge of orgasm. I feel his eyes on my face, on my body, as I gasp and writhe beneath his touch, giving myself to him completely, body and soul...

~ ~ ~ ~ ~

Lauren woke from the dream in a pitch-black room with a throbbing pain in her right arm. *What the hell?* she wondered groggily. Where was she? She knew immediately that she wasn't at home, the lighting was wrong and the mattress she was lying on was too cushy to be her own. She tried to move the arm and found she couldn't. Not understanding, she tried to get up and that was when she realized she was tied securely to the head and footboard of the strange bed. *Oh, God!* She could feel panic welling up inside, threatening to suffocate her, filling her throat like dry cotton. She tugged uselessly at the bonds that held her. They were made of something soft and silky but very strong and completely unyielding.

"Don't you like it? It's from another one of your fantasies." The voice was so sudden and startling that she jumped and nearly screamed. A large hand clamped over her mouth and the voice was back, whispering low and intimate and utterly terrifying. "Don't make a sound, Lauren. Everything we say and do may be watched. Nod if you understand."

A little frantically, she nodded under the hand.

She recognized the voice now. It was Kris, the man who had coerced her into going to supper with him and claimed to be a vampire. No, wait, he *was* a vampire, wasn't he? He had proved it to her somehow—everything in her memory was fuzzy and uncertain. Right now she had a difficult time thinking of anything other than the fact that he had her tied and helpless in a dark room. At least she still had on her clothes, though her shoes appeared to be gone.

"I'll remove my hand but you must promise not to scream. We are in unfriendly territory and you must not do anything suspicious. Nod if you understand me."

Lauren held perfectly still, thinking about it for a moment. If he had wanted to kill her he could have done it already since she had obviously been unconscious for an unknown period of time. If he wanted to torture or rape her, he could have gagged her and he hadn't. She supposed she would have to play it by ear. Reluctantly, she nodded.

Kris removed his hand.

"Is this about the formula? I thought you said I had until tomorrow night," she said.

"Lower your voice, Lauren. While we are here it is very important that you do not speak of our dealings. It would be very…unsafe. Very unsafe indeed."

"Why?" she demanded, but in a lower voice as he had asked. "And why the hell do you have me tied down?" Her eyes strained to see him but he was only an indistinct shape beside her in the blackness. He shifted on the bed, jostling her slightly.

"As to your bondage, I must apologize. It was necessary to keep you from hurting yourself during the treatment. Victims of the Taint often thrash or convulse while the venom is being leached from their system."

"What," Lauren said carefully and distinctly, "the *hell* are you talking about?"

"You are uncomfortable. Perhaps it would help if I turned on the light?" It was maddening the way he talked in riddles and dodged her questions. Lauren felt her fear beginning to give way to anger.

"It might," she said in a tightly controlled voice.

"Shut your eyes. You have been in darkness for two days and the traces of the Taint still in your system may make your eyes light-sensitive."

"Two days? *Two days?*" Lauren could scarcely believe what she was hearing. "I agree to go to dinner with you and you repay me by taking me to a strange place and tying me to the bed for two days and nights? I have to tell you, Kris, you're not exactly making me sympathetic to your cause." What must Henry have thought when she didn't show up to work? Surely there would be a missing person's report filled out on her by now.

"Do not worry about your work, Lauren. I called Henry and persuaded him that you were taking a few days vacation." Kris' deep voice was as velvety as the blackness surrounding them. Damn him, could he read her mind?

Before she could ask, the light came on suddenly. It was a dim glow in the dark room but it seemed to shoot lances of pure, brilliant agony straight into Lauren's eyeballs. She felt as though someone had driven a railroad spike into her frontal lobe. She got a brief glimpse of the room around them, richly furnished in maroon and gold. It looked like something she'd see once on a documentary about Versailles. Then Kris was leaning over her, his pale, handsome features and icy blue eyes filling her vision and blocking most of the light.

"You son of a bitch!" she fumed, enraged by the calm in those unreadable eyes.

"I have asked you before to lower you voice, Lauren. Don't force me to gag you." His voice was low but forceful. "As for the reason I brought you here, that was not my choice. That decision was forced on me when you chose to put yourself in the path of danger. The revenant that attacked you was old and slow. Had you not practically offered yourself on a silver platter I doubt any of this would have been necessary."

"Offered myself...revenant... Are you talking about the old homeless man who bit me outside Le Jardin?" Kris was still close enough to kiss. Lauren did her best to stay angry and look unafraid, though being tied helpless to the bed with him leaning over her did little for her peace of mind.

"That was no man. It was a revenant—a creature who has survived an unsuccessful turning."

"Turning into a vampire? But I thought you said if someone had the wrong blood type it always resulted in death." Lauren tugged at her bonds, which she could now see were made out of some black, silky material, possibly satin. Kris was right, this did indeed figure prominently in several of her fantasies. She wondered if he had picked the satin bindings specifically with her in mind and felt a slow blush creeping into her cheeks as she remembered how most of those fantasies went on.

She cleared her throat. "Are you going to untie me anytime soon?"

"In good time," he said, apparently unconcerned about any mental or physical discomfort she might be experiencing. Bastard. Lauren yanked uselessly on the bonds.

"The process does not always kill when the person being turned has a blood type other than AB positive. Sometimes they survive physically but their mind is stripped away. Nothing remains but the lust for blood with no intellect to control it," Kris continued. "The creature is one of the Half Life—what we call a revenant. The one that bit you outside Le Jardin was Tainted—infected with a very serious and fast-acting disease which attacks the body on a cellular level. Once you were bitten I had no choice but to take you to the nearest safe house for treatment. It was either that or lose you, and I found myself strangely reluctant to do that."

He smiled at her, a white, unsettling smile, and stroked one gentle finger down the side of her face. Lauren jerked away.

"Will you just *untie me*?" she hissed, trying to ignore her body's reaction to this situation, to his nearness and her own helplessness. Damn her submissive fantasies, now was definitely *not* the time.

"When I have finished explaining our situation I will consider it." Kris leaned forward and stroked her cheek again. This time Lauren forced herself not to flinch. "Brave little human," he whispered in her ear in that low, seductive voice. He smelled of something wild and fresh and sharp, like a northern forest after the rain. It was a tantalizing scent and completely inhuman.

"Are you frightened that I might hurt you in some way? Did you think I brought you here to act out another one of your so compelling fantasies? Perhaps this time for real?" He began to kiss slowly along the side of her neck, finding every sensitive spot to suck and nibble as though he had all night to tease her.

"N-no," Lauren stuttered. She felt like her heart was trying to pound right out of her chest and she cursed herself for her body's helpless reaction to Kris' slow, hot kisses. She tried hard not to think about the *Slave Girl* sequence he'd put her through at the restaurant, the way he'd touched her...taken her... Trying to steady her voice and ignore his lips, which had settled at the sensitive spot right where her neck met her shoulder, she said, "If you wanted t-to do that to me...to rape me, you could have done it several times by now."

"But how do you know I wasn't waiting for you to wake up? I receive no special pleasure from making love to unconscious women. I much prefer that my bed partner has a little fight in her." Kris drew back to look at her but she couldn't tell if he was joking or not. The glacier-blue eyes held no laughter in their depths.

"Please," she said tightly. "You said you would tell me what the situation was."

"You may change the subject for now but I promise we will go back to our earlier topic of conversation eventually." Kris propped himself up on one elbow, leaning over her with the comfortable air of a lover who knew her body well.

Lauren yanked on the bonds once more and then gave up and lay still. "The *situation*," she reminded him.

"Ah, yes. It is such fun to tease you that I could almost forget the gravity of our present predicament. Almost. The situation we find ourselves in is this, the nearest safe house to Le Jardin where you were bitten happened to be The House of Pain."

"The House of Pain?" Lauren almost forgot she was tied down and tried to sit up. "But The House of Pain is the kinkiest, weirdest…"

"Yes, yes." Kris waved his hand impatiently. "All that to the side, the club is owned by Simon Travain, one of the most powerful of my kind in the city. He is not a member of my organization, the Brotherhood of Truth, however."

"He's…on the other side? The vampires who don't want to, um, come out?" Lauren felt a stir of fear in her belly. They were stuck in the kinkiest sex club in Houston, God only knew if half the rumors she'd heard about the place were true, and the owner was one of Kris' enemies? Bad news. Very bad news.

Kris seemed unperturbed. "Simon is not affiliated with The Dark Eye, the faction which does not wish us to 'come out' as you say. He declares no affiliation at present and the general consensus is that he is waiting to see which side is more likely to prevail if our disagreements come to violence. He is motivated wholly by self-interest and if he knew who you were or that you possessed…the secret you possess—" Lauren realized he was talking about the formula for NuBlood. "He would not hesitate to use you or your knowledge for his own benefit."

"Then untie me and let's get out of here," Lauren suggested. "We're not prisoners here, are we?"

"Not exactly, no," Kris answered carefully. "But the rules of my society dictate that we cannot leave the house which has given us healing and shelter in less than a fourth of a fortnight."

Lauren tried to make sense out of this. "A fortnight is…what, two weeks? So we have to stay here half a week and you said we've already been here two days and nights. So we have to stay at least another day or two?"

"Roughly," Kris said. "Which doesn't give us much time to prepare for the Gathering only a few nights from now." He leaned over and gave her a soft, lingering kiss on the cheek.

Lauren jerked. "I wish you'd stop doing that," she muttered angrily, her heart pounding.

"I am keeping up appearances. At The House of Pain, one can never be certain who may be watching by fair means or foul. While we are here, you are my human concubine and I must treat you accordingly."

"I'm your *what*?" Lauren couldn't stop herself from yanking on the bonds this time.

"Lower your voice. There is no other reason I would be traveling with a human woman," Kris explained blandly. "Not one I cared enough to save from the Taint, anyhow."

"Y-you arrogant bastard! I will never, ever…"

"Listen to me, Lauren." Suddenly Kris was hovering over her again, much closer than before, his face filling her entire field of vision. Lauren felt his large hand on the curve of her waist. "I do not think you recognize the danger we are in here. Our lives may depend on your ability to play this role and play it well."

His large hand slid slowly up until it was cupping her full left breast. "I want your word, here and now, that you will act the part I have assigned you or I will keep you tied and gagged for the rest of our stay. Of course if I do that, I'll have to say that the Taint you received from the revenant has driven you mad and Simon will wonder why I don't simply destroy you. It will be difficult to explain and make a dangerous situation worse."

The hand that was cupping her breast moved and he captured her nipple in long fingers, pinching just hard enough to draw a gasp from between her lips. Kris smiled at her, the cold smile that didn't reach his eyes. "I understand that you have your pride but you must swallow it, at least for the time being. Do you understand?"

"I…" Lauren swallowed hard, trying to ignore the tingling in the nipple he was still twisting almost idly. Her heart was pounding double time again and there was a growing heat between her legs that she didn't want to acknowledge. "I understand. While we're here I'll do what you say. But once we get out of enemy territory, all bets are off."

"I suppose I will have to take my chances then," Kris said. He released her nipple and stretched up to do something above her head.

"What are you doing?" she asked suspiciously. She was angry, not just at his cold arrogance or his insistence that she obey him, but at the way he had made her body react against her will.

"Untying you. I thought that was what you wanted," Kris said mildly, finishing with her hands and moving his attentions to her bound feet. "There will be plenty of time later for me to tie you up again if you wish."

Swearing under her breath, Lauren sat up in bed, ignoring the pins and needles in her arms and legs, and tried to storm off to the half-open door to her right, which she assumed was the bathroom. She got halfway there before a wave of weakness overcame her and she fell.

Kris caught her before she could hit the floor. As the luxurious room swam around her, Lauren reflected that this fainting and catching routine was getting to be a habit with them and it was getting old fast.

Chapter Eight

He took her into the bathroom and sat her on the closed lid of the commode while he ran a hot bath filled with luxurious bubbles from a small bottle of expensive-smelling fragrant liquid. Of course Simon would have nothing but the best in his guest rooms. It was just another way of strengthening his guest's obligations. Kris didn't even want to think of how he could possibly pay when the bill for his hospitality came due.

He had done everything he could to minimize their debt, even to the point of insisting that the anti-Taint serum injected into Lauren be distilled from his own blood. But that was just a drop in the bucket as far as Simon was concerned. Their guest debt would still be a heavy one.

When the bath was ready he undressed Lauren down to her lacy black bra and panties, amused by her indignant objections. Her pale skin was creamy against the black lace, the softly rounded inner thighs and the curves of her breasts looked succulent in the steamy light. She flushed angrily under his gaze and tried to shield herself from him. Her modesty made her all the more desirable and again he had to remind himself that there would be a better time to fulfill his growing need for her. The little human was definitely getting under his skin.

At last Kris agreed to turn his head while she slipped out of the last few items and climbed into the large marble tub herself, though he refused to leave the room entirely in case she might slip and fall. When he was well satisfied that she was safely in the tub, submerged in bubbles up to her chin, he left and went to see their host.

* * * * *

Simon Travain was lounging in his audience chamber, a large, round enclosure built of rough, gray stone in the second half of the club that only a few select people ever got to see. Several half-dressed human women and one man lounged like pets on large silken pillows at his feet, all of them exotically beautiful, and no doubt completely in thrall to their master.

Simon was one who enjoyed playing his part to the hilt and this evening he was dressed in tight black leather pants, high black leather boots that climbed halfway up his thighs and nothing else. Kris, who was wearing an expensive suit, almost identical to the one he had worn to Le Jardin, straightened his tie and looked with disdain at the owner of the most flagrantly, kinky bondage club in the larger Houston area.

Simon was arguably one of the most powerful vampires in the city as well and although Kris' own power was growing, it was not yet equal to their host's. Soon it would be, his equinox was fast approaching, but not yet.

Kris eyed their host. Simon's long, black hair was a mass of midnight waves that flowed down his back in what Kris considered a ridiculous profusion and his deep, chocolate brown eyes had a soulful quality that human and vampire women alike seemed to find irresistible. Their velvety color masked the cruelty hidden in their depths.

"Well, well, if it is not my esteemed guest, Monsieur Kristov. How are you, *mon cher*?" Simon abruptly switched to Russian. "Enjoying the guest quarters, I hope?"

Kris sighed and bit back a number of sarcastic replies. Simon was French and therefore utterly insufferable, but he was also the host in this situation which gave him the upper hand. He had spent some time in Russia, before the turn of the last century, and so considered himself a linguist. To Kris' ear, his accent was atrocious.

He made an abbreviated bow to Simon's obvious amusement and replied in perfectly accented French. "Your hospitality is above reproach. I cannot thank you enough, Monsieur Travain."

Simon straightened in the large, throne-like chair where he lounged like an indolent cat and gave Kris a sharp look. "Nicely, if somewhat formally put, my friend. I had almost forgotten you were here, you keep so exclusively to your guest chamber. How is your little human concubine? Recovering nicely, I trust?" In English again, a great improvement in Kris' opinion. But his question required care.

"The Taint is slowly leaving her system and she is still very weak," he said carefully. He was on dangerous ground here and he knew it.

"But surely her weakness won't keep her from coming out in company tonight? She was quite beautiful, what little we saw of her. We would be most sorry not to have the pleasure of her company at our banquet."

Kris frowned slightly. When Simon started referring to himself in the third person in any language he was telling, not asking. If Lauren was up and around, there was no way Kris could deny his host the right to her company tonight. It had to be done carefully, however — certain limits had to be set.

"I'm certain Lauren would love to join the banquet tonight," he said. "But she may tire easily. Also, I am afraid the Taint has rendered her blood unfit for a formal Host Tasting which I very much regret."

"Yes, most regrettable. Most regrettable, indeed." Simon frowned, clearly displeased. "We were very much looking forward to the flavor of her blood. You have such impeccable taste, Kris, that she could be nothing less than exquisite."

"She received rather a large dose of venom and I'm afraid it quite ruined the flavor of her blood. I wouldn't wish to offer you such an inferior libation, it would be a poor repayment of your hospitality," Kris said, trying to sound apologetic.

"Well, we expect so. We suppose we will have to think of some other way for you to repay your guest debt then." Simon motioned to one of the half-naked girls at his feet and she crawled forward and began to untie the leather thongs that held his skintight pants together. "We are certain to think of something, *mon cher*. In the meantime, please feel free to order anything you want from the kitchen for your little human. She must be starving and we want her at full strength before you leave us."

That sounded ominous but Kris simply bowed, knowing nothing he could say would change the situation. It was also troubling that Simon had not once asked him about The Brotherhood of Truth or mentioned Kris' affiliation with them. His host was not one to shy away from asking personal or confrontational questions and the fact that he had said not a word about the conflict between The Brotherhood and The Dark Eye was not a good sign.

Kris wondered uneasily if Simon had picked an affiliation. He would not mark Simon as one who clung to the old ways and superstitions but the other vampire was, above all things, an opportunist. He would align himself with whichever faction he thought could benefit him the most, of that there was no doubt.

As he let himself out, the girl Simon had called over was kneeling before him and taking his engorged shaft as far down her throat as she could. Simon stroked her hair absently and nodded at Kris as he left.

Kris walked rapidly down the long, stone hallway reflecting that it was certainly overkill when even the passage to the kitchen looked like a corridor in a medieval dungeon. Whoever Simon's decorator was, he had something of a one-track mind.

* * * * *

Lauren sat in the bath and relaxed for a while, admiring the severe yet chic black and white décor of the bathroom, too tired and weak to do anything else. She supposed it would make sense for her to be weak, especially if she hadn't eaten or drunk anything for the past two days and nights.

The minute she thought of that, her thirst exploded and she sat up weakly, holding on to the slippery side of the huge, black marble tub and turned on the cold tap, taking handfuls of water in her cupped hand until she could drink no more. At last, her thirst quenched, she leaned back against the slope of the tub with a little moan of pure satisfaction. Houston city water never tasted so good.

Her right arm still ached and she took a moment to examine it now in the brighter light of the luxuriously decorated bathroom. A huge purple and black bruise covered most of the underside of her forearm and there were a few faint, green lines radiating out from the center of the bruise. Amazingly though, the skin appeared to be unbroken. Lauren could have sworn that the thing that bit her, what had Kris called it?—oh yes, a revenant, that was it—had broken the skin and possibly even taken a chunk out of her arm. Yet here she was, battered but whole. Her arm looked terrible and was extremely tender, but at least she didn't have a big hole in it.

From what Kris had said, the revenant had injected her with some kind of poison or venom and she eyed the fine green lines on her arm apprehensively, resolving to ask him more about exactly what had been done to her to heal the venomous bite. Being a doctor, she didn't appreciate being given medical attention without her consent and knowledge, though she supposed that in this case it had been unavoidable.

Lauren sighed and decided she was too tired and weak to worry about things until Kris came back to provide the answers to her questions, assuming he would, of course. He was the most maddening man she had ever come in contact with, the way he answered her questions with questions of his own and refused to give her more information than he felt like divulging.

She certainly wasn't crazy about the deal she'd had to make with him in order to get him to untie her. His human concubine indeed! But he had seemed so deadly serious, could they really be in that much danger just being here? She supposed she really had no choice but to play along, at least until the situation became a bit clearer. After all, she knew next to nothing about vampire society. Hell, she hadn't even known there *was* a vampire society before Kris came into her life.

Kris himself would take a bit more studying as well. Remembering the way he had kissed her neck and pinched her nipple was enough to make her shiver all over. And the way he had taken her so thoroughly in the *Slave Girl* fantasy... *What would it be like for real? To submit to him outside my fantasies,* she wondered. Deciding that she would be better off if she put that kind of thinking out of her mind, Lauren ducked under the water to wet her hair, then reached for the bottle of shampoo on the low shelf to her right.

She hissed in pain when she extended her hurt arm too far and felt a stabbing sensation in the bruised area. Pulling it back she cradled the wounded appendage against her chest. *Damn it!* This was a major inconvenience. She wondered how much longer it would take her to heal.

"Here, let me."

Lauren nearly jumped out of the tub. Looking up, she saw Kris lounging in the doorway, a slight smile on those lips that managed to look cruel and sensual at the same time. She sank a little farther into the water, the bubbles having long since dissipated, and stared at him mistrustfully. "What are you doing in here?" she asked, crossing her arms over her chest protectively.

"Helping you, Lauren, if you'll let me. You were about to wash your hair, no?" He took off his suit jacket and hung it neatly on the hook behind the bathroom door then walked towards her, rolling up his shirtsleeves. Lauren couldn't help herself—she watched the large, capable hands and muscular forearms in mute fascination.

Kris sat on the edge of the tub and reached over her. Easily snagging the shampoo bottle he poured a generous dollop into one palm. "Lean back, I won't hurt you," he said in a gentler tone than she had yet heard him use.

Lauren relaxed warily against the side of the tub and sighed as strong fingers massaged the fragrant herbal shampoo into her scalp. Kris took a long time, doing a thorough job of working in the suds. She felt almost hypnotized by the heat of the water and the pressure of his hands, gentle and firm at the same time.

Her Gram used to wash her hair like this when she was a child. Lauren remembered the fun they used to have, shaping her long blonde hair into outrageous styles, horns and curls and Mohawk-like crests when it was stiff with lather. She could almost hear her own childish laughter as she gazed in the mirror at the wild child with a head full of bubbles...

"Time to rinse." Kris' deep voice shattered her memories and Lauren realized that she had been almost asleep, lulled by the gentle motion of his hands in her hair. She scolded herself for such carelessness. Kris was definitely not the kind of man to let her guard down around, despite the fact that he was being so gentle. *Not to be trusted*, a little voice in her head insisted, even as he tilted her head and poured warm water over her hair, cupping one palm carefully at her forehead to avoid getting soap in her eyes. But she felt so tired and weak that it was almost impossible to keep up the angry front when he wasn't provoking her.

Lauren wondered distantly how she had come so far in such a short amount of time. Hadn't she promised herself she wouldn't even have supper with this infuriating man? And yet, here she was, not three days later, letting him wash her hair while she sat naked in a bath. The thought made her cringe inside. The bubbles that had filled the tub were long since gone and Kris would have a clear view of her body through the cloudy water. She crossed her arms over her chest, wincing at the pain in her wounded arm as she did so.

"Don't try to hide yourself from me, *Solnyshko*. You're beautiful and I want to see all of you." His voice was low and soft, like a finger of desire tracing the length of her spine.

"What did you call me?" Lauren pressed her arms closer to her body, determined to cover herself.

"*Solnyshko*—it means 'little sun' in my native tongue. That is what the color of your hair reminds me of, Lauren," he said softly and she felt his fingers slide gently through the wet strands of honey-colored hair that covered her shoulders. "I have not seen it in many years, the sun, but I treasure the memory always."

"S-so at least some of the vampire fiction is right. You can't go out in the sunlight?" She made it a question, hoping to change the subject and get a little more information about him at the same time. His hands in her hair and the low tone of his voice were making her body react again and she could feel her heart pounding too hard in her chest.

"Some of what is said of us is true." He laughed, a hard, humorless sound like swallowing a mouthful of broken glass. Lauren shivered. "The touch of the sun is deadly to us and we prefer to sleep during the day, though it is not a necessity. As long as we keep out of the sunlight we thrive like the creatures of the darkness we are."

He sounded so bitter and, for the first time, unhappy instead of arrogant. "Don't you like being a vampire?" Lauren asked hesitantly, wondering why she was asking. It was just that he seemed more human and approachable somehow, as though he was letting down his guard a little when he let his emotions show.

"It doesn't matter whether I like it or not. I am what I am and have been for nigh on a century," Kris answered simply.

"And how did you become…" Lauren felt she was pushing it but she couldn't help being intensely curious and he seemed disposed to answer questions. "I mean, did someone *make* you a vampire or how did it happen?"

Kris made a small, indeterminate noise and when she turned her head to look up at him, his face was dark. For a moment she thought he wasn't going to answer and then he said, "I never saw the face of he who made me—my Maker. But if I ever do he will have much to answer for."

Evangeline Anderson

The menace in that low tone made Lauren shiver and Kris noticed the movement.

He shook his head, as though pushing aside a dark dream. "Come, it is time to dry you off, the water must be getting chilly." He stood up abruptly. Reaching for a huge, fluffy blanket-sized black towel he held it up to chest level, stretched wide to receive her.

Lauren hesitated. It was one thing for him to see the dim outline of her body through the cloudy water, standing up and letting him see her stark naked and dripping wet in the strange bathroom was something else entirely. She didn't feel comfortable with it, despite the vivid fantasy they'd shared at Le Jardin.

Seeing her hesitation, Kris frowned. "Come, Lauren, remember your role. Your modesty, while charming, has no place in this house. I will see every inch of you eventually. It might as well be now."

His words sent a cold shiver down her spine. His voice didn't seem to hold any kind of a threat, only a matter-of-factness that was more frightening than the most ominous warning. Lauren looked up at him for a moment, into his blue, implacable gaze and realized he meant every word.

Struggling to maintain her dignity, she rose from the water, feeling that cold blue gaze on her body like a physical touch. She stepped down onto a black bathmat and shivered as he wrapped her in the towel.

After she stopped shivering Kris dried her off, his touch impersonal and gentle in a way that was nearly maddening. Lauren wished that if he was going to do something to her he'd just go ahead and get it over with instead of acting icy-cold one minute and almost tender the next. She kept feeling as if she were waiting for the other shoe to drop, as her Gram would've said.

"What now?" she asked in a low voice when Kris had her dried and wrapped in a black satin dressing gown several sizes too big. It had a sharp, clean scent about it that reminded her of him and she wondered if it was his.

"Now you eat. You must certainly be famished after such a long fast."

Kris got her settled back in bed with a tray of steaming soup that seemed to have arrived while she was bathing. He laid a fine linen napkin in her lap and poured her some wine as though they were at a fine restaurant and he was the maître d. Lauren drew the line, however, at letting him feed her.

"I may be weak but I can manage to eat soup on my own," she snapped, taking the antique-looking golden spoon from him.

Kris shrugged, broad shoulders moving easily in the tight confines of his white dress shirt. "I am simply keeping up appearances. While we are here it would be wise for you to get used to the idea of being treated in the manner of that which you portray."

Lauren took a moment to wrap her head around this statement. "You mean a human concubine? Or is it more of a life-sized doll? What else are you going to do with me? Undress me, dress me, bathe me, feed me, fix my hair…?"

"Cherish you." The deep voice was quiet, stopping her in mid-sentence. Kris raised a dark eyebrow at her obvious astonishment. "The relationship between one of the Second Life and his or her concubine can be a very deep and meaningful one."

"Second Life?"

"It is the name we give our existence after the conversion from human to…other than human," Kris replied. "But those of the Second Life do not join together. It is much more common for us to have a long-term relationship with a human—a concubine. The concubine gives life, nourishment, as often as not, love. In return, her master provides security, shelter, and care for the most intimate of needs."

Lauren began to get an understanding of what he was talking about. "So a concubine isn't so much a love slave as a...lifelong companion?" It made her shiver to think of being tied to someone as fascinating and irritating as Kris for life.

"A cherished companion—a lover, even a friend," Kris clarified. "It is a bond much deeper than your human marriage vows for it cannot be broken without a great deal of pain on both sides. A concubine is to be treated with respect and affection. While you are here you will be attended every moment. Either by myself, or a servant if I am not available. Get used to it, Lauren."

There didn't seem to be a correct answer without getting into another verbal sparring match so she simply picked up the spoon and began eating. It was some kind of broth with noodles in it, definitely not Atkins-approved, but she was so hungry she didn't protest.

She could be allowed a few extra carbs, she told herself. She hadn't had a bite to eat since the bloody lamb two days ago. Possibly, she might even be approaching a size twelve. The thought cheered her considerably, though being kidnapped and taken to a vampire sex club where you were tied up for two days seemed like an extreme way to lose a few pounds.

Kris watched with approval as she ate the soup. "Good, you were becoming rather too thin, *Solnyshko*."

Lauren frowned at him and put the last spoonful back untouched. There was that strange nickname again, what had he said it meant? Little sun? "I don't think there's much danger of me wasting away just yet," she said, pushing the tray to one side.

"That depends on your idea of 'wasting away'." He frowned at her. "I suppose you are one of these tiresome modern women, determined to make yourself into an emaciated skeleton."

"Well," she said defensively. "I'm not naturally a size six like some women so I have to work on it."

"A size six?" Kris made a face that conveyed distaste. "I should hope not."

His reaction amused Lauren. "I promise you, I'm nowhere near it. No need to start breaking out the Ho Hos just yet."

Kris gave her a quizzical stare and Lauren reflected that as a bona fide vampire he had probably never sank fangs into a Ho Ho. He shook his head and rose from the bed, taking her tray with him. He pulled a long, silken cord that hung from the ceiling and she heard a brisk tinkling. Honestly, everything about this place was like something out of an old movie.

Presently, a light rapping sounded at the door and Kris opened it. He thrust the tray out into the hall and someone Lauren couldn't see took it away without comment.

"Now what?" she said as he came back to sit on the side of the bed. She felt like some sort of a convalescent, which she supposed in a way she was, if everything he'd said about the "Taint" was true. She glanced at her bruised arm again and saw Kris' eyes follow her own.

"How does it feel?" he asked, not answering her question which was typical for him. Without asking permission, he took her arm in both of his large, capable hands and studied it like a scientist looking at a particularly interesting specimen under a microscope.

"Do you mind?" Lauren tried to snatch her arm away but he clamped down on it with a grip that felt like flexible iron. She had a sudden understanding of his strength, which made her mouth go dry. She would have a better chance of pulling her humeral head out of its socket if she kept yanking than of freeing her arm from that grip.

"Are you done?" he asked quietly when she had stopped struggling. His tone was soft but there was steel buried in the deep voice. The ice blue eyes regarded her with chilling anger.

"Yes," she said, feeling angry with him for being so frightening and herself for sounding like a sullen child.

"Good. Once and for all, Lauren, you will have to get used to being touched, to having my hands on your body. Is it really so distasteful?"

Actually it wasn't, which why she objected so strongly. The feel of those large, warm hands sent a shimmer of pure heat through her body when he touched her. And the way he spoke, in that soft yet masterful voice—it was exactly like her fantasies. But that was all they were—just fantasies. She didn't actually want to submit her will and surrender her body to a stern but loving master, did she?

She became aware that Kris was still staring at her, waiting for her answer. "No," she said at last. "But that still doesn't mean I like it."

"Well, like it or not it is a necessity here at The House of Pain." He went back to his leisurely exam of her arm, a small, thoughtful frown on his smooth features. "There are still traces of the Taint in your system, which is probably one reason for your weakness. I'll have to tend to that before you rest tonight. If you start to feel weak or ill during the banquet you are to tell me immediately, do you understand?"

"Banquet?" Lauren said blankly. "Are you telling me we're going out somewhere tonight?"

"No, the banquet will be held here in Simon's private dining hall. He is our host and he has made it abundantly clear that he expects us to attend." Again he made a face of disgust. "You must be on your best behavior at all times. Do I make myself perfectly clear?"

"I'm quite able to mind my manners in company, thank you so much, Kris," she snapped, fed up with his domineering tone. "Are you ever going to give me back my arm?"

Kris frowned at her and released her arm. "If you really were my concubine you'd have to pay for taking such a tone with me, Lauren," he said, his voice low and dangerous.

"Ha." She kept her voice low as well but couldn't resist taunting him. "What would you do, spank me?"

"Maybe." Those ice blue eyes were suddenly predatory, causing a tightness in her chest and a shortness in her breathing.

"Or possibly, I could devise a more suitable punishment. Based, perhaps, on one of your own fantasies. Hmm?"

Lauren felt her cheeks heat in a sudden flush of embarrassment and she looked away quickly, unable to meet his gaze any longer. Damn him for reminding her that he had read the contents of the Mac and knew all of her most secret fantasies. Then she had a sudden thought. "My Mac, where…?"

"In a safe place," he said, in that cool, infuriating tone. "Don't worry, *Solnyshko*, no one but myself will ever see it and know your true desires."

"You son of a…" Lauren looked away from the amusement in his cool blue eyes.

"Come," he said, rising from her bed and walking to the huge, walk-in closet. "It's time to find you something appropriate to wear tonight."

Chapter Nine

Lauren Wright was the most infuriating woman he had ever met. She was as weak as a kitten from the Taint, which still lingered in her system, but she still insisted on fighting him at every opportunity. Before, he had found her reluctance to be amusing, if somewhat exasperating. Now it was beginning to be more than annoying.

Kris had a proprietary feeling towards her, which he knew was partially caused by the presence of his plasma in her bloodstream. The anti-Taint serum had been made entirely from his own blood, spun down to the pale, straw-colored liquid that could be safely injected into another's veins since AB type blood plasma didn't contain the antibodies that caused reactions between different blood types.

Another part of the attraction was the fact that every time he fed from her, to draw the Taint from her system, he was injecting his essence. The pale blue liquid secreted by his fangs was as unique to every vampire of the Second Life as a fingerprint or a retinal pattern was to humans. It had exceptional chemical properties, carrying both a vampire's strength and weaknesses within it, and it could cause serious complications in his relationship with the human doctor if he wasn't careful.

Then there was the fact that he was marking her every time he fed—marks visible only to another of the Second Life. In all probability, Lauren didn't even see the marks of his fangs on her skin herself. The healing factor in his essence made them nearly invisible to anyone but another vampire. But they were there, branding her as his. Kris couldn't help feeling a sense of ownership when he saw them on the underside of her forearm, even though he knew their Master/concubine arrangement was a pure fiction.

There was no doubt that Lauren would want nothing to do with such a relationship in reality, despite her amusing fantasies. Jenica had certainly wanted nothing to do with it. Kris shook his head, why think of such a thing now? Such memories were almost a century old and he had much more pressing concerns at the moment. He turned his thoughts back to Lauren.

His own vampiric plasma swimming in her veins, the essence he had injected into her each time he fed from her and drew more of the venom from her system, and the marks of his fangs on her body, visible to other vampires if not to Lauren herself, all contributed to his feelings for her. But they couldn't completely explain the strange emotions he was experiencing when he thought of the little human. Emotions he had thought dead and buried in Russia a hundred years ago.

Now she was walking along behind him wearing an outfit he thought was quite becoming, though it had angered her when he insisted on it. A deep green gown made of slithery satin hugged the generous curves he was burning to explore, and fell to her ankles in a swirl of soft fabric. Up one thigh ran a high slit that showed her lovely legs each time she took a step and the top was a low-cut v-neck with spaghetti straps to hold it up. A pair of high-heeled green sandals completed the outfit.

He knew Lauren wasn't so much upset about his choice of outfit which suited her and brought out her catlike green eyes. No, what upset her was Kris' refusal to let her wear any underwear beneath the slippery material. She had raged and protested until he had warned that if she didn't put the gown on herself, he would put it on her and not be very careful where his hands wandered as he did so. That had quieted her, and with a final angry look she had turned her back to him and slipped into the gown.

Kris spared a glance for her now, trotting obediently at his heels just as though she were a proper human concubine. If he was quite honest with himself, he had to admit that he was rather glad she was not.

He had never hungered to have complete control of any human's mind as others of the Second Life did. He scorned such a relationship as inferior, though he knew it didn't bother other vampires in the least — Simon being a prime example. Rather, he preferred a strong-willed woman with a mind of her own. That way her surrender was that much more delicious when it was finally given.

Such a woman was all but impossible to find as all were so vulnerable to vampire mind tricks, which was one reason Kris had never taken a concubine before. He had only been tempted to do so once, and that had been many years ago.

Her immunity to his power was one reason Lauren Wright intrigued him, he supposed. Submission was always sweeter after a struggle and the little human was nothing if not tenaciously stubborn about giving up any part of herself to him.

She stumbled, causing a light flurry of echoes in the stone corridor and Kris was at her side, catching her before she could hurt herself. He held her by her upper arms, careful not to make a bruise with his superior strength. Humans were so delicate, so easily broken, he reminded himself.

"Are you all right?" he asked, feeling more anxious than he liked.

"Fine," she said. He could see the inner conflict going on behind those cat-green eyes. She wanted to struggle away from his grip but she knew they were probably being watched out here in the public corridor. She also knew that she had no chance of getting free until he decided to let her go. Reluctantly she remained still.

"Remember to tell me if you feel ill in any way," Kris told her. He watched her carefully for signs of Taint-induced fatigue. Despite everything he could do, there was still some venom in her system and he wasn't very happy about bringing her out to Simon's banquet tonight. But their host could no longer be put off and so Kris would simply have to keep a close eye on his human charge.

"I'll be fine," she muttered, not meeting his gaze. "These are higher heels than I'm used to. That's all."

"Very well." He let her go, somewhat reluctantly. "Do you wish to take my arm for support?" he asked, holding it out to her but she shook her head. Doubtless she was still angry over the outfit. Kris allowed himself a moment to enjoy the way she looked in the formfitting gown.

"Have I told you how breathtakingly lovely you look tonight, Lauren?" he asked in a low voice.

Her face flushed and he could hear her heart begin to race. "Your skin is so smooth and creamy in contrast to your gown, it makes me want to caress you all over," he told her, letting the truth of his words show in his eyes.

She turned her head, refusing to look at him and he could smell her scent, warm and feminine, perfuming the echoing stone corridor in which they stood.

"I can see the outline of your breasts, your nipples," he whispered, allowing his fingers to trail along her bare arm, enjoying the case of chill bumps his touch provoked. Oh yes, the attraction was there. There was no way she could deny it.

"Don't," she nearly whispered, a soft catch in her voice.

"Don't what? Tell you how beautiful you are? How much I desire you?" He pulled her suddenly from the open stone corridor to a dark, empty room to their left. Enfolding her in his arms, he felt her heartbeat rabbiting against his chest as she struggled to get away.

"Please…"

"Don't struggle. It only makes me want you more."

She turned to wood in his arms, obviously realizing there was no way to be free of him until he let her go.

Amused by her silent protest, Kris let his hands wander over her creamy shoulders and caress her back, left bare by the deep dip in the green gown's silky material. He brushed the soft cloud of honey-blonde hair away from her cheek and buried his face in the smooth curve of her neck. He felt his fangs extend with a sharp little pleasure-pain, pricking lightly along the warm skin at her throat.

Lauren stiffened even more and her heart rate skyrocketed. Kris realized she was afraid he was going to bite her and feed from her right then and there. Of course, he had been taking blood from her for the past several nights as he drew the Taint slowly from her system, but she didn't know that. To Kris it hardly counted, as it wasn't a deep feeding. It was the difference between merely taking nourishment and sitting down to a true feast.

"Relax," he whispered softly, pressing his lips to the throbbing pulse in her neck. He could smell the blood rushing under the surface of her skin, salty and hot. The memory of her unique taste teased him, making his fangs ache.

"Wh-what are you doing?" Her voice was low and breathless and he could taste her heat, rich and heavy on the back of his tongue. He wanted to reach beneath the silky gown and spread her trembling thighs. Wanted to tease her sweet, swollen inner lips apart and stroke her heated cunt. Despite her fear, or maybe because of it, he knew he would find her hot for him. Hot and wet and ready.

"I thought we were going to the banquet," she protested.

"And so we shall," Kris breathed, allowing himself a soft kiss behind her ear. He pulled her pelvis close to his, pleased at the sensation of her soft curves rubbing against his throbbing cock. Lauren gasped and pressed her thighs together tightly but didn't try to move away. Good, she was learning.

"I simply wanted to warn you," Kris told her, letting his hands wander over the round curve of her ass, naked beneath the satin gown. "The feast we will be attending tonight is like none you have ever experienced. You may see some things that frighten you."

"Wh-what do you care if I'm scared?" Her voice trembled ever so slightly and Kris knew she was truly frightened now. Frightened and aroused, he could smell it on her. It was a heady combination for his vampire senses and he longed to take her then and there against the wall of the dark room. To plunge both cock and fangs into her soft flesh at the same time. A deep feeding. But such an action would have irrevocable consequences—would seal the bond that was already growing between them.

"I care because while we are here you are my concubine. My *Solnyshko*. My cherished treasure." His hands roamed over her body, enjoying her curves and the small, animal noises she made in the back of her throat when he cupped her breasts and twisted the erect nipples, causing her to squirm against him.

"What I am trying to tell you, Lauren, is that there is no need for fear," he whispered into the honey-blonde hair. "While you are with me no other shall harm you in any way. Do you understand?"

He waited for a heartbeat and when she still didn't acknowledge him, he nipped lightly at her neck, coming as close as possible to drawing blood without actually doing it. Letting her feel the razor-sharp edge of his fangs.

"I...yes, I understand. Now will you please get your hands off me?" She was trying to sound tough and indignant and was failing miserably. Kris savored the flare of her temper, loving the way she refused to submit completely even though she was helpless in his arms.

"I don't think so," he murmured into her ear. "I think you need to remember who is Master while we are here. Answer me one question truthfully and I shall let you go."

"What?" Her breath was coming in hot little gasps now, her heart beating more rapidly than ever.

"Do you wish me to take my hands off you because you are frightened, or because my touch does nothing to arouse you?"

"Be-because..." He could hear her trying to decide which was safer, the truth or a lie.

"Because you don't do a thing for me. Now let go of me, you promised you would if I answered," she finished in a rush.

"I promised I would let go if you answered *truthfully*," Kris reminded her. "Do you remember in the fantasy we shared at Le Jardin, I told you there would be penalties for lying?"

"Y-yes. But how can you...you don't know..."

"Oh, but I do know, Lauren. I can smell your heat, I can taste your lust like honey on the tip of my tongue. You cannot hide the reactions of your body from me."

"But wh-what are you going to do to me?" She shifted against him, desperate to escape but he held her in an iron grip.

"I am going to touch you, *Solnyshko*. I'm going to spread the sweet lips of your cunt and see if you're wet for me. If you're not then I will know you were telling the truth. But if you are..." He let his words hang between them, unfinished.

"But...no, you can't!" She pressed her thighs together tightly, as though she could keep him out.

"Don't be foolish, Lauren." Kris slipped one hand into the high slit in the silky green material of her dress, just as he had longed to do earlier. "And don't forget that I am your Master here. Your body belongs to me to do with as I choose. Relax and submit." The last words he spoke in a tone of command, letting her know he was on the edge of losing his patience.

He felt her tremble against him again and then, with a soft sob, she spread her thighs, giving in to his dominance. "That's right, my darling," he murmured soothingly, stroking the damp curls that covered her soft mound. "I won't hurt you...just relax."

She shivered against him, drawn tight as a wire while he ran seeking fingertips along her honeyed slit. The soft lips of her cunt were slick and swollen with desire. He parted them gently, hearing her small intake of breath as he stroked along the sensitive bundle of nerves at her center. She was very wet, as he had known she would be.

"So it seems that you lied to me," Kris murmured in her ear, still stroking her gently but firmly. He spread her further and pressed two long fingers into her tight entrance, making her moan low in her throat. The air around them was filled with her delicious fragrance — the scent of a woman in heat.

"Wh-what are you going to do to me?" She was holding onto his shoulders, obviously trying to keep her balance while he kept up the maddening pleasure. Her eyes were wide in the dark room, seeing nothing, he knew, but the dim outline of his face as he touched her.

"For now, nothing," Kris assured her. He stroked into her steadily, feeling her wet heat tighten around his fingers, knowing she was close to the edge. Half of him wanted to make her come then and there, to watch her face while the orgasm overtook her. But he was close to the edge himself — too close. If he watched her sweet face flush with that ultimate pleasure, if he felt her wet cunt spasm around his fingers as she gasped out her pleasure, it might be too much. He might not be able to stop himself from taking her then and there, and he was not yet ready for that.

"N-nothing?" Lauren gasped.

"No." Kris removed his fingers regretfully, finding great satisfaction from her little mewl of disappointment as he did so. "But remember who is Master here, Lauren. And next time you lie or disobey me in any way, there will be the most severe penalty, which I promise. Do you understand?"

"I-I understand," she gasped softly, still leaning against him for support. "Please…just let me go."

He drew back, studying the slanting green eyes, gone wide with fear and desire in the dimness of the room. Her breath was coming in short little pants and he could feel her heart racing madly. Her trembling hands pushed ineffectually against his broad shoulders. "If it is truly what you desire then, I will let you go," he said and placed a soft, openmouthed kiss on her pink, panting lips.

For a moment it seemed she would surrender to the kiss, and then she jerked her head back, turning away from him.

"Please," she said in a low, unsteady voice. "I can't...I don't..."

"Very well, Lauren," he whispered softly into her ear and then let her go. "Come, the banquet awaits."

Chapter Ten

Lauren stumbled after him on legs that felt like sticks. How could he do that to her? When he touched her and used that low, commanding tone of voice it was like she was made out of melted butter. Like he had reached inside her head and found exactly what made her feel hot and vulnerable and needy...

Well, he *had* reached inside her head, in a manner of speaking. He'd read the Mac's entire contents, Lauren reminded herself for the umpteenth time. He knew about her secret, shameful wish to be dominated. But just because he knew, didn't mean she always had to let him get to her like this. She pressed her trembling thighs tightly together, still feeling his long, strong fingers stroking into her, then shook her head, to clear the image. It was time to straighten up and stop letting Kris affect her so much.

"Here we are." He looked back at her briefly and nodded at a set of massive, wooden double doors that looked like the entrance to a dungeon directly in front of them. "Remember who you are while we are here, Lauren." His pale blue gaze burned into her for a moment and then he rapped twice on the heavy wooden doors.

Straightening her spine, she walked tall behind him and tried to look regal and bored instead of confused and half-naked, which was how she felt. The door swung open to reveal a massive chamber done in somber tones of red and black. Gray stone walls were hung with richly woven tapestries that seemed to depict violent and sexual themes exclusively and the black marble floor reflected the scenes of submission and pain in its shiny surface. Lauren thought that whoever had designed the room wanted to be certain that The House of Pain lived up to its name.

To their left, as they entered, was what appeared to be a small stage with a red velvet curtain drawn across it. To their right, the room was filled with a U-shaped table. About twenty-five people, who she supposed must be humans and vampires, sat around it. Although Kris was the only vampire she had every knowingly seen, it seemed to Lauren that she could pick the vamps out of the crowd easily.

The vamps had paler skin and there was a look of coldness in their eyes. The same look she remembered seeing on Kris' face when he first came to her lab and coerced her into joining him for dinner. That night seemed about a hundred years ago now. Lauren couldn't help but remember that when he looked at her now, the pale blue gaze was hot instead of cold. She shivered and tried to push the thought away.

Sitting at the exact apex of the U at the huge table was a person whose appearance simply screamed "vampire". Either that or "deviant", she was beginning to wonder if they were the same thing. The man, who had long, dark hair and cool brown eyes, rose to meet them as she followed Kris into the huge chamber. He smiled courteously and walked around the table to greet them.

Lauren saw he was wearing a pair of skin-tight black leather pants and thigh-high suede boots of the same color. A black leather vest completed the outfit, swinging open to reveal well-developed abdominals and skin that must have been a rich brown when he was still able to go out in the sun. The rock-star outfit would have looked ridiculous on most men, but the person sauntering towards them pulled it off effortlessly. In contrast, Kris' well-tailored black suit seemed even more austere and forbidding.

"Well, Kristov. We're so pleased you were able to join us tonight. And this must be the charming little concubine that has so captured your heart." He turned to Lauren and took her hand in one cool palm, bowing over it gracefully as though they were in a European court instead of the back of a sex club in Houston. "You are most welcome here, *ma chérie*." He had a beautifully cultivated voice with just a hint of a French accent, Lauren noted as he released her hand.

"Lauren, this is Simon Travain, our host. He gave us shelter when the Taint was still strong in your blood. We are deeply in his debt." Kris didn't sound very happy about it but his words seemed to make their host positively glow.

"Now then, Kristov, there is no need to speak of debt. I am certain we can find a way for you to work off your little…ah…obligation in a manner that is not too onerous."

Lauren looked at Kris who had a scowl on his chiseled features and felt her stomach do a slow flip-flop. Obligation? Debt? The words had a certain ominous ring to them and she wondered what the verbal sparring between the two vampires meant. She looked questioningly at Kris, but the ice blue gaze was locked with the deep brown one of their host. After a moment, Simon looked away, a cruel little smile twitching at the corners of his full mouth.

"Come join us at the table, my friends. The entertainment hasn't started yet and we're most eager for your company." Turning gracefully, Simon led the way back to the U-shaped table. He indicated two plush, high-backed chairs with curling scrollwork along the backs and arms and invited them to sit.

Lauren noted that Kris was careful to put her on the far side of himself so that he was sitting between her and their host. A frown passed briefly over Simon's smoothly handsome features as he noticed this as well, but their host said nothing.

There was an empty chair to her right so that Kris was the only person she was close enough to talk to which made her both grateful and perversely irritated. Why did he keep acting like she was entirely incapable of taking care of herself? Human concubine or not it was insulting and, she felt, sexist. Then she reminded herself that he probably came from a time when a man's first thought was to protect his woman. A hot flush crept up her cheeks at the thought and she hastily amended it—not that she really was his woman, of course. Or would ever want to be.

They got settled in their seats and Lauren looked up and down the table. Everyone appeared to be in groups of two or three. She and Kris, she noted, were the only people dressed in remotely normal fashion. If, in her case, you could call wearing no underclothes beneath your dress normal.

Everyone else at the table had on costumes that appeared to be Renaissance Festival meets upscale sex shop. Leather and chains mixed with ribbons and lace to give a bizarre effect. She felt like Alice at the Mad Hatter's tea party if the Mad Hatter had been heavily into S&M. Did vampires and their concubines always dress like this or was it a nod to the formal occasion of the banquet?

The general rule seemed to be one vampire to one human, though several of the vamps appeared to have more than one concubine. Simon, she noticed, appeared to have four — three women and one young man seated to his left. The quartet was eagerly hanging on every word their Master said, ridiculously eager to please. Mildly repulsed by the display, Lauren looked further.

At one end of the table sat two women, one tall and cool and much blonder than Lauren was herself. Beside her sat a woman who was obviously of Latino heritage. From the way the blonde was running her fingers through the other woman's long dark hair it was obvious they were together.

At the other end of the table was a girl who looked to be no more than fifteen but from the coldness in her gaze, Lauren thought she was probably much older. Beside her, wearing a conservative suit with no shirt underneath, was a man with black hair which was going a distinguished silver at the temples. Out in the city together, Lauren supposed they would be mistaken for father and daughter but their body language told a completely different story. The girl reached up to caress the man's face, her lips parting to reveal a set of fangs that would make a piranha shudder and he smiled down at her, whispering something Lauren couldn't quite catch.

Perhaps the most visually arresting couple at the table was halfway down on the right side of the U. Lauren literally did a double take when she saw the two men with identical features speaking quietly together. They both had long, golden brown hair and broad shoulders but one of them had skin so pale it was almost white while the other had a dark, even tan. As she watched, two sets of identical sky blue eyes looked at her and then the tan man reached for the pale one and planted a deep kiss on the other man's full red lips.

Lauren gave a little gasp and turned away from the public display, embarrassed to have been caught staring.

"I see you've noticed Stephen and Michael." Kris' deep voice held just a hint of amusement and Lauren realized that he had been watching her to gauge her reaction to the other people at the table.

"Are they...look so much alike they could be twins." Lauren spoke softly, out of the corner of her mouth, still looking carefully away.

"Indeed, so they are," Kris told her with a perfectly straight face. "It is not always easy once one enters the Second Life to leave behind all that was dear to one in the First. Stephen chose to keep his beloved brother close to him. He is not the first to have done so."

"I...see," Lauren whispered, still looking down at her hands twisting helplessly in the confines of the deep green gown.

"No, you don't, but you must," Kris replied. "They are still putting on a display for you. Look at them, Lauren."

"I don't want to," she hissed back fiercely.

"You must." There was steel in the deep voice. "It's considered very rude in my culture to provoke a display and then not watch it. Now *look...at...them*."

Unwillingly, Lauren turned her head again to watch as the twins kissed each other deeply and thoroughly. The pale twin, she could see, had sprouted a set of fangs that were grazing delicately along his brother's throat in a teasing fashion. It was exactly what Kris had been doing to her in the dark room before they entered the banquet hall. Vampire foreplay, she supposed.

She shivered involuntarily, remembering the sharp pricking along the vulnerable, sensitive skin of her throat and the hard press of his cock against her belly. She risked a quick glance at Kris. He was watching intently as the twins, one vampire and one concubine, she supposed, continued to make their display. His fangs, she noted, were conspicuously absent now. Did they only come out when he was hungry or aroused? The scientist in her was intrigued by the possible implications and she made a mental note to ask him later if she could think of a nonsexual way to bring it up.

At last the twins broke apart with a final rough and luscious kiss and Lauren felt free to drop her eyes. There was polite clapping up and down the length of the table and she realized she and Kris had not been the only people observing the display.

"That was...strange," she confessed to Kris under her breath. A strong hand took hers under the table and squeezed once before letting go.

"If a little incestuous love play is the worst thing you have to witness tonight you may consider yourself very lucky, *Solnyshko*. Now come here."

"What—?" Lauren began, but then he was pulling her close, pulling her to him and large strong hands were roaming all over her body. Kris was touching her the same way he had just before the banquet. But that had been in a private room, not in front of God and everybody. Or whatever deity these people worshiped.

"What are you doing?" Lauren protested in a low voice as he trailed slow, hot kisses along her neck. She could feel every eye in the place on them as Kris continued the humiliating display.

"It's unspeakably rude to provoke a display and then not return one in kind," he breathed in her ear as he nibbled at her earlobe.

"B-but everyone is watching us!" she hissed back, feeling a red blush of mortification creep over her face at the thought.

"That's the idea, Lauren. If it helps you just close your eyes and pretend we are alone." His large hand cupped her breast and pinched the nipple straining against the green satin.

Lauren gasped and shut her eyes tightly, fighting both the urge to struggle in his grasp and the deeper, more primal urge to submit utterly. She tried to remove herself mentally from what he was doing but it was hopeless. She could feel his fangs pricking along her neck again and the big hands on her body made her hot and needy in a way she couldn't deny.

"You want this, Lauren. Don't try to pretend you don't." His voice was low and rough, meant only for her, as he took her mouth in a deep, almost bruising kiss.

Unable to help herself, she opened her mouth and let him in, feeling his long fingers tangle in her hair as he demanded her complete submission. His fangs were razor-sharp as they grazed against her tongue but he didn't draw blood to her mingled relief and disappointment.

Kris kissed her thoroughly, establishing his complete ownership of her mouth, of her body and soul. *This is the way he would fuck. Slow...hard...relentlessly.* The thought came unbidden to her brain and Lauren tried unsuccessfully to push it away. She could feel her nipples tightening into painful points at the tips of her breasts and the slow, wet heat growing between her thighs...

He relinquished her mouth at last and then his lips were traveling down her neck again, fangs nipping at her unprotected throat as he went. Lauren gasped as he reached up and slid one of the thin spaghetti straps down her shoulder, baring her right breast and its jutting pink nipple, already hardened by need and desire.

He teased her nipple with his tongue for a moment before sucking it into his mouth. She could feel his fangs again, grazing against her lightly, a gentle threat of what he could do if he chose to. Lauren moaned, eyes tightly shut and tried not to think about everyone else at the table who must be watching this display. It was beyond humiliating for Kris to treat her like this, to establish his dominance and demand her submission right here at the table…

But then the delicious sensation of his hot mouth on her bare flesh pushed everything else out of her mind. Lauren buried her fingers in his thick, chocolate brown hair, pulling him towards her, thrusting forward to get more of her breast in his mouth. The intense sensation was shooting little sparks of heat to her sex, already wet and hot from the way he had touched her before they even entered the banquet. God, she could almost come just from the feel of his mouth on her…

Kris stopped abruptly, drawing away from her as suddenly as he had pulled her to him. Smoothly, he slid the thin green spaghetti strap back up into place to cover her exposed breast and resettled himself in his chair.

"What…why did you…?" Lauren was left feeling breathless, ravaged. She stared at him uncomprehendingly, noticing that his fangs were fully extended.

"The display is over." His deep voice was little more than a growl. "Or did you wish me to continue?" He turned back to face her and she could see that the fire was back in his pale blue gaze. "Do you wish me to take you here and now, in front of everyone? Even I have my limits, *Solnyshko*. Don't push me."

A light, polite smattering of applause brought her back to reality and Lauren realized she had literally forgotten everything else while he kissed her, including the watching eyes of their impromptu audience. She dropped her eyes in confusion. What was happening to her?

"Ah, the first course. Lovely." The voice belonged to Simon and she risked a quick glance at their host, who was smiling and nodding as several white-gloved servers brought a large steaming tureen to the table. It was obviously some kind of soup but looking down at her place setting, which was fine bone china with a thin golden edge around the rim, Lauren realized she had no bowl. Kris, however, did.

When the lid was lifted and the contents of the huge tureen came into view Lauren began to understand. "Blood," she whispered unsteadily as one of the servers ladled a generous helping into Kris' bowl. She wondered how they managed to heat the stuff without actually cooking it.

"Of course," he said, picking up a gold-plated spoon and beginning to stir his "soup". "What else would you expect, Lauren? We are, after all, vampires. Nothing else can sustain us." Again his voice had that faintly bitter ring to it and she wondered how he really felt about what he was. But now was definitely not the time to ask. Instead she stared at the cream-colored tablecloth and tried not to wonder who the blood in the tureen rightfully belonged to.

She was concentrating so hard on not looking at anyone else eat that it was a bit of a shock to see a white-gloved hand suddenly appear in front of her, placing a tray that held a fist-sized mound of little black globules.

"The finest Beluga."

Lauren looked up and saw that their host, Simon, was talking to her. He leaned around Kris, who was sipping his soup stoically, to do so.

"We realize that our concubines cannot be expected to share our rather...esoteric taste in food but we try to provide something that is pleasing to everyone's palate here at The House of Pain." He gave her a little nod.

"I...thank you," Lauren said uncertainly. Beside the small tray of caviar the server had placed a plate of white toast points and a bowl of *créme fraîche*, pale and frothy, with a tiny golden spoon to scoop it with. A fluted champagne glass filled with sparkling liquid was set before her and she took a long drink to steady her nerves.

"Eat up, *ma chérie*. We want you to regain your strength as soon as possible." Then, with a rather predatory grin, Simon went back to his blood soup.

Caviar was far from her favorite food but Lauren had been to enough parties for potential investors on behalf of Century Labs to at least know the proper way to eat the stuff. Although she had never felt less hungry, she scooped up a dollop of caviar and ladled it onto a toast point then finished the concoction with a blob of *créme fraîche* and took a bite.

At least no one could say that Simon spared any expense for his guests, she reflected. She estimated that the mound of caviar in front of her was more than five thousand dollars worth and she was betting that the champagne in her glass was the finest vintage. Simon, as her Gram would have said, enjoyed putting on the dog.

The ominous thought of the "obligation" Simon and Kris had both spoken of wandered across her forebrain. Kris had spoken to her of vampires being wealthy beyond imagination so money must mean little or nothing to them. How would you pay for the finest accommodations and the most expensive food if money was not an option? Lauren hoped she wouldn't have to find out.

The second course for the vampires was a large, jiggling mound of what looked like blood Jell-O. The humans were served a pale broth that Kris told her was watercress soup and a small plate of escargot. Lauren ate the soup and left the snails, trying not to watch as their host raised a jiggling spoonful of the second course to his mouth. She was beginning to feel more than a little queasy, her head and her hurt arm throbbing in time. She considered telling Kris she felt unwell and then decided not to give him the satisfaction of seeing her weakness.

"And now it is time for dessert and entertainments." Simon clapped his hands briskly and at once everyone's plates were whisked away. The servers brought out trays of golden goblets with small, icy scoops of deep maroon sorbet and placed one in front of everyone, humans and vampires alike.

Kris took a small scoop of the sorbet, letting the maroon concoction melt on his tongue. Lauren felt utterly revolted. He looked over at her, apparently noticing that she hadn't lifted her spoon.

"Lauren, take a bite. It's rude not to at least try the offered course," he said softly, nodding at the small golden spoon that came with the sorbet.

"Kris, I *can't*. Blood sorbet…" Lauren struggled not to let the revulsion show on her face.

He laughed, a deep rumble that seemed to vibrate her bones. "Oh, I see the problem. But your dessert is made of blood *oranges*, *Solnyshko*, not blood. Try it—I'm certain you'll find it quite good."

Hesitantly she took a small spoonful and let it melt in her mouth. The flavor was bitter and tart and sweet all at once, a surprisingly pleasing taste that she found she wanted more of. She ended up enjoying the dessert course most of all. Or she would have if the entertainment hadn't started just then.

Simon clapped his hands again and the large room darkened. On cue, the wide velvet curtain drawn across the small stage that faced the U-shaped table parted. The stage was dark at first but then, gradually, a pale, glimmering light began to grow. Lauren gave a little gasp as she saw what the light revealed.

Strapped to a strange metal frame was a large, muscular black man with his arms spread apart to bare his broad back. He was completely naked and the dim lighting glistened along his ebony body as though he had been oiled from head to foot.

As everyone at the table watched, a petite Asian woman— Lauren thought her Japanese—with pale skin and long, black hair that brushed her bare hips strolled in from stage right. High-heeled boots clacked hollowly on the stage's wooden floor as she walked and the red leather bustier she was wearing cupped the tiny swollen buds of her small breasts lovingly. She wasn't wearing anything between the bustier and the boots and her neatly trimmed pubic thatch was very dark at the pale intersection of her thighs.

The woman raised one hand, gloved in black leather, above her head and there was a creak of leather as a long black whip she'd had coiled in her fist uncurled. Lauren tried to bite back a gasp and didn't quite succeed. She hoped like crazy that what she thought was going to happen wasn't really going to happen.

As the tiny woman drew back her whip with a low whisper across the wooden stage, Lauren found herself groping for Kris' hand under the pale cream tablecloth. From the corner of her eye she saw him looking at her quizzically but most of her attention was riveted on the "entertainment" about to take place on the stage before them.

With a low "crack" the whip snapped through the air and lashed at the muscular ebony back. There was a muffled cry from the huge man bound on the metal rack and a sigh of satisfaction from the audience. The woman spared them a brief, cruel smile with blood-red lips before she went back to her task.

Lauren wanted to get up, wanted to say something. The doctor in her was outraged to see the deliberate harm being inflicted on another human being. Apparently sensing her urge, Kris leaned down and whispered, "Relax. He's a willing participant. The woman is his Mistress and they do this often. Don't forget where you are."

Oh right, The House of Pain. She gave him an incredulous look, but he only nodded briefly and directed her attention back to the stage.

Again and again the whip cracked, not only leaving welts but drawing thin rivulets of blood as the flogging continued. All her time in the ER and the surgical suite as a resident at St. Luke's couldn't prepare her for this spectacle of blood and pain. Lauren wanted in the worst way to look away but it seemed she just couldn't. It was like watching a train wreck—both horrible and compelling. Also, she was pretty sure it would be considered "rude" not to watch the carefully prepared entertainment. So she forced herself to look, though her head and arm throbbed worse than ever and she was beginning to feel weak and nauseous.

Under the table she squeezed Kris' had so hard she was sure he would complain, anyone else would have at any rate. But he simply gave her another unreadable glance from those cool blue eyes. Lauren remembered vaguely that she probably couldn't hurt his hand by squeezing it. In fact, being run over by a truck probably wouldn't hurt it. She tried to distract her mind with the idea as she speculated about vampire physiology. She wondered exactly how strong they were, if they had different bone structure, anything to take her mind off the spectacle still going on in front of her but it didn't work.

The hiss and crack of the whip, the muscular man's groans, the approving murmurs from the audience and the soft patter of blood as it dripped onto the stage went on and on, filling her ears. She could smell a faintly sweet, metallic scent of fresh blood. It lodged under her tongue like a copper penny she couldn't spit out and the room they were sitting in began to feel decidedly too warm. Still, she might have lasted rest of the night without fainting if she hadn't had to witness the rest of the entertainment.

When the black man's back was a bloody mess of tattered ribbons and he was hanging limply in his bonds, groaning low in his throat, the petite woman threw down her whip. With a glance at the audience, she manipulated a lever to crank the rack the man was tied to so that he was in profile to the audience at the U-shaped table.

Incredibly, Lauren saw, the naked, bleeding prisoner was sporting an erection that was truly impressive. So Kris had been right—he *was* a wiling participant. Although, how anyone could get off on that much pain was beyond her. She could actually see the white knobs of bone protruding like small, bloody islands from the ridge in the center of his dark brown back.

As they watched, the woman walked around to his bleeding back. Ducking down while keeping her eyes on the crowd, she licked a long, wet furrow up the center of the black man's spine. A shiver of ecstasy ran through the huge muscular frame strapped to the rack and his lean hips pumped helplessly as his Mistress continued to lick up the fruits of her labor.

Lauren had been feeling warmer and warmer, and less and less oxygen seemed to be making its way to her brain as she tried to breathe. She was dimly aware that her arm was throbbing in the spot the revi had bitten her and huge black stars were beginning to explode before her eyes. Vaguely she felt Kris squeezing her fingers and realized he was trying to say something to her. But her attention was riveted to the stage where the bloody tableau continued.

She had been leaning back in her chair, wanting instinctively to get as far from the spectacle on the stage as possible, but now she felt herself falling sideways. She heard Kris utter a low curse in guttural Russian as he caught her. For once she didn't mind.

Chapter Eleven

~ ~ ~ ~ ~

"Do as I say, now, Lauren. I expect your complete obedience." Large, warm hands are positioning me while he talks. Putting me in the exact center of the bed on my hands and knees. My breasts are like ripe fruit, the sensitive nipples brushing the red silk sheets as he presses my shoulders down so that my bare ass is elevated. I feel those hands on my inner thighs, parting my legs, getting my body arranged to his satisfaction.

"I'm frightened," I whisper, in a voice so low I almost can't hear it myself. But he hears me anyway.

"Don't be, my darling. Only submit to me and everything will be all right." Those large warm hands caress me now, petting along my spine as though I was a cat that might arch my back and purr. His pleasure in my body is apparent and I feel the helpless shiver of anticipation as he cups my full breasts, tugging at my exposed nipples.

"So beautiful—so sensual. You were made for this, Lauren. Made to be fucked." His voice is deep and rough, his words echoing inside me, shattering my self-control. Those hands travel to the spot between my thighs again. This time I can feel him framing my sex with both hands, his thumbs poised to spread me apart.

"Please…" I cannot bear to look, cannot bear to be in this vulnerable position while he takes his time exploring me, claiming me.

"Are you wet for me, Lauren?" he asks, in that same deep, quiet voice. "When I spread the lips of your pussy will I find you slippery and hot and ready for my cock?"

"I-I don't know," I gasp although I know perfectly well that he will. But there is no point in answering in either the affirmative or the negative because he's going to check to be sure either way.

"Let's find out," he almost whispers, and then I feel him parting the lips of my sex, exposing my soft, pink inner cunt to his probing gaze. I can feel his breath on me, hot and eager, as he leans forward to take a closer look. My exposed clit throbs with need. I am utterly bare, completely open to him and there is nothing I can do about it.

"So sweet," he murmurs and then, with no warning, I feel his mouth on me there. His tongue, wet and hot and demanding is entering me, filling me, pressing inside me in a way that makes me need to scream. I wriggle against him, unable to hold still, but his hands clamp down on my hips like an iron vise, holding me in place. He takes his time, delving into me, exploring my wet depths as though we had all the time in the world. I cry out. I can't help it, as he builds my desire, pushing me higher and higher towards the peak. Just when I feel myself tipping over the edge, he withdraws his tongue and kisses me once, softly, on my open sex.

"Delicious, my darling. Nothing could be better than eating your sweet little pussy…except perhaps fucking it."

"Please…" I gasp, needing him so badly despite my fear. I am helpless on the bed before him, on my hands and knees, legs spread wide, my sex open and defenseless. I don't know how he will take me…sometimes he is gentle, using long, slow strokes to open my body, building my orgasm until the pleasure overflows inside me. Sometimes he is harsh, forcing himself inside me, fucking deep and hard, mastering me thoroughly with each deliciously rough thrust.

I feel him move behind me, I hear the rough purr of his zipper coming down. Then I feel the blunt head of his cock, nudging against the opening of my unprotected sex. He parts my lips, swollen with desire for him, and rubs the wide shaft slowly along the length of my slit, rubbing over my aching clit, not entering me yet but teasing me—getting himself wet enough to enter me.

"Please," I moan again. My hands are clenched in the red silk sheets, bunching the slippery material between my fingers, bracing myself for his entry.

"You just can't wait, can you, Lauren?" His voice is deep, almost a growl. "You need it so badly—need to be fucked…"

~ ~ ~ ~ ~

She woke from the fever dream to see a pair of concerned blue eyes staring into her own.

"Damn it, Lauren, why didn't you tell me you were feeling weak?" The angry words were belied by his soft, concerned tone. A cool, damp towel was laid across her forehead, bringing a soothing relief from the pounding heat that seemed to have taken over her skull.

"Din want you…t' think…'m weak," she said, realizing she was slurring as she spoke. Maybe she'd had too much champagne. She'd never been much of a drinker. She opened her eyes and realized they were back in the luxurious bedroom and she was lying in the middle of the massive bed. The lights were dim but even so she could see the look of worry crossing Kris' usually stern features. His ice blue gaze was almost soft.

"I'm sorry," she whispered. On impulse she reached up with her unhurt arm and cupped the pale cheek in her palm. Without looking away from her eyes, Kris turned his head slightly and pressed a gentle kiss into the center of her palm, just as he had after their first dinner together at Le Jardin. Lauren felt a tremor run though her belly at the feel of his lips against her skin. She tried to sit up but he held her in place easily with one large hand.

"Lay still, *Solnyshko*. You're still not well." His free hand caressed her unhurt arm.

"I'm fine," Lauren insisted although she felt anything but "It was just that…*scene* on the stage that got to me." She struggled to get up again, suddenly incensed as she remembered the horrible brutality she had witnessed. "What ever happened to that man? Did he receive medical attention after the show?"

Kris looked mildly amused. "If you had watched a little longer you might have seen that he was quite well by the end of their little act."

"Quite well? *Quite well?* What the hell are you talking about, Kris? Injuries like that would take weeks, even months to heal." She was so angry she felt dizzy.

He shook his head. "Not so. Did you not see her licking his back?"

Lauren shuddered at the memory. "Did I see it? I feel like it's burned into the back of my eyes. I'll never be able to forget it."

Kris frowned. "Yes, I suppose from a human perspective it would seem rather…shocking."

"Shocking? Kris, she flogged the skin off his back and then licked up his blood. It was hideous—*repulsive*."

His white face went very hard and still and he withdrew the hand that had been absently caressing her arm. "Yes, I expect so. I suppose I cannot blame you for being repulsed. However, the act they were putting on for our amusement was just that, an act. I assure you that the man is quite well as we speak."

Looking at his white face, Lauren understood that she had offended him somehow. But, damn it, she'd been plenty offended too, having to watch that sick spectacle these people considered "entertainment". And how the hell could the man possibly be healed? She opened her mouth to ask but Kris was already talking again.

"You're weak but not in any real danger. You need to rest." He sighed, running a hand through his fall of thick, chocolate-colored hair distractedly. Lauren thought he looked different with his usually neat hair rumpled, more human somehow. "How does your arm feel?"

Remembering his saying before the feast that he would have to "tend to her", Lauren felt a sudden rush of apprehension. What exactly did "tending" involve?

"Feels fine," she said, tucking the arm in question, which was still throbbing strongly, into the folds of the bedspread on which she lay. She hoped he wouldn't insist on examining it again.

Kris shook his head. "I wish I could stay with you, but etiquette dictates that I must go back and watch the end of the entertainments."

"Entertainments…right." Lauren tried and failed to suppress a shiver.

Kris pulled back one sleeve and examined the face of a gold Rolex. "I expect to be back in time to check on you before the dawn. In the meantime, Simon has been gracious enough to loan you one of his pets to keep you company."

"Company?" Lauren struggled to sit up and this time Kris sighed and helped her, making sure she was propped up on the pillows comfortably. "I don't need any company," she said, once she was situated. It made her feel better, less vulnerable, to be able to look at him eye to eye instead of looking up from flat on her back.

Kris frowned. "I told you, Lauren, that while we are in this house you must get used to being attended. Naturally you should watch what you say, but I believe the girl is harmless enough. I don't want to leave you alone when you're so weak."

"I'm fine," Lauren insisted stubbornly. To be honest, she felt as if she tried to get up she might fall down but she wasn't about to admit that to Kris. Another of her Gram's sayings flashed through her mind. *Feel like I been rode hard and put up wet.*

A small smile that might have been admiration crossed his face and then Kris rose and went to open the door. At once, a petite girl with long brown hair and rosy cheeks entered the room and ducked her head in a brief nod. Lauren didn't recognize her from the feast but she supposed she might have overlooked her. The girl was wearing a pale rose dress with a cream leather corset on the outside that pushed her small round breasts up and out.

"Lauren, this is Sophia, one of Simon's concubines, I believe?" Kris looked at the girl for confirmation and she nodded nervously.

"Yes, sir."

Kris nodded back. "Very well, I'll leave you two. Sophia," he said sharply, making the girl jump. "If my concubine becomes any weaker or begins to feel ill I must be notified at once. No one is to attend to her but me. Do you understand?"

"Y-yes, sir," the girl stuttered. Plainly Kris made her nervous. "No one but you. I'll see to it, Monsieur Kristov." She ducked her head again.

"Very well. If anything happens to her while I am gone I'll hold you personally responsible. Is that clear?"

"V-very clear, sir." The girl could barely get the words out and she was so red Lauren was afraid she'd burst a blood vessel.

Kris nodded and with a last imperious glare at the hapless girl he left, closing the door behind him. The girl sighed deeply, a relieved sound. She looked around and found a carved wooden chair which she dragged over to the side of the bed.

"Hi." She grinned charmingly and held out a hand. "I'm Sophia, but you can call me Sophie. Phew—your Master's a scary guy, isn't he?"

Lauren took the offered hand in her left one since the right where she'd been bitten still throbbed and ached. "Scary? Kris?" She thought about it for a moment. "Yes, well, I guess he can be when he wants to be. Thank you for coming to sit with me," she added as an afterthought although she would much rather have been alone.

"Oh, no problem," Sophie said carelessly. "I wanted a chance to meet you anyway."

"You did?" Lauren struggled to sit up a little higher and Sophie obligingly adjusted her pillows. "Why?" she asked when she was settled.

Sophie shrugged rose-pink shoulders and tugged at the cream corset. "You mind?" she asked Lauren. "This thing is killing me."

"Be my guest." Lauren indicates she should take it off if she wanted to. "Do...um, do you all dress like that all the time?" she asked, nodding at the leather and lace contraption that now decorated the high carved back of the chair.

Sophie grinned. "Well, for banquets and to promote the club we do. I'd rather wear jeans but Simon doesn't like them. He entered the Second Life back in the eighteen hundreds—thinks women in pants look too masculine or something."

Lauren was surprised. "So you wear whatever he tells you to all the time? Even if it's uncomfortable?"

Sophie shrugged again. "It's part of the deal, you know? Besides, doesn't your Master tell you how to dress?"

Lauren opened her mouth to refute such a ridiculous idea and then remembered the argument about the green gown she was currently wearing. An argument which Kris ultimately had won. She settled for shrugging instead and winced when the motion hurt her arm.

"Are you all right?" Sophie was immediately concerned. "Please tell me if you're not. I really don't want your Master mad at me."

"I'm okay," Lauren assured her. "You don't have to be so nervous about Kris, I won't let him hurt you," she added, realizing even as she spoke that she wasn't at all sure if she could keep her word.

"Thanks." Sophie looked relieved. "You're really lucky, you know? It must be amazing to have a Master that cares about you so much. I mean, to save you from the Taint the way he did and everything."

Lauren felt surprised, especially in light of the love, honor, cherish routine Kris had been giving her about the vampire/concubine relationship. Maybe every relationship was different though. "Wouldn't Simon, I mean, *your* Master, save you?" she asked.

Sophie shrugged again. "I guess it would depend on his mood. I know one thing for sure, he wouldn't have the anti-Taint Serum made exclusively from his own blood. That's what lesser vamps are for—their blood isn't so strong. Your Master is almost as powerful as Simon but he was very specific about that, you know. Nobody's blood but his was to go into the batch of serum they made for you."

"Kris has been...injecting me with his *blood*?" It made her ill and the halfway warm emotions she'd been feeling for him earlier completely evaporated. She'd know she was receiving some kind of medical treatment but she'd never dreamed there was anything like *that* in it.

"Well, yeah." Sophie looked like it was no big deal. "But just the plasma. There's only so much of the Taint they can suck out. The essence helps some and the serum takes care of the rest, ya know?"

"Oh, just the plasma. Right." Lauren's voice sounded far off and distant in her own ears. "Universal Blood and Body Fluid Precautions" rose in her mind, swamping her with the possible ramifications of such a treatment. Not to mention all the effects she would have no idea about because she knew next to nothing about vampire biology. What kind of diseases did they carry? For a moment she tried to sit all the way up, forgetting about her hurt arm. She gave a little gasp of pain when it reminded her that it wouldn't bear any weight, and sank back against the pillows.

"Hey, are you okay? You're looking worse since we started talking." Sophie leaned over her, the big brown eyes widening with worry.

"Fine...I'm fine. Just a little tired is all." Lauren made an effort to keep her voice light. The last thing she needed was

Sophie calling in Kris again. "I'm kind of new at this whole," she waved her unhurt arm in a vague gesture, "concubine thing. And I've never had the, uh, the Taint before. Do you know…with this serum they've been giving me. Do you know if there are ever any adverse reactions? Any contraindications or complications?"

"Adverse…?" Sophie's brow knitted for a moment in incomprehension. "Oh, like side effects?"

"Yes." Lauren nodded strongly.

Sophie laughed and patted her arm reassuringly. "Oh, don't worry about that. No more than just the usual effects of their essence when they inject it into you while they feed. It's just, um…" She seemed to be searching for the right word. "Concentrated, ya know? Like, it causes a stronger bond, longer life span, stuff like that."

"I'm sorry, did you say a 'bond'? And what is essence?" Lauren looked at her, wondering if she'd heard correctly.

"You know—the blue stuff that comes out of their fangs when they bite you? That heals the bite marks afterwards?" Sophie looked confused. "Say, don't you know *anything*?"

"I-I think the Taint must have wiped out some of my memory," Lauren said, thinking fast. She shifted on the bed, trying not to wince as her hurt arm throbbed warningly. "Don't mind me if I ask stupid questions, all right?"

Sophie grinned, apparently satisfied. "Sure. Hey, I'm the *queen* of stupid questions. Simon has been teasing me about it from the first minute he bonded me to him. He's always like, 'I didn't pick you for your brains, Sophie'. And like that." She grinned.

Lauren tried to grin back. There was that word again—bond, bonded. It troubled her greatly. "So do you and Si…your Master have a very strong bond?" she asked, hoping the question wasn't anything out of the ordinary.

"Well, let me think…" Sophie got up and fixed her a drink of water without asking. She held the cup to Lauren's lips who sipped gratefully at the cooling liquid as she waited for the reply.

"I don't guess my bond with my Master is nearly as strong as the one between you and your Master 'cause Simon only feeds from me every fourth or fifth night. So I don't have nearly as much of his essence in my blood as you probably have from your Master."

"He feeds…" Lauren's voice trailed off as she realized that really would be an odd question. Of course Simon fed from this girl. That was part of the vampire/concubine relationship, wasn't it? Even Kris with all his doubletalk didn't try to deny that. She shivered, imagining life as some monster's blood bank. Her arm throbbed.

"'Course he wouldn't feed on me at all if I had the Taint," Sophie rattled on, clearly oblivious to Lauren's slip. She made a face. "Everybody knows how nasty Tainted blood tastes, but your Master wouldn't let anybody else help him draw out the venom."

Lauren felt ill all over again. Here she had been thinking of how sad it was for this girl to live her life as a human blood bank, always open for withdrawals, and Kris had been treating her the same way, while she was unconscious. Feeding on her. Injecting his mysterious "essence" whatever the hell that was, into her as he sucked her blood like some huge leech. Not to mention injecting his own body fluids straight into her veins…her head throbbed and she wondered if she was going to be sick.

"Hey, you *really* don't look good. I better go get your Master." Sophie's big eyes swam in and out of focus and Lauren was dimly aware that the throbbing in her arm had transmuted itself into a fire. She felt as though she'd been injected with a forty-cc syringe of liquid magma.

"No," she tried to say and shake her head, but all that came out was a slight noise of negation that sounded like, "Nnnn."

"I'm going right now!" The look on her face was truly frightened this time and then she was gone, leaving Lauren to slip in and out of darkness.

* * * * *

She was pale and sweating when he reached her, damning himself for ever leaving her in the first place. If he had been any place but The House of Pain he could have flouted convention and stayed with her, but Simon Travain was not one to insult. Besides, Kris already knew that Simon perceived his affection for Lauren as a weakness, one that could conceivably be used against him in the future. Refusing to return to the banquet would have enforced such a notion. He refused to admit, even to himself, that there might be any truth to the idea.

"Lauren," he called softly. Bending down, he raised her right arm, the one that had been bitten. The bruise was fading but there was an angry green blister pulsing just beneath her skin. It was the last of the Taint leaving her system—something he hadn't expected for hours.

He turned angrily to the little concubine that cowered behind him as though waiting for a blow. "Why didn't you come get me earlier?" he demanded. She opened her mouth, brown eyes wide, but apparently couldn't think of anything to say. "Never mind, get out of here." He motioned impatiently at the door and the girl fled, banging it shut behind her as though fleeing a haunted house.

"Lauren?" he said again. Her eyelids fluttered and her lips parted but no sound came out but a low moan. There wasn't a moment to lose. Raising her arm to his lips he prepared to bite.

"No!" His movement had brought her back to a sluggish, semi-dazed consciousness. She tried weakly to pull her arm away from his grip.

"It will only hurt for a moment, I promise," Kris soothed, seeing the fear in her green cat eyes.

"Not...not your blood bank," she muttered, still yanking feebly at the arm which he held so easily.

Kris felt his face tighten even as his fangs extended. So that was how it was—she wasn't only concerned about the pain. "Nevertheless, this is necessary," he said, trying to keep the hurt from his voice.

Not allowing himself to look at the revulsion twisting her lovely features, he pulled her arm to his mouth roughly and bit down, tasting the bitter venom of the Taint only faintly as her cries echoed in his ears.

Chapter Twelve

"No...wait...what—" Lauren felt the words torn out of her throat as he bit her, those sixteen gage needle teeth sinking into the tender, bruised flesh of her arm. There was an instant of searing pain and then it was gone just as suddenly as it had appeared. For a moment there was nothing but sweet relief as the tightness and throbbing in her arm eased almost immediately. Then an entirely new sensation began.

"Oh...*oh!*" It was as though a large hand had reached inside her body and was stroking every major pleasure center at once. Lauren felt her nipples harden under the slippery fabric of the green dress and her sex was suddenly aching and wet with need. What the hell was he doing to her?

"Stop...*stop!*" she begged, but it did no good whatsoever. Kris only continued to suck, to feed on her, she supposed, although even that didn't repulse her as it had only seconds before. *This must be why they don't mind,* she thought breathlessly as the pleasurable sensations continued to grow, threatening to block out all cognitive thought. *This is why the concubines put up with it, being fed on. This feeling, this pleasure...*

And then all logical thought was lost in the sudden overwhelming wave of orgasm that washed over her in a drowning flood.

* * * * *

She was dimly aware that she was crying and that Kris was bathing her forehead with a damp washcloth for the second time that night. The overwhelming pleasure had drained reluctantly from her body but the mortifying display she'd put on, the easy way he'd manipulated her, was still more than fresh.

"There, *Solnyshko*. It's gone now, the Taint is out of your system. You should have no further problems." His voice was low and soothing but it had no effect on her.

"G-get away from me." She sat up, only dimly aware that her arm didn't hurt anymore. Grabbing the wet washcloth she threw it across the room.

Kris sat back, withdrawing behind that blank, white mask that passed for his face when he was offended or upset. "Problems?" He raised one eyebrow sarcastically, making Lauren want to punch him. Not that it would do any good.

"You're Goddamn right I have problems," she raged. He put one finger to his lips and shook his head warningly but Lauren was over her limit for bullshit that night, as her Gram would have said.

"I don't give a damn about being quiet!" she shouted in his pale, handsome face. "You've been lying to me all this time! You told me I was receiving some kind of medication for this...this disease, this Taint, whatever it is. And instead, you're been injecting me with some sick mixture made with your own blood and feeding on me every night like some kind of a..." She couldn't finish the sentence, she was so angry. "I demand to leave here *now*! I demand proper medical attention. You can't keep me here like this."

"Oh, but I can." He was on her suddenly. In a move too fast for her eyes to see, he had her pinned to the bed, his body long and hard and utterly unyielding on top of her own. Lauren struggled but it was like being trapped beneath a fallen stone pillar. "Are you quite done?" Kris' eyes seemed to glow in the dim light, the pale blue fire of his irises had eaten the pupils entirely and seemed deep enough to drown in.

"No!" she hissed, angry despite her fear. "You *lied* to me."

"While I can understand your feeling of betrayal, I never actually lied to you. I only withheld some information that you didn't need to know. Information which, I suppose, that brainless little concubine, Sophia, tangled into a confusing mess which is why you are so upset."

"I'm more than upset —"

A large hand descended over her mouth. "Lauren, lower your voice or I will be forced to gag you. I will not warn you again. Now tell me what has you so...more than upset. Besides my 'feeding' on you, of course." He removed his hand.

"You...you..." Lauren forced herself to lower her voice at the warning she saw in his face. "Sophie said you injected me with a serum made of your own blood. Is that true?" she demanded in a furious whisper.

Kris appeared to consider for a moment and then nodded. "Yes, but then anti-Taint serum is always made using the blood of one of the Second Life because we are immune to the venom. Would you rather have another's blood flowing through your veins at this moment? Someone besides myself, whom you did not even know?"

"I..." Lauren found she didn't have an answer to that. "Are you telling me there's no other way to cure it? Why should I believe you?"

Kris shrugged. "Why should I care whether you believe me, Lauren?" Abruptly, he rolled off her and sat up, still looking perfectly composed. "If it is some disease process that you fear might have passed to you in my blood, you need not worry. We of the Second Life are immune to any and all human ailments. And your next accusation?"

Lauren opened her mouth for a moment, then sat up, glad to be free of his crushing weight. "You've been biting me — feeding off me."

Kris' face was hard and still but he only nodded. "Yes, that was necessary to draw the Taint from your system. Much like drawing out a snake's venom after it has bitten you. Please forgive me for saving your life. I can only promise never to feed from you again unless you invite it." His voice was dry and emotionless.

"Saving my life." She said it with as much sarcasm as she could muster. "If you 'save' me much more you'll drain me dry. I'm probably dangerously anemic already."

"That is not so. Chemicals produced by my body actually encourage the production of red blood cells in your own. If you don't believe me, look at your nail beds."

Unable to stop herself, she glanced down at the healthy pink that colored her fingernails. If her red count had been truly low, they would have been pale instead. "You...I..." Lauren felt her face flush red with anger. He was twisting what she was trying to say. "What about those *chemicals*? Every time you bit me you injected me with your...Sophie called it essence. What else does it do besides encouraging red cell production? What are the side effects? Why did you have to inject me at all?" She threw all the questions to him in a rush but Kris was utterly unflappable.

"Injecting you while I was drawing the Taint from your system was unavoidable. Whenever I bite, my body automatically produces essence. Besides raising your blood count, it also promotes healing. Without it you would still have a large ragged hole in your forearm instead of just the bruise." Kris rose from the bed and got the glass of water Sophie had left on the nightstand. He held it out to Lauren. "Drink."

She started to refuse, but the stern look in his eyes made her shut her mouth. Unwillingly, she took the glass, cool and heavy, and brought it to her lips. She was surprised at how thirsty she was. She drained the entire glass and then handed it back to Kris with a muttered, "Thanks."

"You are most welcome." He sat beside her on the bed again, not touching, but still near enough to be invading her space. "These things are not the only issues that are troubling you, Lauren. Why don't you make a clean breast of it?"

She realized he was asking her to finish her accusations. Feeling suddenly shy and angrier than ever because of it, she tried to think how to phrase her next statement. "Sophie said...she told me that...that..."

Kris raised an eyebrow. "Yes?"

"She said that it formed a bond. When you...when a vampire injects his essence into you." She paused for a moment. "I guess essence is the pale blue liquid I saw on your fangs?"

"It is." Kris opened his mouth briefly and, as though to illustrate his point, two tiny beads of the pale blue liquid appeared on the sharp points of his fangs before he shut it again. "It is a remarkable chemical compound that both pleasures and heals at once. It helps us protect the identity of those who feed us by smoothing away the marks left behind by our fangs and it makes our 'victims' more willing to succumb to our monstrous appetites." His voice was distinctly sarcastic now, though his face remained blank.

"Oh." Lauren felt faint. She looked down at her arm, now only a little bruised but still tender. The faint green lines running up her forearm had completely disappeared. And even though it defied all logical explanation, there were no marks where his fangs had entered her body either. At least, none that she could see. The essence must also be the answer to her rapid healing.

"But the bond," she protested weakly.

"I see that is the 'side effect' which you most fear." Kris frowned. "What Sophie told you was correct but such a bond is useful only if the human being injected plans to stay with the vampire who is doing the feeding and injecting. It takes a period of time for such a bond to grow and certain...actions must be taken in order to seal it—that is to make it permanent. Actions which I have not taken with you.

"I will admit, my plasma in your bloodstream will accelerate the process of bonding and would form a more powerful bond between us if you were inclined to seal it or make it permanent. However, you have made it abundantly clear you are not so inclined."

"I-I hardly know you," Lauren protested, wondering how he could manage to twist everything she said to his own advantage. "And I don't even know what would be involved if we…were to bond."

"Nor do you need to know, as we are not planning on taking that step together." Kris' voice was dry and hard. He moved closer, looking her in the eyes. "But this is still not all that is bothering you. Come, Lauren, confess."

Lauren felt her breathing grow shallow and she wanted in the worst way to look away, yet found that she could not. "When you fed from me, injected me, I felt…" She swallowed, not sure how to put it. "The way my body reacted…" She tried to sound clinical, tried to put the terrifyingly strong orgasm that had been forced from her into dry, medical terms but Kris saw through her.

"Ah yes, the way you came for me, sweet Lauren." His voice was softer now, inviting, tempting. The same voice the snake must have used on Eve in the garden, Lauren thought faintly.

"That," Kris continued, moving even closer to her, "was your body's natural reaction to my essence in your system. It must have been frightening for you to feel such intense pleasure without understanding the source. My apologies for not warning you."

"I…" Lauren wanted to draw away from him but she felt as if she was rooted to the spot, as her Gram would've said.

"Do you know what your problem is, Lauren?" Kris threaded the fingers of one hand through her hair and drew her closer, to whisper in her ear. His breath was warm, with a faint hint of copper and cinnamon, against her neck. "You dream of being dominated and yet you fear to lose control. Were I really your Master, we would spend much time on such issues."

Warm lips brushed along the tender, vulnerable column of her throat, making her breath grow short, making her nipples into hard little points at the tips of her breasts. But behind those lips she could feel the sharp point of his fangs.

"I would teach you to give yourself to me utterly and without reservation," Kris breathed. "How I would savor your submission when it finally came."

"You..." Lauren finally found the strength to pull back from him, from those warm lips, from that large, frighteningly strong hand that was caressing her so gently. "You're not my Master, though, Kris. And you never will be."

"Oh?" He rose and gave her a look so hot it would have melted steel. "We shall see, *Solnyshko.*"

And then he was gone.

Chapter Thirteen

~ ~ ~ ~ ~

"Come here, Lauren," Kris says softly and I come and stand in front of him, still dressed in the schoolgirl plaid with the white shirt and knee socks. He pats his lap softly.

"Sit with me," he tells me and I fold myself gratefully into his lap. No one who knows his ruthless side would believe it, but he is very affectionate. He seems to understand my need to be cuddled and he holds me to him, pressing my head down under his chin so that I can hear his slow, steady heart beat in my ear. I sigh contentedly and give myself up to him entirely, surrendering to the pleasure of just being close and feeling safe.

One of his hands caresses my back, warm and slow and the other reaches up to stroke my breasts. My nipples stiffen against the thin fabric instantly as he swirls his fingertips almost lazily along the front of my blouse.

"Unbutton your blouse, Lauren," he murmurs softly into my hair, which has come mostly undone from the French braid I put it in earlier and is curling around my face in soft tendrils. Fumbling a little, I do as he commands. When the shirt is completely unbuttoned, I pull it open and feel my nipples harden even more from the cold air slipping inside my blouse.

Kris strokes my bare breasts softly, he knows how sensitive I am and just how to make me moan. His featherlight touch makes me gasp and I cry out softly when he pinches first one nipple and then the other, mixing a little pain with the pleasure he is giving me. I shift restlessly on his lap, feeling the crotch of my white panties getting damp all over again. The bulge of his cock against my ass lets me know he is aroused as well.

"What's the matter, Lauren? Am I hurting you?" he asks softly, twisting a nipple between his thumb and finger and watching my face intently for my reaction. His gaze captures mine and will not let me go. He kisses me softly, never releasing my nipple as he waits for my reply—but I find I cannot talk.

"I asked you a question," he says sternly. "I said, am I hurting you?" He gives my nipple another fierce little twist that makes me gasp. "Answer me, Lauren," he instructs me in that low, commanding tone.

"A-a little," I confess, squirming on his lap, loving the sharp little pain he inflicts.

"Do you want me to stop?" he asks, twisting the other nipple now, causing me to arch my back and thrust my breasts outwards, like a cat that wants to be stroked.

"No," I whisper in a small voice.

"What? Speak up," he demands, pinching harder.

"No, Master," I say more loudly, pressing my ass hard against his cock and loving the protective, possessive way he is handling my body.

"Does this arouse you, Lauren? Are you excited?" he asks me, his voice low and intense, pinning me with his pale blue gaze.

"I...yes. It does, I mean, I am," I admit. He kisses me again, never closing his eyes as he takes my mouth gently but thoroughly.

"Let's just see about that," he whispers and his hand moves down from my breasts to my thighs which he spreads open so that he can feel under my skirt. His warm hand cups my damp mound, separated from my sex only by the thin barrier of my cotton panties. Slowly, his fingers begin to work under the elastic side of the underpants so that he can stroke my sex.

"You're wet, Lauren," he says in my ear and I moan as his fingers spread my moist folds and begin to stroke my overly sensitive flesh.

"Yes, Master," I tell him, pressing my pelvis up to meet his fingers and spreading my thighs a little more for him.

"I think you like it when I touch you this way," he murmurs, kissing me again and then trailing a line of burning kisses down my throat. He sucks one nipple into his mouth, nipping me lightly while his fingers continue to rub my folds and press inside my wet sex.

"Yes…oh God. Yes, I do, Master," I moan, writhing on his lap, feeling his cock hard against my ass and wanting it inside me again. Abruptly he stops what he's doing and removes his hand from beneath my panties. I moan with frustration but he only smiles.

"What time is it, Lauren?" he asks me, softly. I look at the clock on the wall.

"Nine o'clock, Master," I whisper, wondering where he is going with this.

"Time for your bath."

Since I'm already in his arms, he simply stands up holding me and carries me upstairs to the room where he took me the first night, the first time he mastered me. I love this room because it is the first place we ever made love and also the place where I finally gave myself to him completely, body and soul as I had waited so long to do. This room is all about submission and beauty and growth.

He lays me gently on the bed and rolls up his sleeves as he fills the tub with warm water. I lie back, watching him, knowing he will want to undress me himself.

At last the tub is full and he comes back to me and undresses me slowly, pulling a piece of clothing off at a time and kissing my body as he does, tenderly and sweetly until I am completely exposed before him.

"Lauren, you are so beautiful," he whispers, raising me naked in his arms and then depositing me gently into the full tub. He pours warm water over my head, being careful not to get any in my eyes and washes my hair with strong fingers, massaging my scalp until I relax utterly, my breasts floating gently on the surface of the water, my nipples hardened by the cool air currents blowing over them.

He rinses my hair and then takes a natural sponge and lathers it with a special herbal soap he ordered just for me. He claims I have sensitive skin which needs special products to keep it smooth and supple but I think he just likes the exotic herbal fragrance which lingers on my body for hours after he bathes me.

He washes me thoroughly from head to toe, paying attention to every part of my body, my neck and back, my fingers and toes, the curves of my buttocks and breasts and the tender cleft between my legs. When he is satisfied that I am clean, he has me stand and pats me dry with a large, fluffy towel. Then he gently caries me back to the bed and lies down beside me, pulling the long white drapes closed around us.

"*Solnyshko*," he whispers and I relax in his arms, knowing he will do whatever he wants with me, whatever he thinks is best. "You're so beautiful," he tells me again. "Tonight I'm going to kiss you everywhere."

One of the things I love about being with Kris is that the spankings, while very stimulating, aren't the sum total of our sexual relationship. There is a loving, tender side to him as well and he tends to my body as carefully as though I were a beloved flower. When he washes me and caresses me it is with the careful air of an owner with a cherished possession or a gardener with a rare blossom. Every word he speaks to me, every touch of his hand on my body, every caress of his mouth on my flesh speaks of his complete ownership of me. And I am more than happy to give up control and let him own me this way.

"Raise your arms over your head, Lauren and don't lower them until I tell you to," he instructs me and I do as I'm told, arching my back and feeling the cool play of air over my naked nipples. Kris has slipped off his shirt but he is still wearing his pants. It makes me feel even more naked and vulnerable when I know he is still clothed.

I feel his mouth cover mine, kissing me thoroughly, tasting me, possessing me. He kisses a trail down my neck to my shoulders, his mouth hot and moist on my flesh. The hollow of my throat receives special attention as do the curves of my breasts. I think I will go insane with wanting before he finally sucks my nipples, one at a time into his mouth. I cry out and thrust my breasts up to meet him, arching my back even more and loving the feel of his wet mouth and hot tongue making maddening swirls around each nipple in turn.

"I love the noises you make when I taste you, Lauren," he tells me. "I'm going to taste you everywhere tonight." His mouth continues to explore my body as he leaves soft, wet kisses along my ribs and belly, making me squirm a little because I'm ticklish, which, of course, he knows. He then bends lower and takes a long, sweet eternity kissing my calves and thighs, running his cheeks, a little scratchy now with five o'clock shadow, along the tender flesh of my inner thighs until I feel like I might scream or beg or both.

"Are you getting hot now, Lauren? Are you getting aroused?" he asks, in that intense voice I have no choice but to answer.

"Yes, Master," I tell him. "I-I can't help it."

"I don't want you to help it, my darling," he answers, amusement obvious in his deep voice. "I love it. In fact, I want you to spread your legs for me so that I can taste how aroused you are right now."

"Oh, Master, I don't know," I whisper in a small voice, squeezing my thighs together. He knows I'm still a little reluctant in this area. It makes me feel nervous, vulnerable in a whole new way. Slowly, he is teaching me to enjoy it but it's still hard to get used to. I begin to lower my arms, for what reason I don't know. To cover myself? But he catches both my wrists in one of his strong hands and pushes my arms firmly back above my head.

"Did I tell you to lower your arms, Lauren?" Kris asks quietly, intensely.

"No, Master," I say in a small voice.

"What did I tell you to do?" he asks me, leaning over my supine body and looking intently and seriously into my eyes.

"...spread...spread my legs," I say in a voice so small it's little more than a whisper.

"What?" he demands, quietly.

"You said to...spread my legs for you, Master," I tell him a little louder.

"Then why haven't you, Lauren?"

"I don't know," I confess. "I think maybe I'm feeling..." I shrug inarticulately, as well as I'm able with my hands pinned above my head.

"Shy?" he suggests, with the barest hint of a smile playing around his mouth. I nod with relief. He understands. My Master always understands me.

"Shy." I echo the word and he smiles at me and kisses me softly on the forehead, nose and mouth oh-so tenderly.

"I know we've talked about this before, Lauren. Sometimes you have to overcome your shyness, and I'm going to help you do that right now. Now spread your legs for me or do I need to discipline you again?" His ice blue gaze is stern—he is leaving this entirely up to me.

He can taste me now as he wants to do or he can spank me first and then taste me, but either way he will end up between my thighs. The thought of a spanking makes me hot but I also adore our more tender lovemaking sessions. Besides, Kris will most likely punish me for my reluctant behavior later on this week, probably tomorrow, so I'll get to have my cake and eat it too by cooperating now. And truly, there's never any real question about submitting to his demands. When I am with him, my body is not my own. I am his own private possession and he does what he pleases with me.

"Yes, Master," I whisper, spreading my thighs for him.

"Good girl," he murmurs. "You're a good girl, Lauren. Spread your legs wide for me, I want to taste you…"

Moaning a little with mingled shame and pleasure I do as he tells me, fighting to keep my arms above my head as his hands and mouth move slowly, teasingly down my body. In truth, this little power struggle, however minor it was, has increased my arousal exponentially — something my Master surely knows.

Nothing excites me more than having him reassert his dominance over me whether he is doing it by whipping me or tenderly touching me as he is now. I never feel that I belong to him so completely as when he is pushing the limits of my comfort, forcing me to relax while he does something to me I would never voluntarily think of or ask for.

My breath catches in my throat for a moment when I feel him finally position himself between my spread thighs. His breath is hot on my naked sex and he spends a few moments just rubbing his cheeks softly against my lower belly and inner thighs, making me ache for him despite my lingering anxiety.

"I'm going to taste you now, Lauren," he tells me softly in that low, intense voice that makes me melt under him. "I'm going to taste you until you come for me. Do you understand?"

"Yes, Master," I whisper, feeling utterly exposed, utterly aroused.

"Good," he whispers, his breath blowing softly against my hot flesh. Then he lowers his head and I can feel him kissing me so tenderly. Kissing my sex the same way he kisses my mouth. I gasp and writhe beneath him and he holds me still, his strong hands on my thighs pressing me even more open for him as he begins to spread my folds with his tongue, exploring my wetness while I cry out under him, softly.

"Oh Master…" I moan as his tongue makes magical figure eights around the throbbing bud of my clitoris. He loves to drive me crazy this way, though it's still hard for me to understand why he enjoys it so much. He says he loves the taste of me, of this most intimate and secret part of my body. And I think he also enjoys pushing my boundaries. He savors my reluctant submission and enjoys punishing me for my reluctance later on.

He is spreading me even wider now, if that is possible, sucking my clit and then pressing his tongue inside me, penetrating me gently but forcefully. Despite my initial reluctance to let him taste me, I have to admit that Kris is excellent at this. He seems to know exactly how my body works and what causes me the most pleasure or torment at any given time.

"Oh…God." I am moaning, tilting my hips up to his mouth, losing control as I'm sure he knew I would. His tongue laps at me gently but firmly and I am unable to keep my arms over my head anymore. Despite the eventual punishment I know it will entail, or perhaps because of it, I have to bring them down and bury my hands in his thick, silky dark chocolate hair.

"Oh…oh…" I am riding his tongue now, pressing against him fiercely, squeezing my thighs tightly against the sides of his head and feeling the stubble on his cheeks scrape my tender flesh raw. That little bit of pain magnifies the pleasure he is giving me a thousand times and I peak suddenly, grinding against his tormenting mouth shamelessly and crying out my pleasure in a throaty, breathless voice while I clench my hands in his hair.

Kris gives me a moment to come down and then he slowly raises his head from between my thighs and looks at me. There is an undeniable heat in his eyes. He likes giving me pleasure as much as he likes giving me pain. Sometimes I just think he likes making me lose control.

"Lauren." He frowns at me and his voice is deep and intense. His tone is severe. "You lowered your arms before I told you to."

"I…yes, Master, I did," I admit softly, struggling to regain my normal breathing. I am still tingling all over with pleasure and it's hard not to pant.

"I'm going to have to punish you for that, Lauren," he tells me, blue eyes blazing. "Once again I'm afraid your behavior has been very bad. Unacceptable."

"I-I couldn't help it." I whisper, trying to meet his gaze and failing. Kris has climbed back up the bed now and he is lying almost on top of me, between my still spread thighs. This position makes me feel so exposed, so vulnerable and I think he knows it. With one quick thrust he can be inside me and I can feel his hardness pressing insistently against my thigh even through his dark trousers.

"You disobeyed me and there's no excuse for that," he tells me sternly. "Bad behavior must be punished."

"Wh-what are you going to do to me?" I ask him softly.

He sits up abruptly. "I'm afraid I'm going to have to spank you to teach you a lesson. Come here and lay over my lap facedown, Lauren," he instructs. I shiver as I comply.

My prone position has put my belly against the crotch of his wool pants and I can feel his cock digging into me mercilessly as he shifts his legs under me and prepares to strike. I wiggle and squirm nervously but he surprises me by holding me firmly in his lap and caressing my ass instead of slapping it.

"You've been a naughty girl, Lauren, but I don't want to hurt you," he tells me softly, running his hands from my tender ass cheeks and upper thighs to the small of my back. "So I'm going to give you a few good slaps to teach you a lesson and then I'll let you suck me a while for the rest of your punishment. Do you understand?"

"Yes, Master," I whisper, trying to restrain my excitement. I love to suck him, to take him in my mouth and give him back some of the pleasure he has given me. I can hardly wait to taste him and lick the salty droplets from the head of his cock and then take it as far down my throat as I can.

"Good, Lauren. I'm going to spank you now. You know you deserve this."

Kris spanks my bottom hard and I cry out in mingled pain and pleasure as he punishes my tender flesh. I writhe against his lap and feel his cock throb strongly against my belly again. I know how much it turns him on to punish me like this even though, as he says, he is careful not to hurt me too badly. His hand connects with my ass again and I can't help arching my back and spreading my thighs while he does this, he just makes me so hot when he punishes me.

"Oh, Master…" I gasp, as he continues to spank me. "I'm sorry my behavior was so bad. I know I need to be punished. Let me…suck your cock. Put your cock in my mouth. Show me how bad I've been…"

He groans when I say this and the spanking stops abruptly. He buries one strong hand in my hair and pulls my face commandingly down to his crotch. I hear the harsh grate of his zipper going down and then his hard flesh is rubbing against my cheek.

"All right, Lauren," he tells me, his voice barely above a whisper, he is straining so hard to keep control of himself. "I want you to suck me now and you'd better do a good job."

"Yes, Master," I whisper before bending my head to inhale the spicy, masculine scent of him and rub the large, plum-shaped head against my lips. I swirl my tongue expertly around his hard shaft, eliciting a muffled groan to my satisfaction before I take him fully into my mouth.

"Oh, Lauren…" he whispers, pressing his hips up to me so that more of his cock slides between my lips. "You do that very well," he tells me, threading his fingers through my hair as I suck him, feeling the familiar pleasure of submission twisting in my lower belly as I do. This is something Kris taught me, how to suck him just right and I take great pleasure in practicing my skills and proving what a good teacher he is.

Remembering his lessons makes me even more aroused and I suck harder, taking more of his cock in my mouth and down my throat and feeling my tender nipples brush against his thigh as I work on him. Kris groans and thrusts between my lips.

His shaft is thick and the salty-sweet bitter taste like tears at the back of my throat tells me he's very close.

Suddenly, his hand in my hair is pulling me back and his cock is sliding out of my mouth. I make a small sound of protest and disappointment. Why did he stop me?

"I want to finish inside you, Lauren," he tells me, by way of explanation. "Lie on your back and spread your legs for me. I need to fuck you hard and deep tonight."

Moaning, I roll over feeling the cool bedspread tickle my back again. I love it when he tells me exactly how he's going to fuck me. I spread my thighs wide to receive him and then he is over me, on me, and I feel his slick shaft pressing against my wet sex as he penetrates me deeply with a single, rough thrust.

"Oh, Master!" I shout, feeling him ride me hard and fast, pressing my legs over his shoulders to get as deeply inside me as he can. "Fuck me hard, punish me!" I beg him.

He answers me with a particularly sharp thrust and he leans over to kiss me while he takes me. I continue to beg for his cock inside me while he presses deeper and deeper, claiming me, filling me, fucking me.

We can't last long, going at this frantic pace. The position he had me in ensures that he rubs against my swollen clit with every thrust and I am already sensitive due to the orgasm he gave me earlier. Soon I feel myself falling over the edge of pleasure again, crying and scratching his broad back as I do, marking him the same way he has marked me with pain and love. He buries himself to the hilt inside me and pulses into me, filling me completely...

"Lauren," he whispers, "I love you so much."

"Kris," I gasp, loving the taste of his name on my lips. "I love you too...my Master."

~ ~ ~ ~ ~

Lauren woke the next morning from a most disturbing dream to find herself in the huge bed and her first thought was *Where the hell am I?* Then a barrage of images and memories came rushing back—waking, tied to this same bed, Kris' pale blue eyes as he told her the roles they must play while they stayed at The House of Pain, the banquet and the horrific "entertainment" afterwards, and the way her body had reacted when he bit her…it was almost too much. *At least I didn't wake tied up this time.*

She twisted her head to see if the black satin ties were still hanging from the bedposts. They were—and lying on the floor beside the bed was a crumpled piece of stiff parchment. Her stomach did a lazy flip-flop when she remembered what was written on that piece of paper.

Kris had sent Sophie back with a note after he had left, presumably for his bed or coffin or wherever it was he slept, the night before. In a faultless cursive that looked antique to her eyes, used to modern handwriting, which was little more than a scribble, were these words:

Lauren,

I will come to you at sunset tomorrow night. Under no circumstances are you to leave your rooms. Ring the bell for anything you require and it will be brought to you. Do not disobey me unless you are prepared to pay the consequences. If you are wondering what these might be, look no farther than the bedposts and your own imagination. I believe that particular scenario was entitled Love Bonds, *was it not?*

K.

The note from her "Master" had been the final straw. Reading it, she had been alternately hot and cold. How dare he threaten her with her own fantasy, which he had read without her permission? It was one of her favorites too—filled with hot, unwilling submission. Lauren had read the words twice more before balling up the note and throwing it over the side of the bed. It was a long time before she could get to sleep, and the heat building between her thighs each time she thought of his warning didn't help. That was probably what had brought on the strange dream…the dream Kris had a starring role in.

Now she sat up, her head spinning with all the crazy things that had been happening to her lately. She examined her arm in the strong sunlight coming through the small windows to the right of the bed. It looked perfectly normal, as though nothing had ever happened to it, even the bruise was gone. She shook her head, was her quick and efficient healing all due to the "essence" from Kris' bite?

The scientist in her wondered about the chemical composition of the pale blue liquid, not that she planned to stay around here long enough to get a sample. She had known last night, after reading his note, exactly what she had to do.

Lauren Wright intended to get the hell out.

Slipping to the floor, she checked her watch, which was placed on top of her neatly folded pile of clothes on the nightstand. She saw with some dismay that it was well past one in the afternoon, why had she slept so late? Could it have something to do with Kris or had she just been tired out by her recent illness? Actually, she felt remarkably well but she was going to have less of a head start than she'd hoped. Still, her mind was made up.

Squaring her shoulders, Lauren rapidly shed the silky green dress, which she was still wearing from the night before, and slid into the black blouse and skirt combo she'd worn to Le Jardin what seemed like a million years ago. Someone had thoughtfully washed and pressed the outfit and she wished briefly that she had time for a quick shower before dressing. She hated to put on clean clothes without feeling fresh herself, but there was no time.

Before she left, she searched the room rapidly for the Mac, hoping against hope that Kris had hidden it somewhere in the room. But she had no luck. Once more, the Mac with all her private fantasies was gone. At this point, though, Lauren was less concerned about her laptop than in getting out of this freak show in one piece. Kris could post her fantasies on the internet or hang them on a billboard by the side of the highway for all she cared—she just wanted *out*.

It wasn't just the weird and horrifying things she'd witnessed at Simon's banquet last night either, that made her so anxious to leave. It was the way Kris touched her, the sound of his voice, low and commanding in her ear, the way he made her melt when she felt his hands on her body, his mouth on hers.

Could it have something to do with the "bond" that must be forming between them as a result of his essence and plasma in her bloodstream? But to Lauren, that felt like a cop-out, an excuse. She was too honest to lie to herself about this—the way she felt around Kris frightened the hell out of her. She might dream of submission to a stern and loving Master, but that didn't mean Lauren ever wanted those dreams to become a reality. She was walking much too close to the line here and it was time to leave while she was still her own person.

Making a final sweeping glance of the opulent bedroom, she slipped out the heavy wooden door and found herself in a long corridor made of gray stone. Trying to remember the way she and Kris had taken the night before, she walked confidently forward, glad that the place seemed to be deserted. The click of her heels echoed against the stones, bouncing the sound back to her and making her feel more like she was in a catacomb under some ancient city instead of in the back of a Houston sex club.

Soon Lauren found herself at an intersection she didn't remember from the night before. Choosing arbitrarily, she took a right and found herself at yet another crossway in barely a minute. Frowning, she took another right and kept going. The hallway had to lead somewhere...it did, to another hallway. After making several more turns, she decided maybe she should go back. But there were no landmarks to go by, no doors or windows, not even a painting she could remember to help her find her way back. Impossible as it might seem, she was lost.

"Well, well, my dear. And how lovely to see you this fine day."

Lauren whirled around, looking for the source of the soft, oily voice. She would have sworn she was perfectly alone. The long echoing corridor stretched out ahead of her and behind her like an empty stone throat.

"And what might you be looking for, *ma chérie*? You appear to be most distressingly lost."

Lauren turned again and found herself suddenly face to face with Simon, their host. "Oh! Y-you startled me." She put a hand to her chest and took a step back.

"Ah, but such was not my intention, my dear. My most sincere apologies." Smiling, he took a step forward to fill in the gap she had put between them. Lauren wondered if all vampires were so pushy about invading your personal space or if it was just because both Simon and Kris were European. At least the tall vampire wasn't referring to himself in the third person today, a trait she found intensely annoying.

Simon was dressed in plain black jeans, a black silk shirt open to the waist that showed a smooth expanse of muscled, hairless chest, and a magnificent jeweled collar that appeared to be solid gold and was a good three inches thick. There was a diamond at the center of the collar that was too huge and vulgar to be anything but real. For a moment, Lauren wondered how he could possibly be up at this hour and then remembered that Kris had told her that while vampires preferred to sleep during the daytime, it wasn't a necessity.

"Might I inquire again exactly what you were seeking? You *want* to tell me, no?" The soft, oily voice held just a hint of menace and there was a coldness to his deep brown eyes. Lauren realized she'd been just standing there, staring at him for the past minute without saying a word.

"I...uh..." she fumbled. Just then her stomach rumbled loudly, saving her the trouble.

"Ah, but you are hungry." Simon's face softened a little. He flicked his heavy mane of black curls over one broad shoulder and offered her his arm. "Let us go to the kitchen, *ma chérie*, and see what we can find for you to dine on."

Completely against her will, Lauren found herself taking his arm and heading down the long stone corridor again. Only this time, instead of being an impenetrable maze, the moment they turned the next corner, they found themselves walking into a wide, airy kitchen. It was spacious and well-appointed, but the kitchen had no windows or doors other than the one they had just come through and Lauren would have sworn that it hadn't been there before.

"It's like the looking glass house," she murmured to herself, feeling confused.

"Pardon?" Simon raised one perfectly shaped eyebrow at her in a polite question.

Lauren cleared her throat, feeling silly. "Your club reminds me of a book I read when I was a little girl — *Through The Looking Glass*."

"Oh yes, I know the book well." Simon nodded for her to continue, leading her to a large butcher block table with several chairs placed around its clean wooden surface.

"Well, you know the part where Alice is trying to get to the little hill at the top of the garden but she keeps getting sent back inside the house every time she tries? And the harder she tries, the less success she has in getting where she wants to go. That's the way it was when I was trying to get...when I was trying to find your kitchen," Lauren finished rather lamely.

"Indeed." Simon smiled politely. "A most fascinating concept. Lewis Carroll had quite the most vivid imagination of anyone I was ever privileged to meet."

Lauren felt her mouth go dry. "Y-you knew Lewis Carroll?"

Simon laughed, a rich sound that was almost tangible. Lauren felt like she should have been able to break pieces of that laugh off and stuff them in her mouth like chocolate. Her stomach rumbled again.

"I cannot claim to have known him intimately, *ma chérie*, but I did meet him on several occasions after his books became popular. Remind me to tell you sometime of how he came up with the idea for his poem, *The Jabberwocky*. A most amusing anecdote." Simon nodded and turned to the stove. "Now, what might you be craving for your lunch, my dear?"

"Oh, no, I couldn't possibly ask you to go to any trouble," Lauren protested, realizing he intended to cook for her himself. She was very much afraid she might end up eating duck with crimson sauce or mashed potatoes with corpuscle gravy if Simon did the cooking. "Why don't you let me?" she said, half rising from her seat.

Simon waved her back down. "Nonsense, my dear, you're my guest. I *insist*. Now then, what will it be?"

"Nothing fancy or imported," Lauren said quickly. "Maybe just a sandwich?"

Now her host looked almost insulted. "*Mon Dieu*, I spent years under some of the finest chefs in the court of the Sun King himself and she asks me for a *sandwich*?" He shook his head, a disgusted look on his handsome face. "The modern American palate has truly gone to hell."

"Ah…what would you recommend?" Lauren asked, hoping to avoid offense. She reached for an excuse. "I'm just still feeling kind of under the weather, if you know what I mean, and I'm not sure if my stomach can handle anything too rich."

"Well, then," Simon looked almost mollified. "I'm certain I can make you something that will settle your stomach and tempt your senses at the same time, my dear. How about a delicious plate of fluffy scrambled eggs?"

"Oh, that sounds just perfect." Lauren nodded eagerly. Eggs sounded safe enough and hopefully wouldn't be too much trouble.

"With just a few delightful slivers of black truffle and a touch of Gruyére cheese," Simon finished, going to get the necessary ingredients out of the huge, brushed steel refrigerator which looked like it could hold enough food to feed an army.

"Oh…" Lauren didn't know what to say to this but apparently her input wasn't required.

Simon closed the refrigerator door with his hip and laid his armful of ingredients on the counter. "Would you like to help, my dear? That is, if you're feeling well enough."

"Oh yes, I feel much better," Lauren said without thinking, then when he raised a quizzical eyebrow at her, she added quickly, "I mean, much better than I was last night, anyway."

"Excellent." Simon nodded for her to join him at the counter. "Now then, you may grate the cheese while I prepare the eggs. It's been a very long time since I had such a lovely sous-chef to order around." He smiled at her charmingly and Lauren actually found herself smiling back. She had to remind herself sternly that no matter how charming and personable he seemed, Simon was still the same person who had orchestrated last night's bloody "entertainment" at the banquet.

"Were you...did you really cook at the court of the Sun King?" she asked, taking the lump of pale cheese and beginning to grate.

"I was a nobleman, actually. One of Louie's favorite lackeys, in fact. But I had developed an interest in cooking from my old nurse and it pleased the King to indulge my whims. So I was 'apprenticed' to one of his head chefs. I used to make him the most amusing dishes, strictly for entertainment value, you understand." Simon smiled fondly at the memory. "That was back when I was mortal, long before I entered my Second Life." He sighed. "Though I was there in jest, I managed to pick up much that was useful in my time spent in the kitchens of Versailles. Are you done with the cheese, my dear?"

"Oh, yes. I think this is plenty." Lauren nodded to the fine, white pile of cheese and he nodded approvingly.

"Excellent, then you may start on the truffle." He produced what looked, to Lauren, like a roundish, dirty black root that fit in the palm of his neatly manicured hand and a very sharp little knife. "Have you ever worked with black truffles before, my dear?"

"Well…no." Lauren was afraid he might get offended again if she admitted she'd never worked with any kind of truffles at all. The thing in his hand was giving off a pungent earthy aroma that she didn't find at all appetizing.

"A pity. They're far superior to the white truffles one finds in Italy. True black truffles of the finest quality grow only in French soil. Now, like this…see?" Simon demonstrated by shaving off a tiny sliver of the black root-like thing with the sharp paring knife and then handed them both to Lauren. "Just a touch, mind you, my dear. A very little goes a long way."

Lauren was glad to hear that as she planned to eat around the black slivers of truffle as much as possible. She thought of her diet, probably blown to hell after last night's banquet. Eggs and cheese were Atkins-approved but… "You wouldn't happen to know how many carbs are in this, would you?" she asked, gesturing with the knife at the truffle.

Simon raised a dark eyebrow delicately. "Pardon?"

"Never mind." Lauren felt her face go red and went back to shaving tiny black slivers.

"So," Simon continued, adding heavy whipping cream and some mysterious spices she didn't dare ask about to the egg mixture which he was beating in a blue china bowl. "You must be a very special woman to have so captured the heart of the elusive Nickoli Kristov. However did you two meet?"

Lauren shrugged, feeling distinctly uneasy. This part of their "story" was something she hadn't discussed with Kris and she wasn't sure exactly what to say. "The usual way," she said at last, deciding to try and make a joke about it. "I was working in a blood bank and he came in and ordered a nonfat double tall O negative with extra foam."

"Ah." Simon eyed her, still beating the eggs vigorously. "You do not wish to speak of it. I understand why the attentions of such a one as Monsieur Kristov would make you shy, *ma chérie*. He is a most intriguing figure. Tell me, have you known him long?"

"Not…very long," Lauren murmured, pretending to concentrated on shaving the truffle just right. She had a feeling she was on very thin ice here.

"And yet you have captured his heart, though he has never been known to take a concubine before. I confess that I find it most singular." Simon had stopped beating the egg mixture and was staring at her with intense concentration.

"We just…hit it off." Lauren shrugged uneasily and showed him the truffle shavings. She'd made a lot more of the pungent little slivers than she wanted to out of pure nervousness. "Is this enough?"

Simon nodded, not answering her question verbally, and went back to the eggs, which he began to pour into a large, cast iron skillet. "He has told you of his tragic past, I suppose," he said, almost offhandedly as he poured. A cloud of fragrant steam rose around his head.

"Tragic past?" Lauren watched with fascination as he whisked the eggs delicately, adding the tiny black truffle shavings at intervals. It was beginning to smell delicious, little black specks notwithstanding.

"Indeed." Simon watched the eggs critically, never looking at her as he worked them into a fluffy mass. "It is a sad tale, but I am sure you would rather hear it from him. Wouldn't you?" He said it with finality, giving her a sidelong glance.

Lauren had the feeling she was being tested in some way but she wasn't sure how. And the chance to learn anything about the mysterious man she'd spent the last few days and nights with was too tempting to resist.

"I'm sure Kris won't mind if you tell me, he probably just hasn't gotten around to it yet." She handed Simon the cheese he was reaching for, and watched as he sprinkled the mixture over the yellow, black-speckled mass of scrambled eggs. "That is, if it's common knowledge," she added.

"Very well." Simon looked at her sharply and then continued adding cheese. "It is not, as you say, common knowledge, but I will tell you anyway. Perhaps when I have told you what I know you can answer some questions for me as well. And exchange of information as it were."

Lauren looked at him warily. "Well, you can ask but I can't promise I'll answer." Was this exchange of information another bizarre vampire custom or just Simon "fishin' for trash" as her Gram might've said? She thought it might be a little of both.

Simon nodded. "That is fair enough. I admire honesty in one so lovely. I will give you a taste of my information and then, perhaps, you will give me a taste of yours. First, however, tell me what you wish for a drink to accompany your eggs. Perhaps some champagne? I have a very dry, lively vintage that would complement this dish quite well."

"Uh…it's a little early for me." Lauren smiled, hoping she wouldn't offend him. "Maybe just unsweetened tea?" she asked hopefully.

Simon made a face but no comment. He plated the eggs which smelled very good indeed, and set the plate along with a steaming cup of hot tea on the butcher block table. "Eat."

Lauren picked up the fork which he had placed beside the plate and took a hesitant nibble of the eggs. To her surprise, they were delicious, even the tiny black speckles of truffle. "These are *wonderful*," she told Simon, who watched with approval as she dug in. "The best eggs I've ever had."

"But of course." He gave her a little smile and sat beside her at the table. "But my culinary skills are not the most fascinating topic of conversation, are they, *Solnyshko*?"

Lauren looked up sharply, but her mouth was full. By the time she managed to swallow, Simon was already continuing. She listened and ate the eggs as the soft, oily voice flowed over her in a semi-hypnotic steam.

"Your Monsieur Kristov has an interesting past. Involving, as all interesting pasts do, a failed and heartbreaking romance."

"How do you know about Kris' past? No offense but he isn't exactly the most open kind of guy and I didn't get the impression that you two were confidants." That was putting it mildly but she couldn't think of a more delicate way to skirt the issue of the deep animosity between Kris and the other vampire.

Simon raised one dark eyebrow and shook back his luxurious mane of hair. "As to that, *ma chérie*, I have my sources. Monsieur Kristov is, as you say, most mysterious but his past is perhaps less hidden than he would like to believe." He laughed softly. "As are many things."

"But...why do you care?" She forked up more eggs.

Simon smiled unpleasantly. "What is the old saying? Keep your allies close but your enemies closer. I find it pays to be informed, my dear. It pays very well indeed, in fact."

The look on his face made Lauren distinctly uncomfortable and she made an effort to get back to the earlier topic of conversation. "So, what happened with his romance? Did the girl die?"

"Not immediately, would you like more tea?" Simon rose and considerately refilled her glass before sitting down again.

"The romance?" Lauren reminded him, curious despite herself. She wondered if she could believe one word in ten that Simon told her.

"His family did not approve. She was not the one his father had chosen for him." Simon shrugged. "Arranged marriages were common in that day—no one thought of marrying for love. It simply was not done."

"So his family broke them up?" Lauren was beginning to think that his information was more general than concrete. Turning to a subject she was more interested in anyway, she asked, "If you know so much, who turned Kris into a vampire in the first place?" She remembered Kris saying that he had never seen the face of the vampire that turned him. If Simon pretended to know she could probably discount everything else he'd told her, not that it had been that much in the first place. Who *didn't* have a failed romance in their past?

But Simon only frowned. "Now *that*, *chérie*, is a question for the ages. Certainly it was someone very strong, perhaps even one of the old Masters—one who was born to the Second Life without ever having passed through the First."

Lauren frowned, the scientist in her having difficulty with this concept. "So they just spring into being? Full-blown vampires as it were?" she asked skeptically. "Like toadstools shooting up after a rain?"

Simon looked distinctly uncomfortable. "No indeed. They are created when a woman late in term is bitten and turned. The vampiric essence penetrates the womb and the child is born to the Second Life, as I told you, without ever having lived the First." He made a face. "They are monsters—hideous to look upon but very strong. Centuries ago the Council declared them anathema and forbid their creation so the only ones heard of now are, of course, very old."

"What makes you think it was one of those that made Kris like he is...a vampire, I mean?" Once more Lauren found herself fascinated by a whole other branch of science and physiology.

Simon frowned. "He is too strong, your Master. Too strong for his age, which is quite young among our kind, to have been made by any other than such a one." He sighed. "But whoever Kristov's Maker was, I was unable to learn his or her identity, and it is certain that he does not know himself."

"Why?" Lauren wondered how he'd come to that conclusion, though she knew it to be true.

"Because." Simon's face darkened. "If he knew the identity of his Maker he would surely have attempted to kill him by now."

Thinking about the bitterness in his voice when he spoke of what he was and the faceless vampire who had made him that way, Lauren was inclined to agree. But she wasn't about to let an opportunity to learn more about vampire society pass her by, especially when Simon was being so much more free with his information than Kris had ever been.

"Is that...something you do? The, uh, ones of the Second Life?" she asked, taking a sip of her tea.

"Kill our Makers?" Simon looked amused. "As a rule, no. But then, most of us are given a choice as to our eternal fate as your Monsieur Kristov was not. There exists a bond between the Maker and the Made that provides a bit of...shall we say *vulnerability* on the Maker's part. We have a saying among us, when the time is right only the Made can unmake his Maker."

"I would have thought it would be the other way around, that the Maker would be stronger." Lauren took another sip of tea. "And I thought you couldn't use your powers against each other. Kris told me something like that when he was trying to convince me vampires were real."

"There are exceptions to every rule." Simon made a dismissive gesture. "And there are many ways and sayings that we keep, we of the Second Life, that are mostly from the old country. I am certain Kris has told you that we vampires are not romanticized there as we are here in America." He smiled.

"Is it that way all over, uh, the old country then? Because I know Kris is Russian and you're French..." Lauren looked at him, an eyebrow raised in question.

Simon nodded. "Indeed but after my time at Versailles and my conversion to the Second Life I wandered the world a bit. I found your Master Kris' country most amusing." He smiled charmingly.

"Do you know that even today Russian peasants are suspicious of strangers and any they suspect might be outsiders or creatures of the night? They have rituals to protect themselves from us. For instance, before burying a corpse, they will likely as not insert a long sewing needle into its navel. They believe this will keep it from becoming a vampire."

Lauren put a hand to her mouth. "Still, in this day and age? But how can people be so..."

"Ignorant? Superstitious?" Simon grinned at her, and for the first time she caught a glimpse of razor-sharp fangs beneath his full red lips. "It is foolish, no doubt, but at least they try to protect themselves from such as us. While the modern world marches on, blissfully unaware of the evil that stalks their nighttime streets. What is the quote I am looking for? Ah yes… 'When ignorance is bliss, 'tis foolish to be wise.' Would you not agree, *ma chérie*?"

"I-I'm not…" Suddenly Lauren's mouth was dry and there was a bitter taste on the back of her tongue that had nothing to do with the swallow of tea she'd just taken. Simon's brown eyes, so calm and charming at the beginning of their conversation, had grown huge in his pale face. They reminded her of Kris' eyes the night before, when the iris had eaten the pupil of his eyes, leaving nothing but a sea of blue fire. But in Kris' eyes, she had seen desire and need.

In the bottomless brown depths of Simon's eyes there was only a cold curiosity, as though he were wondering what she might look like if he pulled off her arms and legs, the way cruel boys pulled the wings off flies. It was as though he had been wearing a mask of charming good humor for their entire encounter and had suddenly decided to drop it and show himself as he really was.

"There are some who believe the world at large should remain ignorant of us, of those of the Second Life that walk among them," Simon went on, still staring at her in that cold, calculating way. "But of course, your Monsieur Kristov is not one of those. Is he?"

"N-no," Lauren whispered through numb lips. She wanted to lean away from him but she felt frozen to the spot.

"Now." Simon leaned even closer, pushing her plate and glass to one side. "I have told you my information about your precious Master. You will tell me everything you know about the Brotherhood of Truth. Because you *want* to, don't you, my dear?" He took one of her hands in both of his and stroked it gently, sending a shiver of pure revulsion up Lauren's spine. The disgust gave her a measure of courage she hadn't had before.

"I don't know anything about the Brotherhood," she said, sitting up and away from him and extracting her hand from his grip with some difficulty. "But even if I did I wouldn't tell you. I don't know where you stand and my first loyalty is to Kris." Even as she said the words, she realized they were the truth. Kris might be maddening, irritating, and vaguely insulting but she trusted him. Trusted him to take care of her and not to hurt her or let anyone else in this crazy funhouse of a club hurt her. It was an emotion Simon could never inspire in anyone.

He sat back, brown eyes going back to normal, and gave her a look that was clearly surprised. "Well, you *are* a special one, aren't you, my dear? Such a strong-willed child. I begin to see why Kristov is so taken with you."

Lauren glared back at him, her heart beating in her throat, hoping he wouldn't try anything. "I-I'd like to go back to my room now. Thank you for the lovely lunch," she made herself say. Back to her room to wait for Kris. She shuddered when she remembered his note and the possible consequences for this little outing. But there was no other choice.

Escape was plainly impossible.

Chapter Fourteen

~ ~ ~ ~ ~

The door is rough, a wooden plank, no more. Not richly carved like the ones in his father's house. There is no fine carpet underfoot and servants do not stand ready to tend his every need but he doesn't care. Has never cared for such luxuries, such trivialities.

All that matters is that beyond the rough wooden door is the woman he loves, the woman who professes to love him above all others. She is willing to come away with him even though it will mean hardship and poverty. She is used to such things. He is not, but he knows he will feel neither hunger nor cold if she is with him.

He has changed since last they met, a clandestine meeting in the woods at twilight because her father's shop was being watched. A meeting to plan their escape — their future. He was taken and changed on the way here, taken by a creature with no face that he could see.

A whisper of cold breath, a bright pain at the side of his neck, as though someone was pressing there with a pair of daggers. He tried to cry out and could not. A pleasure unlike any other, sweet and deadly, was flowing through his veins. And the taste of some cold nectar, the taste of damnation, he now knows, was pressed to his lips. A voice, low and grating, like the hinges of an ancient door clotted with dirt, whispered in his ear.

"Drink. Drink, Nickoli, and if you survive my dark communion we shall see how your father and family will care for you, how your sweet Jenica will love you when you are one of the damned." He tried to resist, to refuse, but when he opened his mouth to speak, the cold, salty tide rolled in, drowning the words on his tongue. His body convulsed, caught fire in a sweeping tide of pain that felt like death. That was death. Then, the pain was replaced by pleasure, a sweeter fire in his veins, causing a rude hunger to awaken.

He is different now, new in ways he cannot understand but the love remains. They had spoken the vows to each other, though there was no priest to see—had sworn eternal love despite poverty and illness, had vowed to let nothing divide them from each other. "I love you so much." The setting sun—the last sunset he ever saw—was turning her honey-gold hair to fire when she spoke those words, his Jenica. They are the words that give him the courage to knock on the rough wooden door despite his change.

She comes at once, summoned by the hollow sound. She is dressed in her best cloak, a bag of provisions, securely tied, in one hand. Ready to leave, to start a new life with him.

"Where were you? I was getting so worried!"

"Jenica…"

At the sound of her name she looks up at last, stops fussing with her pack and her cloak. He knows what he must look like to her, blood on his throat, blood on his lips. Blood looks black in the moonlight but there is no mistaking the stain of that unforgivable sin.

"Holy Virgin!" She takes a step back, her hand fumbling at the neck of her simple, homespun dress, reaching for her crucifix.

"Jenica, it's only me. I'm changed now but I'm still me. I still love you…" He takes a step forward and she stumbles back. Finally finding the carved wooden crucifix, she yanks it free, the leather cord around her neck snapping with her haste to get it up and between them. A shield against him. A shield against evil.

"Back! Get back! You're not Nickoli! Y-you're an abomination!"

Monster, she calls him. Evil, undead, unclean…unwanted.

He tries to explain how it happened, that he never chose it, that he would never hurt her...but her shrieks split the night and there is a loud clatter of footsteps from the stairs inside her house, the hoarse shout of her father's voice, angry and protective.

He runs into the night, rejected, alone, damned. Driven more by her revulsion than the puny crucifix he runs until even his changed body cannot keep the pace anymore and he collapses, a broken thing, all his reserves of energy exhausted. There in the darkness he feels the thirst for blood for the first time. The insatiable need to feed. And he knows she was right about him.

Right about everything.

~ ~ ~ ~ ~

Kris woke suddenly, feeling the last threads of sunlight leave the sky as he always did, awake or asleep. He rose, pushing back the lid of Simon's plush guest coffin, and greeting the new night. But the darkness around him, usually so comforting, was still tainted with the vivid images. He shook his head, it was more than forty years since the dream had tormented him. Why should it come back to him now?

You know why. He frowned, trying to push the thought aside. Jenica. She had been the only woman he ever loved. He could have taken Jenica that night, could have Clouded her mind and tied her to him using all his new tricks. Tricks that now were so very old. Even now she could be living by his side, for a concubine could live as long as her Master, and those of the Second Life were immortal unless consumed by sunlight or fire.

But it wouldn't have been living—it would have been merely existing. To keep one who does not want to be kept, who longs for freedom, who hates and reviles her keeper...no, Kris had vowed never to do that. Once he had seen that look in her eyes, the fear and disgust, he knew she could never be his.

Old thoughts, old hurts. He hadn't thought of Jenica in so long and now the dream came to him again, opening the old wound. Why now? Again the answer came—*You know why*. It was Lauren Wright, so much like the woman he had once loved. Not so much in appearance, though the luxurious blonde hair was much the same. But in disposition and personality. Hot-tempered, beautiful, willful, intelligent, strong—all the things he craved in a woman, in a concubine. And add to that, she was completely immune to vampire mind tricks. There could be no forcing or coercing her submission—it would have to be a gift freely given. A gift she would never give...

Kris frowned. There was no point in thinking such things. Lauren had shown, beyond a shadow of a doubt, that she had no interest in such a relationship. No more than Jenica had so long ago. *I'm not your blood bank*, she'd said to him the night before. Very well, he would not feed from her anymore, although, in truth, he'd only been sucking the Taint from her system, not actually feeding in the way natural for one of the Second Life.

That kind of feeding, a deep feeding, could be a most pleasurable experience for all involved. To make love to her as he drove his fangs into her body, into the sweet, pulsing vein that throbbed in her pale, vulnerable throat. To drink from her as he thrust inside her wet, willing cunt, filling her with himself, with his cock, with his essence. To master her and taste her submission as she gave herself utterly to him...but such an action would seal the bond between them—a bond she wanted no part of.

There were other things to think of. For one, payment must be rendered for Simon's hospitality. Another worry was getting safe passage to the headquarters of The Brotherhood where he could pass along his information before the Gathering. And the Gathering itself was only a few nights away. There was barely enough time to finish their obligatory stay here at The House of Pain and get to Prague where it was being held.

Kris ran a hand through his hair. He must be prepared, with the formula for NuBlood on hand. It was his greatest ambition to once more be a legitimate part of society. To take back what had been taken from him on that dark night, by a vampire whose face he had never seen.

It was important to keep these goals in mind and not let himself be distracted by a ridiculous infatuation with a woman he could never have.

Kris resolved to put it out of his mind and went to find their host to talk about payment.

* * * * *

"Ah, Kristov, so pleasant to see you." Simon was, as usual, being attended by several human concubines of either sex. "But I see you have something on your mind, no?" He sat up a little and leaned forward in the stone throne when Kris made an abbreviated bow.

"Indeed. I am here to discus the matter of payment." Kris found it best to get straight to the point in such matters. If allowed to do it, Simon would mince around the issue all night, simply for the fun of watching his guest squirm.

"Payment? But you cannot be thinking of leaving so soon." Simon shook his head in mock disappointment.

"Indeed. But Lauren, while still weak, is mostly cured and a fourth of a fortnight is almost up. We cannot possibly intrude upon your hospitality any longer," Kris said firmly. "So I have come to ask the price of your generous shelter and succor as tradition demands."

"Alas, that such things are necessary." Simon made a rueful face as though he truly regretted having to charge Kris anything for the use of his safe house. "But it is, as you so cleverly point out, tradition. And who are we to break with tradition, *mon cher*?" He tapped one long finger against the side of his cheek as though thinking hard. "Well, as you say that your sweet Lauren is cured of the Taint, I suppose I will be happy to accept a Host Tasting as my fee for the use of my guest room." He cast a sly glance at Kris, as though waiting for him to react.

Kris frowned. "I very much regret it, but Lauren is still weak from blood loss and her system is currently flooded with my own essence. Perhaps there is something else I can do to repay our debt?"

Simon frowned petulantly. "It is difficult to think of anything we would rather have more than a taste of your strong-willed concubine, Kris. We had the distinct pleasure of her company today at an impromptu luncheon and were most taken with her."

"Even in your own house you cannot enter the room of another without asking. I forbid Lauren to leave her room and I cannot imagine her inviting you in for any reason." Kris struggled to keep the possessive rage out of his voice. Surely Simon was lying or in some way bending the truth.

"Well, she might have invited us in if we had asked her correctly but as it happens, she was wandering in our little maze, *outside* her room, and such tactics were not necessary. Not that they would have been useful even had we attempted to employ them." Simon smirked at him, lounging in the gray throne like a lazy cat.

"What…exactly do you mean?" Kris felt his heart grow cold in his chest. Surely she hadn't disobeyed direct orders and wandered out of her room. Surely not…

"Oh yes, *mon cher*, she came to me." Simon was clearly enjoying his dismay, so much that he slipped and referred to himself in the singular sense. "She came and we had a most enlightening conversation. I begin to see, I think, why you are so very taken with her. She is an exquisite creature and so headstrong. So perfectly immune to our little tricks, no?"

Kris opened his mouth and closed it again. There was no point in denying anything. Simon knew about her immunity to Clouding but at least he hadn't mentioned anything about artificial blood. As long as he simply thought Lauren was a lovely human with immunity to vampire mind tricks and had no idea of her secret there was some hope, however slim.

Kris promised himself there would be hell to pay if he could get her out of The House of Pain safely. Simon's next words made that seem much less likely.

"Yes, a lovely concubine and so very *unique*. I dare say she would prove quite invaluable in many ways to any one of the Second Life lucky enough to own her."

"Lauren has a mind of her own," Kris said, determined not to give anything else away.

Simon nodded. "So she does, so she does. I suggest, Monsieur Kristov, that you think of a suitable payment for your stay here or I will be more than glad to claim both her mind and the luscious body that contains it. Do I make myself perfectly clear?" He sat up, lifting an eyebrow, his face coldly calculating.

"Indeed." Kris made another abbreviated bow and turned to go, his mind in a whirl. How the hell was he going to get them out of here now?

Chapter Fifteen

"What did you tell Simon?"

His voice was low and forceful enough to send a shiver up her spine. Lauren sat up in the bathtub so suddenly that she splashed water all over the black- and white-tiled floor. A bath to relax her had seemed like a good idea at the time, but she hadn't planned on Kris catching her in it.

"Do you mind? Can't I get any privacy around here?" She clutched at the tiny black washcloth, trying ineffectually to hide herself from his angry, ice blue gaze.

"Not until you tell me what was said during your little foray into the club today. You remember, the one you took, though I specifically told you *not* to?" He strode up to the side of the tub and Lauren saw that the white dress shirt he was wearing was unbuttoned at the throat and the sleeves were rolled up to his elbows. He looked like a man who was about to do some serious and difficult work.

"Y-you can't order me around. I'm my own person," she shot back. Her defiant reply was somewhat spoiled by the way she hunched lower in the tub, trying to hide herself from him.

"How many times do I have to explain this, Lauren? While we are here you are *not* your own person. You belong to me. Stand up." His gaze was positively glacial.

"No." Her voice came out smaller and a lot less confident than she would have liked but her refusal did her no good at all. Kris simply reached down and pulled her up with one strong hand hooked under her arm. Water splashed and spattered all around them.

"Do you not think that if I ask you not to do something, I have a good reason for it?" he demanded in a low, intense voice.

"I asked you not to leave the room for your own good, because I was afraid you would do exactly what you *did* do."

"W-what are you t-talking about?" Her teeth were chattering as her naked, heated body was suddenly exposed to the cool air. She could feel her nipples hardening into tight little points. "S-Simon asked me ab-bout The Brotherhood of Truth and I t-told him I d-didn't know anything!" She thought about telling Kris how eager Simon had been to share his own information with her and then decided he was already angry enough. How much more pissed off might he be if she told him that a rival had been gathering tidbits about his past for whatever reason?

"Here." He made her step all the way out of the tub and began to rub her down with a large towel. His motions were smooth and quick and somehow managed to convey his anger much more effectively than his words had.

Lauren felt like her heart was beating somewhere in the vicinity of her throat. "I didn't tell him *anything*," she protested again, in a low voice.

"And that is precisely why he knows you are different and the reason he is demanding such an outrageous host fee—because you told him nothing when another human would have spilled all they know." Kris wrapped the damp towel around her shoulders and propelled her out into the bedroom.

"W-wait!" Lauren protested. "Different how? What are you talking about?"

Kris sat her firmly on the bed and began pacing, running one large hand through his dark chocolate hair distractedly. Lauren longed to reach for something drier and less revealing than the towel but didn't dare to move. She had never seen him this angry and upset before. Finally he stopped pacing for a moment and looked her directly in the eye.

"You want to make love with me right now, Lauren," he said in a low, firm voice.

"*What?*" Lauren felt her cheeks color crimson with embarrassment and anger. "I most certainly do *not!*"

"Do you see?" Kris gestured at her, no longer bothering to lower his voice. "*That* is how you are different. You are immune to our mind tricks as no human should be. When I put a suggestion in your mind it should instantly take root and grow into an absolute certainty. But you shrug off my Clouding as though it was of no consequence, just as you shrugged off Simon's. He knows about you now, knows of your unique ability."

Lauren stared at him, a lot of things were beginning to make sense. "The way you talked to me when we first met...the way Henry was so convinced you represented a legitimate pharmaceutical company..."

Kris nodded impatiently. "Yes, yes, all of that was my doing. But on you it didn't work, perhaps because of your rare blood type, who can say? The point is that a human who is immune to vampire mind tricks would be a precious commodity indeed in our community. Your value for espionage alone would be immeasurable. You could be sent to a rival's house and he or she would never dream that you were only pretending to follow orders, that you were listening to their most intimate secrets..."

Lauren wrapped the towel more tightly around herself. "My *value*? You're talking like I'm just some piece of property to be bought and sold."

Kris whirled to face her. "And that is exactly what you would be in the hands of our host."

"But he can't...I mean I don't belong to him. You said while I was here I belonged..." Lauren bit her lip to stop the words but it was too late.

"Yes, while you are here you belong to *me*. But how can I protect you if you will not do as I say?"

"I don't understand. I-is Simon going to try and take me away from you?" Just the thought of those cold brown eyes and

Evangeline Anderson

those perfectly manicured hands on her body made her feel ill, almost nauseous.

"Not if we can pay his price," Kris muttered darkly. "Which *you* have raised immeasurably with your arrogant disobedience."

"What price?" Lauren asked, apprehensively. She vividly remembered her speculation about the nature of the "obligation" Simon and Kris had spoken of the night before.

"The host price—our debt of obligation to Simon for letting us stay here and helping me save your life." Kris ran a hand through his hair again and shook his head. "Without the shelter of this house, and the use of Simon's medical facilities to make the anti-Taint serum, you would be dead right now."

"All right..." Lauren ran a hand through her own hair, which was coming down in damp waves from the loose chignon she'd put it in to keep it from getting wet in the bath. "So I made the price higher, I'm sorry. But didn't you tell me th-that the people in your community are wealthy beyond human imaging, that money was no object?"

"That," Kris grated, stalking over to her. "Is precisely why we will be expected to pay in an entirely different coin. This isn't a matter of emptying your bank account, Lauren, unless you count your funds in blood and pain."

"Blood and...what are you saying?" Her lips felt numb and she clutched the towel closer.

Kris leaned over her, one hand planted firmly on either side of her body, invading her space. "Do you remember the little 'entertainment' we saw last night that made you so very ill? The pain...the exquisite agony that the concubine being flogged had to endure before his Mistress finally healed him?"

"Y-you don't mean that. You can't!" Lauren wanted to back away from him, but somehow he had caught both her wrists and pinned them neatly to her sides. Fighting him was like fighting a brick wall and his eyes were like a river of blue fire.

"Oh, but I do. Consider the name of this place, Lauren. Do you think that Simon calls it The House of Pain because of the paltry human sex play that goes on in the front of his club? Only a concubine bonded to one of the Second Life can survive true suffering—pain without the surcease of death. Only here can agony be made into an art form."

"Oh, my God!" Lauren struggled wildly to be free, heedless of the way her towel fell away, exposing her breasts. She felt cold all over—terrified. "Just because you could heal me afterwards doesn't give you the right t-to torture me!" She gasped out the words, not wanting to cry but the tears were very close to the surface despite her best efforts.

Then Kris was taking her in his arms. Lauren didn't make it easy for him. She stiffened her body as much as possible but all the efforts were completely useless. She still found herself folded neatly into his lap while he stroked her damp hair. "Hush, my darling. Be still, *Solnyshko*. I will never harm you like that—I could not and would not." The slow, strong rhythm of his heart filled her ears and his large hands stoked her gently.

At last the words, spoken in a low, soothing voice, penetrated her fear and she felt herself relax, very unwillingly, against his broad chest. His wild, fresh scent filled her senses and the crisp white shirt he wore felt good against her hot cheek.

"I-if you don't intend to do that to me why bring it up?" she asked at last. She was still angry but so tired, the emotion he'd put her through was exhausting. She realized that, for whatever reason, she trusted Kris. A part of her had nearly broken when she thought he would really betray that trust.

"I simply wanted you to understand that this is no game we are playing, Lauren." His large hand continued to stroke soothingly through her hair as he spoke. "The secret that you hold is in hot contention among my kind, which was already a difficulty. I had hoped to get you well and get the both of us out of here quickly and easily." He sighed. "But nothing is ever easy with Simon Travain. Now that he knows you are special— unique—he will stop at nothing to own you, to make you his.

One way of doing that is to make the host price so high that we cannot possibly pay it."

Lauren sat up, pushing away from him and he allowed it. He was still looking at her seriously, his pale blue eyes filled with genuine worry. "I don't understand," she said again, yanking nervously on her towel. "What is he asking for? Be-besides me." Her voice faltered on the last word. The idea seemed so foreign—so crazy.

Was she, Dr. Lauren Wright, the top of her class at Baylor Medical School, holder of degrees in hematology and oncology and the inventor of the world's first all-inclusive artificial blood substitute, *really* talking about being sold into some kind of sexual slavery? It wasn't possible, was it? And yet the grave look in Kris' ice blue eyes told her that it was.

"The only things that have value to Simon Travain are blood, which all of us of the Second Life value, and entertainment." Kris spoke slowly, and his chiseled, pale features were knotted into a mask of deep concentration. "Under other circumstances, I would allow him a Host Tasting and that would be the end of our debt."

"A…tasting? Of me—my blood?" Lauren's voice quivered, despite all she could do to stop it. The thought of Simon sinking his teeth into her…it was worse than revolting, it was terrifying. "Kris, I don't think…I could stand that."

"Of course not, I know very well how you feel about being fed upon." His voice was cold and slightly sarcastic. "And it would not solve our problem. Simon will be even less willing to let you go once he has tasted your blood. But even if you did not have such strong feelings on the subject, there is too much of my essence in you right now to make such a tasting any less than agony for you."

"What do you mean?" Lauren looked at him a little fearfully.

Kris looked at her directly. "Do you remember the way you reacted last night when I sucked the last of the Taint from your arm?"

Lauren felt her cheeks go red at the memory of the searing pleasure and the almost frighteningly strong orgasm that had rushed over her. Wordlessly she nodded.

"It was like making love in a way, do you not think?" Kris caressed the side of her face with one gentle finger, brushing back a strand of honey-blonde hair that was hanging in her eyes.

Lauren ducked her head, not wanting to look at him, not wanting to feel the fire his touch stirred. "Yes...I suppose in a way."

"That was because your body has absorbed so much of my essence and the part of my blood that was in the anti-Taint serum."

His voice hardened and he withdrew his hand. "There is a bond starting between us. Whether we wish for it or not, it is the direct consequence of my actions to cure you of the Taint. It is by no means complete, nor do I intend to let it become so. But while you are so closely tied to me if another vampire was to feed from you it would be much different from the sensations you experienced last night." His voice grew softer, but no less intense. "If Simon, or any other was to bite you now and inject their essence into your bloodstream, it would not feel like making love—it would feel to you very much like rape."

Lauren sucked in her breath and looked at him, frightened. "So then...if le-letting Simon bite me is out, and some horrible display of pain for his entertainment is out, what are we going to do?"

Kris shook his head. "I told you he values entertainment. But pain is not the only form of entertainment, *Solnyshko*."

"Th-then what?" She clutched the towel closer to her breasts, already afraid she knew the answer.

Kris gave her a look that was deadly serious. "Sex."

Chapter Sixteen

"Huh-uh. No way…" She was backing away from him, the flimsy towel still clutched to her chest and he could smell her fear, hot and vivid in the air between them. But there was another scent riding the air currents between them, tickling his vampiric scenes like a rare spice—desire.

"Come, Lauren," he said, trying to control both his irritation and his lust. "There is no other way."

"I thought I made it clear when we met that I'm not into that kind of thing." Her voice was sharp and the slanted green eyes were wide with fright. Kris knew her need was hidden so deeply that she probably couldn't even perceive it herself.

"Well, I think it is something you will have to 'get into' very quickly if I am going to be allowed to leave here and take you with me," Kris said sternly. "There is another banquet tonight. After the meal we will perform for the audience and tomorrow evening we will be on a plane to Prague where the Gathering is to be held. You will participate with me in this or you will stay here, languishing in The House of Pain, until Simon grows tired of you, which would in all probability take a very long time. Am I making myself clear?"

"But, Kris…" Her eyes were suspiciously bright and it was obvious she was struggling not to cry. "You're only giving me three options," she protested. "Let th-that monster bite me and inject his…" She shook her head, then forced herself to go on. "Let Simon taste my blood, allow you to whip me half to death and then heal me, or have sex with you in front of an audience. What am I supposed to do?"

"Pick one." He knew his voice sounded harsh, but the little human had to understand that there were no other choices if they were going to make it out of here together and alive. "I am very strong, as my kind go, Lauren," he said, trying to make her understand. "And I grow stronger as the century mark of my entry to the Second Life—my equinox—draws near. But even I cannot fight off a whole house full of angry, vengeful vampires. And, as you found out today, no one Simon does not wish to leave can get out. The stone maze you found yourself in is part of his defenses. It keeps his prisoners in and his enemies out. Even I cannot defeat it. We will leave only when he allows us to."

"B-but…" She was still making excuses, he saw wearily. "But why should he let us go at all then? What's to stop him from saying it's not good enough…whatever we do, I mean?"

Kris ran a hand through his hair. "There is a code among us that is not to be broken. If most of those seated at the table tonight are entertained, they will indicate their pleasure and Simon cannot go against the majority. And if Simon himself is sufficiently impressed, he will have nothing more to say."

"But *why*? Why does it have to be sex?" She crouched against the head of the bed, a stubborn look of incomprehension in her eyes.

Kris' patience snapped. "Because that is the way it is between those of the Second Life!" He leaned forward, taking her by the arms to make his point. "I do not understand why you are making such a protest about this, Lauren. It is, after all, one of your own fantasies. "'Forced to Perform' is, I believe, the name you gave it."

"How dare you!" she struggled against his restraining hands. "Stop throwing up to me the fact that you read all my most private thoughts! It's unconscionable and unethical and…and…completely despicable, you son of a bitch!"

"Wait…" Kris released her so suddenly that she fell back on the mattress in a most undignified way. While she was still struggling to right herself he was thinking furiously.

"Y-you..." Lauren's green eyes were narrowed to slits and she looked mad enough to bite him.

Kris turned to her, a smile spreading over his face. "I think I can solve our little difficulty, Lauren."

She drew away from him warily, her blonde hair in a gorgeous disarray around her bare shoulders. "What are you talking about?"

Kris felt the sharp pleasure-pain as his fangs extended in excitement, he saw her eyes grow wide at the sight. "I said, I think I know how to get us out of our impossible situation. And I can do it without giving you to Simon, or whipping you, or making love to you in front of an audience." He smiled at her again, showing the perfect white points of his fangs.

She frowned distrustfully. "I don't understand."

"The answer lies," Kris told her, "in your much-valued fantasies."

Chapter Seventeen

"No way…you're not feeding on me. I told you last night, I'm nobody's blood bank." Lauren said the words as forcefully as she could, keeping her eyes on his fangs, while backing off the bed. But before her feet could hit the floor, he had her by the arm and was pulling her back.

"Don't be silly." He looked mildly annoyed. "I said the answer lies in your fantasies, of which, I have read every one. None of them involve allowing anyone to drink your blood." He stroked a soothing hand over her arm. "Although, it can be a very erotic act between a Master and his concubine, I have promised you that I will never drink from you again until you ask me to. It is a promise I intend to keep."

"Well…good," Lauren muttered, not certain what else to say. She wasn't exactly sure why she felt so strongly about letting Kris feed from her again, after all, it wasn't exactly an unpleasant experience.

Maybe it was just that the act would make her too vulnerable. It felt dangerous somehow and besides, hadn't he told her that every time he bit her he injected his essence and strengthened the bond growing between them? So far she hadn't seen any evidence of that bond, except for her strong aversion to letting another vampire touch her or drink from her, but she was afraid that other signs might manifest themselves very shortly.

"If you aren't going t-to break your promise, then what do you have in mind?" she asked him, moving away from the hand still stroking her arm. It was easier to think when he wasn't touching her.

"I told you, we will be using your fantasies. One in particular, I think, *Naughty Girl*." He smiled at her charmingly, the ice blue gaze full of fire. "It was one of my favorites, as I recall."

He got off the bed, leaving Lauren to gape after him, and pulled the long, silken cord hanging from the ceiling. A brisk tinkling accompanied his action and soon a light tapping sounded on the heavy wooden door. Kris went to it and opened it only a crack. He murmured something to the person on the other side of the door and then closed it again.

"There, it should be here shortly." He came back to sit on the bed, a very satisfied smile on his face. Lauren, however, wasn't feeling quite so cheerful about the whole situation.

"I thought you said we could do this without having sex," she said at last, stating the matter bluntly.

Kris raised an eyebrow at her, maddeningly superior. "And so we shall. Why do you ask?"

"I ask because I wrote that fantasy and I know how it ends." Lauren felt as though her whole body was blushing but she refused to drop her gaze. "In that particular scenario it ends with th-the Master bending the girl…"

"You," Kris said.

"What?" She looked at him.

"You," he repeated quietly. "You write all of your fantasies in the first person, Lauren and they are beautiful, poetic visions of pure lust. Own them."

"Fine," she snapped, finally goaded into speaking plainly. "At the end of the *Naughty Girl* fantasy, my Master bends me over the arm of the couch a-and…"

"And fucks you." Kris' deep voice was quiet but expressive. It seemed to reach inside her body and stroke her like a physical touch. His gaze raked over her until she wished the inadequate towel she was wearing was made of lead. Anything to shield out his intense stare.

"I…" Lauren shivered. If her face got much hotter from blushing, her hair might catch fire. "Yes," she said at last. "That's what happens."

"And that is what will *appear* to happen," Kris assured her. "I will have you in the proper position and everything will appear to be as it is in your fantasy but I will not actually…" he hesitated, "make love to you, however much I may wish to."

Lauren swallowed, thinking of the vulnerable position she would be in, of being bare and having nothing between her naked sex and the thick cock she'd felt throbbing against her thigh when he'd pulled her close and kissed her the other night. "How do I know you won't?" she asked, trying to keep the tremble out of her voice.

Kris smiled at her, a lazy smile full of unspoken promises. "You'll just have to trust me, Lauren."

She opened her mouth to say she would do no such thing, but a light rapping at the door interrupted her.

"Ah." He got up and went to the door, opened it a crack and took whatever it was he had called for earlier. Shutting the door, he turned back to the bed, holding a large bag. "These should do nicely," he remarked, sitting the bag on the bed beside her and beginning to examine its contents. "Trust Simon to have such things already on hand."

Lauren still couldn't talk. Out of the crackling paper bag, Kris had pulled an entire schoolgirl outfit, exactly like the one she'd described in her fantasy. There was a scratchy, stiff, white button-down shirt that went with a short, blue and green pleated, plaid skirt. A pair of white knee socks and some Mary Jane shoes completed the outfit. There was, Lauren noted with a sense of complete unreality, no panties or bra.

At last she found her voice. "Are you…" She swallowed and made herself go on. "Are you serious about this?"

"Indeed, deadly serious." Kris nodded. "The idea is to direct the audience's attention to the content of the scenario rather than the actual mechanics of it. We will distract their eyes with props and capture their imaginations with your so-compelling fantasy which will be much more interesting and arresting than a simple show of sex would be. It is the story which makes the sex interesting in the first place, don't you think?"

"I must think so," Lauren heard herself saying. "Or I wouldn't have written it."

"Very true." Kris' brow was knotted in thought. "Now, I believe the Master in your little scenario is wearing a formal business suit, which is not a problem for me as I have several..."

Lauren realized she'd never seen him wear anything else. "Do you ever dress in anything besides suits?" she asked, her curiosity momentarily overcoming her worry about acting out her fantasy. "I mean, do you dress like the other, uh, vampires I've seen around here?"

She looked at him, trying to imagine him in the rock-star clothes Simon always seemed to be wearing and just couldn't picture it. Kris was always going to be more *GQ* than *Rolling Stone.*

Kris raised an eyebrow at her. "In the time that I came from a gentleman was always dressed correctly," he said, his voice a bit cold. "It was disrespectful to do otherwise. Do you dislike my mode of dressing?"

"Well, no." Lauren shrugged. "I was just wondering if you ever wore anything less, I don't know, formal." She tried to imagine Kris shopping at The Gap or Old Navy and couldn't do it.

"I see no reason to dress any other way. Here, speaking of dressing..." Kris handed her the outfit which she grasped awkwardly in both hands. "The banquet will be beginning shortly and I had to guess at your sizes. Try it on."

"Fine." She turned to march into the bathroom with the armload of clothes, but he stopped her with a word.

"No. You will get rid of that ridiculous towel and put it on here," he commanded. "How many times do I have to tell you not to hide yourself from me?"

Would he never stop ordering her around? Knowing it was an argument she would ultimately lose, Lauren settled for a compromise. Keeping her back to him she dropped the towel on the plush maroon carpet and started to get dressed, relived when Kris said nothing.

Either he was an excellent judge of women's clothing or it was just a lucky guess but the schoolgirl outfit fit her exactly as she had imagined it would when she wrote the *Naughty Girl* fantasy. The stiff white cotton shirt felt scratchy against her tender nipples, still hard from the chilly air of the room, and the pleated skirt was so short it barely covered the tops of her thighs. Even the shoes and socks were the right size.

"There." She turned to face him, gesturing at herself impatiently. "Do I meet with your approval, *Master*?" She meant the word to come out sarcastically but she found, to her dismay, that just saying it caused a warm rush of heat throughout her body and a quivering in her belly. She had never called him that outside her dreams.

Kris sat forward on the bed and smiled at her, as though he knew the effect her own words had on her. "Almost, but let down your hair."

"Oh…" She had forgotten that half of her hair was still up in the loose chignon on top of her head. She reached up and released it, shaking it out around her shoulders. "Now?" She looked at him questioningly.

"Now raise your skirt."

Lauren licked her lips nervously. "What?"

"I said raise your skirt, Lauren." The fire in his eyes and the low, commanding tone twisted something inside her, made her feel hot and cold at the same time.

She shook her head, unable to make herself speak.

"Come here." He gestured for her and almost against her will, she found herself stepping closer to the bed until she was standing between his spread thighs. She wasn't sure why she obeyed. Maybe it was the effect of actually wearing an outfit she had fantasized about for so long or maybe it was simply the way his low, masterful tone seemed to melt her will to refuse.

Though he was still sitting on the bed and she was standing, their eyes were about level. Kris' had gone that deep, drowning blue, the pupils almost completely swallowed up in an ocean of icy fire.

"Don't make me ask you again to do as I say." He raised a hand and pushed the silky fall of blonde hair out of her face, almost tenderly. "The time for pretending is over. While we still remain in this place, I am your Master and you will act accordingly. Do you understand?"

Unable to make herself talk, Lauren simply nodded.

"Good." Kris nodded approvingly. "Then do as I told you."

Feeling like she was standing outside herself, watching a woman who looked exactly like her do things she would never actually do, Lauren slowly reached down to grasp the hem of the pleated skirt and raised it.

"Very good." The warm approval in his voice sent a shiver of desire through her. "Now spread you legs, I want to touch you." Feeling like her knees might buckle at any moment, Lauren did as he asked.

He reached out to stroke her, cupping the soft mound of her naked sex in one large hand. "So soft...so sweet," he murmured.

Lauren felt like her heart was trying to get out of her chest it was pounding so hard but there was still the strange feeling of watching someone else. She wasn't really doing this, was she? Standing here with her legs spread, watching Kris caress her— touch her this way?

"You're wet, Lauren." With one long finger, he parted the lips of her cunt, now swollen with need and desire, and stroked gently over her sensitive clit. Lauren gasped, feeling a fire race through her body at the light, teasing touch.

"Come closer, I want to kiss you while I touch you," he whispered. She leaned forward, bracing her hands on his broad shoulders and he wrapped one arm around her waist while keeping the other between her legs.

Just like the night before, he took her mouth with a fierce hunger and a possessiveness that took her breath away. He kissed her as though he had every right to her body and soul— as though he owned her.

As he parted her lips, demanding entrance with his tongue, two long, strong fingers slipped deeply inside her wet cunt, pressing upwards into her passage with hot, rhythmic thrusts that made her moan. Kris devoured her mouth ruthlessly, hungrily swallowing the soft noise. She knew that if she hadn't been holding on to his shoulders she would have fallen from the intense pleasure, the hot sensation of his fingers inside her.

At last he pulled back from the kiss although his fingers remained buried deep in her body. He kissed a slow trail from the hollow of her throat to the sensitive, ticklish spot behind her ear. "Do you like this, *Solnyshko*? Does this feel good? Can you imagine how much better it would feel if you submitted to me entirely and it was my cock inside you instead?"

Lauren gasped at those hot words, murmured low in her ear. Under her grasping fingers, the crisp white linen of his shirt was wrinkling as she held on tight, trying to stay upright.

"Don't," she gasped as he thrust inside her, slow and hot and utterly sure of himself and the effect he was having on her. "Don't…" But she didn't know if she was begging him to stop at once or to never stop.

Without warning, he suddenly slipped his fingers out of her, making her bite her lip against a cry of frustration. Kris put a little space between them, devouring her with his eyes.

"I see you're blonde all over," he said, lightly stroking the dark blonde bush that nestled between her thighs. "It is lovely but I'm afraid it doesn't quite match up to your fantasy."

"Wh-what do you mean?" It was an effort to make herself talk, to say anything while she was aching from the heat of his touch. She wished she could have more of his hands and mouth on her body and yet she knew she was on a treacherously slippery slope. It amazed her that Kris was able to sit there and speak so calmly while she felt as if she was going to shake herself to pieces.

"I believe in the fantasy you were bare." He stroked her soft mound of blonde curls again. "Shaved."

"Oh…oh, no!" His words sank in and it was as though the spell she was under had been broken. She tried to back away from him but the arm around her waist held her fast.

"Let me go!" Lauren insisted, determined not to go any farther with this madness. "Fantasy or not, I don't intend to do that to myself."

"I know." Kris' grin was hotly predatory and the needle-sharp points of his fangs glistened in the dim light of the room. "I am going to do it to you."

Chapter Eighteen

He could tell by the rapid beat of her heart and the wild look in her eyes that he had hit upon some deep fear or desire, perhaps both.

"No!" She struggled ineffectually to get free, but he held her easily.

"Be still, Lauren," he commanded and was gratified when she quieted in his arms. "I think," he said softly, reaching up to kiss away the single silver tear that had made its way down her cheek, "that it is time for a lesson in submission."

"I'll submit to you any other way but don't…" She took a deep breath, her green eyes still wide with fright. "Don't do that. I…Kris, I'm frightened."

"You need never be frightened of me," he told her tenderly. "But soon it will be time for the banquet and everything must be exactly right. I want you to play your role to perfection, but how can you if you are not properly in character, hmm? Besides—" he kissed her gently on the mouth, relishing the taste of fear and desire on those soft pink lips. "I believe I owe you a punishment for the way you behaved today when you left the room against my orders. Do you remember what I wrote to you in my note?"

She nodded, soft blonde hair falling around her face and shoulders in a wild, beautiful mane. "Yes, b-but I thought you were just kidding. Just threatening me to keep me in line."

"Perhaps it is time you learned that I never make idle threats." He cupped her cheek tenderly and gave her another kiss before releasing her to get up and fix the bed to his satisfaction. "Take off your costume," he said over his shoulder as he worked. "I wouldn't wish to ruin it."

He didn't watch her to be sure she was following orders, but he heard soft rustling noises behind him as he straightened the covers and spread the towel in the center where she would be sitting. He could feel her eyes on his back as he arranged the pillows and tested the black satin ties, to make sure they were still firmly affixed to the bedposts.

"Come to me, Lauren," he said at last, when he had everything in readiness. He patted the bed invitingly and gave her a stern look. "Don't make me come and get you."

For a moment it looked as though she would resist. She shook her head, her arms crossed protectively across her full breasts and her thighs pressed tightly together, too frightened to talk.

"Do you really think I will allow you to refuse?" Kris asked her, meeting her anxious gaze with his own. "Do you?"

Hesitantly she shook her head, and with a little sigh of resignation, she came to him.

He thought he had never seen her look more lovely than when she climbed naked into the center of the bed and positioned herself on the black towel. There were tears standing in her eyes and a slow, sexual flush had crept up the soft, creamy valley between her full breasts. Her nipples looked painfully erect.

"Please," she whispered, her soft voice trembling ever so slightly. "Don't...at least don't tie me up."

"But that is part of it," Kris told her gently. "Don't cry, my darling. You know it is true—you wrote it, not I." He reached above her head to fasten first one and then the other slender wrist firmly in place with the strong black satin. She didn't resist him, but the wide green eyes finally overflowed in tears of shame.

"Come, *Solnyshko*, don't cry. At least I will not bind your feet." He took her face in his hands and kissed the tears away gently, savoring the sweet taste of her submission and need. If she had truly not wished him to do this, Kris would have stopped at once. But under her frightened protests and embarrassed tears, there was another emotion that his vampiric senses could not fail to pick up. Her desire hung heavy in the air around them, a sweet, musky scent that came from her every pore and called to him in a way he could not disregard.

He went to the bathroom to fetch the necessary items, a bowl of warm water, a razor and some shaving gel, and returned to the bedroom to find her quiet and almost resigned.

"Now, spread your legs for me and don't move," he instructed. She did as he asked, turning her head to bury her face in one shoulder, not willing to watch as he lathered the small blonde bush between her legs. Carefully, Kris began to shave, baring her sweet sex as she moaned softly in her throat and trembled beneath his touch.

"That's right, my darling, hold very still," he murmured, enjoying the feel of her soft, slippery skin beneath his fingertips. He was almost done when his knuckles brushed over her deep pink interior, causing her to gasp and buck her hips. His grip on the razor slipped slightly and the blade nicked her, just at the very top of her sweet wet slit.

Lauren cried out and bit her lip against the small pain and Kris put down the razor and stroked her trembling thigh soothingly by way of apology. He patted her dry, admiring the way she looked so much more naked now, so much more vulnerable and bare. The soft lips of her sex were smooth and exposed, as naked as a little girl's, but the hot pink center and the swollen clit he could see throbbing with need was all woman. He took a deep breath, filling his senses with the rich aroma of a female in heat. She needed this, though she could not admit it to herself. And yet, there was still the matter of her small injury to deal with.

It was a tiny cut, no more than a scratch, but as Kris watched the small crimson drop of blood well up in the minute wound, he knew he could not resist. This, too, was part of her fantasy. And he had been longing to taste her sweet sex almost from the moment he laid eyes on her.

He could feel Lauren's eyes on him, wary and watchful. Now that he had finished shaving her, she seemed anxious to close her legs, which he could not allow.

"No, Lauren," he said sternly, placing his hands on the inside of her thighs. "Spread your legs for me, darling. Let me tend you."

"Y-you promised you wouldn't...wouldn't feed on me again unless I asked you to." Her voice was tight and small and there was fear in her eyes. But it was what she said twisted Kris' heart with pain.

God, he couldn't remember every wanting another woman as badly as he was growing to want Lauren Wright. But she wanted no part of it—no part of him. She might submit to him now, but he knew in the long run she longed for freedom and a future that did not include him in any way.

"I am not going to feed on you—I am going to heal you," he said, as gently as he could, knowing his voice sounded rough and unhappy.

"Y-you're sure it won't make a difference? Won't strengthen the bond?"

Kris closed his eyes briefly, fighting to master his emotions. "I will not need to bite you to heal such a little wound. My body produces essence whenever my fangs are extended and the small amount needed to heal this tiny cut will strengthen the bond between us an insignificant amount."

Still she looked at him, undecided, and he knew what she needed—remembered the next part of her fantasy.

"Spread you legs, Lauren," he said again, using a more commanding tone this time. "Submit to me now or bear the consequences."

With a shuddering sigh, she did as he ordered. Kris felt her thighs part under his hands and she leaned back against the pile of pillows he had arranged for her at the head of the bed.

Her hair was tumbled around her shoulders in a blonde cloud and her cheeks and breasts were flushed with desire, the hot blood pumping under her smooth skin. Her body was all cream and gold. Full, lush curves that made his cock and fangs ache to see. Her freshly shaved sex seemed to invite him, the plump lips of her cunt swollen with desire, the single tiny bead of blood at its apex like a jewel. He thought he had never seen any sight so lovely as this sweet picture of Lauren's submission.

"My darling," he whispered, unable to help himself. "My *Solnyshko*." He bent his head to lap at the single droplet of blood and felt her sudden intake of breath as his tongue made contact with her hot, wet flesh. Her flavor exploded inside his mouth and Kris closed his eyes briefly to savor it—her uniquely delicious blood and the rich, salty-sweet taste of her sex.

He felt his fangs drip essence, preparing to feed although he had no intention of biting her. He was thirsty though, there had been no blood since the night before when he had sucked the Taint from her system. Not that he hadn't had the opportunity. Simon had offered him several concubines as a snack but Kris had turned them all down. It was foolish, he knew, but if he could not have the unique flavor of Lauren's blood, he did not desire any other.

He worked his tongue over the top of her slit, tending the small wound and spreading his essence over the area thoroughly. He wasn't injecting it directly into her bloodstream this time, so the effect wasn't quite so dramatic. But it did increase her pleasure and soon she was gasping and moving under his mouth, seemingly unable to help herself.

He licked lower then, paying special attention to her swollen clitoris, which he sucked between his lips and tortured sweetly with his tongue. He felt he could never get enough of her beautiful flavor.

"Oh, God! *Oh!*" Her voice was breathless and needy and she was pulling helplessly against the black satin bonds, as though she wished she could touch him. Kris suddenly wished he had left her untied. He wanted to feel her slim fingers tugging at his hair as he buried his face between her legs and tongued her hot little cunt.

Wanting more, he lifted her hips to his mouth and plunged his tongue directly into her sweet, wet passage. She cried out and writhed under him, pressing her inner thighs tightly against the sides of his head, riding his face as he fucked her orally.

He could hear her heart pounding and her breathless little cries were one long continuous moan now. She was close, so close. He wondered briefly if he should let her come now but that would be too easy. He needed her hot for him at the banquet tonight. Hot and willing and ready. She had to trust him, had to open both her soul and her body to him and desire was needed to inspire that kind of trusting submission.

Just as she was nearing the final peak, he forced himself to pull back. Lauren was gasping and moaning, her creamy skin was flushed all over with near-orgasmic arousal and her small hands were fisted in the satin ties that bound her to the bed.

"What…why?" She opened her eyes, the pupils so dilated they were nearly black. She looked disoriented and was out of breath. "Why?" she asked again and then bit her tongue, obviously unwilling to ask why he had stopped.

"You are healed," Kris said, answering her question anyway. He nodded at the top of her wet slit where no trace of the tiny cut now remained. "Surely you would not wish me to continue to foist my unwanted attentions on you when my purpose for such has already been accomplished?" He grinned.

She shook her head angrily. "Do you ever speak normally? I've met PhDs who talked less mumbo jumbo than you."

"Fine." He leaned forward, looking her in the eye. "Do you want me to finish eating you, Lauren? Do you want me to fuck you with my tongue until you come?"

She blushed hard, a very dark red, and looked away at once.

"Look at me." Kris caught her by the chin and forced her to meet his gaze. "You wanted me to be blunt, I am very capable of that. There is nothing I would like better than eating your sweet cunt until I felt you shaking and quivering under me, coming under my tongue. Nothing except sinking my cock into you to the hilt and filling you with my seed, that is."

She closed her eyes, a shiver running through her at his words. Kris kissed her suddenly and she opened her mouth to him at once, welcoming him inside. He shared her own hot taste with her, reaching down to tweak her painfully erect nipples while he did. She gasped and thrashed under him, her pelvis thrusting blindly upward, begging mutely for what she was afraid or ashamed to ask for verbally.

"You want it," Kris said at last, pulling back from her and looking deep into those slanted green eyes. "You want my cock inside your body as much as I long to put it there. You need to be fucked, Lauren, though you try to deny it, to deny me."

"I-it's just the bond between us. You said it yourself, that it was growing." Her voice was soft and tentative and there seemed almost to be a question in her eyes, as though she wasn't sure of what she was saying. But her words enraged him, caused him pain like he had never known. He felt his face grow stiff and cold.

"That is as it may be." He rose from the bed and untied her in a series of quick, jerky movements. "Now get dressed again. I will be back shortly to collect you for the banquet."

He left her, not trusting himself to stay. But inside his head a voice whispered, *abomination.*

Chapter Nineteen

Lauren was relieved that she was allowed to eat some soup in the kitchen, rather that being forced to sit at the table in the schoolgirl outfit. Although she hadn't had anything since Simon's gourmet scrambled eggs much earlier in the afternoon, she found she wasn't in the least bit hungry.

She kept seeing the look on Kris' face, the cold anger that had passed over his smooth, pale features when she spoke about the bond. Why did it make him so angry when she talked about it? They hadn't even known each other a week yet, surely he didn't want her hanging around for eternity, or however long it was vampires lived. He had said himself that he didn't intend to let the bond grow, so why?

"Lauren, are you nearly finished?"

His voice behind her made her snap up her head and the spoon dropped to the floor with a clatter. It was a golden spoon again, she noted distantly. She hadn't seen any real silverware since she got to this place. Did that mean that vampires really were allergic to silver?

"Lauren?" His voice was a little softer this time and the look on his face was concerned rather than cold. "Are you all right? It's nearly time."

She swallowed hard, trying to make the lump in her throat that had nothing to do with the soup she'd been eating, go down. "I-I'm fine," she finally managed, trying to look nonchalant when she felt like she was about to crawl right out of her skin. Just the look in his eyes, just being near him like this...she remembered the hot feel of his mouth on her sex and shivered.

Did she really need another reason other than this not to want to bond with him completely, as he put it? If she was this much under his spell with only a partial bond, what would she do if he ever completed it? She wasn't about to be some brainless sex toy, even if it was for the most handsome vampire she'd ever met.

"I'm fine," she said again.

Kris looked at her sharply, as though he could read her mind, and then shook his head. "I know you are nervous, there's no need to lie to me about such trivialities. Come, I hear them."

He took her arm, helping her up from the butcher block table where she and Simon had sat so recently. For the first time, Lauren really thought about the story Simon had told her of Kris' past. How much of it was true?

But there was no time for such speculation. Kris had her by the arm and was leading her through the maze of echoing stone tunnels. Apparently it wasn't too hard to find your way around The House of Pain as long as you were going in a direction Simon approved of, which was anywhere but out.

They found themselves in front of a small wooden door, bound with dull brass finishing. A small golden plaque gleamed softly on the door. It said one word, "Stage". Lauren felt her heart start galloping in her chest. Was she really going to do this? Was she really going to go out on the small wooden stage that was on the other end of the banquet hall and simulate sex while acting out one of her kinkiest fantasies in front of almost complete strangers? Kris' iron grip on her arm told her that she was.

"I know we have had no time for rehearsal." His voice was low and tense. "But if you follow my lead, I swear everything will be all right."

"Kris…" She turned to him, feeling all the blood rush out of her face, leaving her cold and almost as pale as him. "I-I don't know if I can do this."

"You can and you will," he said firmly. "If you want to leave this place when I do, you must. Lauren—" he took her chin and tilted her face up to his as though he was going to kiss her again. His eyes were drowning deep. "I want you to focus all your attention on me, not the crowd. I am the one you must please. I am your Master. Do you understand?"

She nodded her head, unable to speak.

"No." Kris frowned, his blue eyes sparking with disapproval. "I want to hear you say it, Lauren. Say, 'Yes, Master, I understand'."

Lauren licked her lips nervously. A part of her wanted to object and say she would never call any man that, despite her fantasies. But another part, a much larger part, wanted to say it exactly as he had commanded. It made her knees weak, that word, Master. Made the soft vee between her legs, so bare under the pleated plaid skirt, throb with need and anticipation. She opened her mouth, uncertain of what was going to come out.

"Yes, Master. I understand," she heard herself saying.

Kris nodded, a small smile of approval twitching at the corners of his full mouth. "Very good, *Solnyshko*. Very good indeed. Now go on stage and I will be there shortly."

He turned the brass handle and opened the door which led up a short flight of steps and onto the wooden stage.

"But…" Lauren tried to protest, but he gave her a firm push that propelled her up the steps and into another world.

* * * * *

Her protest died on her lips when she found herself on the small wooden stage, now dressed with a couch and rug like someone's living room. Someone's living room if they happened to have access to genuine Edwardian furniture and expensive Persian rugs, she thought blankly, looking around her. Even Simon's props had to be costly antiques. She tried desperately to keep her mind on that and not to notice the semicircle of eager, blank faces that stared at her from the banquet table below. She had never felt so naked before, or so vulnerable, as standing here on this stage wearing no panties or bra under this ridiculous uniform.

Suddenly the lights in the banquet hall were lowered and a half-ring of footlights she hadn't noticed before flared into life. Lauren breathed a little sigh of relief when she realized that the new lighting offered her a sense of privacy. The audience might still be able to see her, but she could barely make them out at all, a condition that suited her just fine.

"Lauren." His voice behind her made her jump guiltily, just as though she was a naughty schoolgirl, caught doing something she shouldn't. Touching herself, perhaps, when she knew it was wrong.

"What have you been doing today?" His question was stern, exactly like it was in her fantasy. He looked every inch the forbidding Master in his black business suit and dark maroon tie. Without thinking about it, Lauren found herself falling into it, into the hot scenario she had written herself, but never expected to act out.

"Nothing, Master," she whispered, keeping her eyes down. The word came from her mouth easily this time, sending a cool shiver of lust down her spine as it dropped from her lips.

Kris walked around the couch to stand over her, staring down the collar of the scratchy, white, cotton blouse at the heaving swells of her breasts. Lauren felt herself flush, as though this was the first time he had seen her. In a way, up here on the stage and acting out one of her hottest fantasies, it was.

"Why aren't you wearing a bra?" His voice was low and dangerous. She shivered and he let one long finger glide down her shoulder to the swell of her breast where her erect nipple pressed against the stiff fabric.

"I-I don't know." She gasped as he traced her nipple through the shirt, sending chills down her spine.

"Is it that you wanted me to touch you like this?" Kris' voice was still low and commanding but not quite as harsh now. He pinched both her nipples, making Lauren gasp with need.

She pressed her legs tightly together, feeling the hot moisture that was gathering there against her will.

"M-maybe," she whispered, glad she hadn't given herself many lines. In this fantasy, the Master did most of the talking.

"Unbutton your blouse, I want to see your breasts." Kris' order was curt and he stepped back from her, arms crossed over his broad chest, waiting.

Clumsily, with fingers that felt utterly numb, Lauren did so. When the white, cotton shirt was hanging open on both sides, exposing her full, naked breasts completely, she stood and waited.

"Good girl, Lauren." Kris stepped forward and leaned back against the arm of the couch so that he was in profile to the audience. "Now come here. I'm going to suck your nipples for punishment. You know you get what you deserve when you go around all day without a bra."

"Yes, Master." She came forward without hesitation, completely lost in the fantasy now, and stood between his legs. His position, half sitting on the arm of the couch, put his head level with her chest and he sucked one ripe, aching nipple into his mouth at once.

The sensation of his hot mouth on her sensitive breast was intense. He sucked harder, taking as much of her breast into his mouth at one time as he could, and Lauren gasped again to feel the sharp points of his fangs pricking her gently. He didn't draw blood, but it was clear that he could if he wanted to, if he hadn't promised not to feed on her. For a moment Lauren couldn't remember why she had objected to having him draw her blood. It suddenly seemed like an amazingly erotic act. *The bond...don't forget the bond...it would be wrong...dangerous*, she told herself hazily.

Kris let her go and then reached for her second breast, giving it the same treatment as the first. Dimly, Lauren was aware of soft noises coming from the audience, murmurs of approval and lust, but she couldn't pay them any attention when Kris was doing this to her, making her so achingly, incredibly hot.

At last he stopped, just when she felt like she could almost come just from his hot mouth on her nipples. Panting, she stepped away from him, but one large hand shot out to draw her close again.

"Lauren, I can tell by the way you're acting that you've been having a lot of bad thoughts today. Have you been misbehaving in any other ways besides forgetting your bra?" he demanded in that low, commanding tone. Lauren was beginning to think of it as his "Master voice".

She looked down at the carpet, scuffing one black Mary Jane shoe in its rich nap and shook her head.

"Answer me, Lauren, and you'd better tell the truth." Kris' eyes were a river of blue fire when she looked up into them.

"No," she said in a small voice. "No, Master."

"I don't believe you." His voice hardened and his grip on her arm tightened. "Lauren, spread your legs for me and raise your skirt."

She gasped, and wanted with all her will to refuse. It was one thing to do this in the relative privacy of the bedroom, but something else altogether to do it in front of an audience. But Kris' blue eyes were full of warning and that deep voice was making her want to melt. Hanging her head, Lauren obeyed.

"Lauren, what's this?" Kris looked at her, as if in disbelief, and she thought distantly that he wasn't a half bad actor. He was looking pointedly at her exposed sex, shaved bare so recently by his own hand. Lauren felt her face blush crimson. She had never known how naked she would feel, how vulnerable without the soft nest of blonde curls that usually framed her sex.

"Answer me!" Kris demanded, pulling her away from her speculation. He took her roughly by the shoulders and turned her so that she was facing the audience, the pleated plaid skirt still raised.

"It's..." Lauren felt her voice breaking. "Please, Master, it's my..." She couldn't make herself finish, but Kris finished for her.

"It's your pussy, Lauren, your soft little cunt." He reached around her from either side and spread her trembling thighs even wider, giving the audience a better view. Lauren turned her face to one side in shame, feeling the hot blush of mortification spreading over her cheeks.

"Now," Kris continued. "Can you tell me why it's on display like this instead of decently covered by the nice, cotton panties I bought you?" His large hands framed her sex as though showcasing her shame.

"I-I..." Lauren struggled to remember the correct answer but nothing would come to her lips. To her horror, Kris was now spreading the swollen lips of her cunt open, showing the audience the hot pink inside. Exposing her throbbing clit and showing them how wet she was, how ready for him.

"Did you do it to provoke me, Lauren?" Kris growled in her ear, pulling her back against him so that she could feel the hard bulge of his cock digging into her unprotected backside. "Is that why you did it?" He was touching her now, touching her in front of everyone. Two long, strong fingers rubbed along the sensitive side of her swollen clit, making her gasp and jerk in his hands, and then they were entering her, pressing into her wet channel slowly, deep and deliberate. Violating her in front of everyone watching. Penetrating her, fucking her, making her hot, making her helpless.

"Answer me," Kris growled in her ear, his long fingers fucking her relentlessly.

"I don't know," she gasped, closing her eyes tightly to the hot lights of the stage and the blur of indistinct faces beyond them. If he didn't stop this soon he was going to make her come, come in front of everyone like a common slut. And she was finding it harder and harder to care.

Suddenly, the fingers were removed and Kris pushed her away. Lauren almost groaned with disappointment. But surely she didn't want him to make her orgasm in front of the audience. Did she? *Did she?*

"Turn around, Lauren. I want you to face the arm of the couch and pull up your skirt from behind." Kris' voice was low and heated and she realized suddenly that this was affecting him too. It wasn't all just an act then, he really liked her fantasy, liked acting it out with her. The knowledge rang warning bells inside her head and all up and down her spine and Lauren looked at him, motionless.

"Why?" she asked, trying to keep the trembling out of her voice.

"You know the punishment for provoking me, Lauren." His voice was little more than a growl. "I'm going to fuck you, little girl. Going to fuck you hard and fill your sweet cunt up with my hot cum. Isn't that what you wanted all along? Isn't it?"

"I-I don't know," she said, falling back on her standard reply. But honestly, she didn't. Kris had promised her that he would be simulating this final act of sex but did she really want him to?

"Lauren, I'm waiting." The menace in his voice was unmistakable and Lauren shivered as she did as she had been told.

"Yes, Master," she whispered through numb lips. She turned, keeping a profile to the audience and leaned against the high arm of the couch, feeling a material that was both rough and silky brushing against her tender nipples. Then, she reached back and raised the pleated skirt, baring herself for him as he had commanded.

"That's very good, Lauren." His voice was softer now and his hands on her bare bottom were gentle and possessive. "Bend lower, my darling, and spread your legs wide for my cock."

The hot, dirty words sent a shiver of pure lust through her veins and Lauren did as he asked without protest. She heard the low, purring sound of a zipper being lowered behind her and then there was a silky heat as the blunt probe of his cock nudged against her inner thighs.

Oh God...she moaned inwardly, feeling him rub against her thighs, now wet with her own moisture. She had never felt so exposed and vulnerable. Kris had promised he wouldn't really fuck her, but was he telling the truth? He hadn't lied to her yet that she knew of, not really, but as she felt the broad head nudge against the swollen outer lips of her wet cunt, she wondered. Could any man come so close without actually doing the deed? Without actually fucking her?

"Is this what you need? My cock inside you? Is this what you want?" Kris' voice was low and stern but Lauren couldn't answer him. He was rubbing the head of his cock lightly over her swollen clit, pressing teasingly against the unprotected opening of her wet sex. She gasped as she felt him press inside her, just enough that she could feel the broad head of his shaft beginning to stretch her entrance.

Oh God, he's going to do it...he's really going to do it...

"Master, please...you promised..." she moaned softly, for his ears only.

"Yes, I know what I promised you." He held absolutely still, with just the head of his cock buried inside her. "I promised you a good fucking, Lauren, or didn't you hear me?" He spoke these words louder and she gasped, feeling another inch of his thick cock slide into her unprotected sex.

He leaned forward, keeping the position, and stroking along her trembling back. "Trust me, Lauren, I will not violate my promise to you, but I need to enter you once, in order to make my shaft wet enough to maintain the illusion of sex. But I will not actually fuck you or come inside you, do you understand?" These words were lower, meant, she understood, only for her ears.

Lauren nodded, unable to speak, unable to protest. She understood that he needed to get his cock wet enough to glide against her without too much friction, to make it look like they were fucking for real. But oh God, he was barely inside her now and she wasn't sure she could handle his massive length and thickness, even for a moment, all the way inside her.

As though sensing her anxiety, Kris petted her back softly and whispered, "Relax, *Solnyshko*, you're wet enough to take me and I won't hurt you."

The odd nickname made her relax, somehow, and she realized that she still trusted him. Even on stage, in front of a crowd of strange vampires, with his thick cock half buried in her quivering, exposed sex, she still trusted him.

"Tell me if this is the way you need to be fucked," Kris ordered, sliding another thick inch of his cock into her trembling pussy and Lauren understood that it was time to get on with the show.

"Yes, Master," she managed to make herself gasp and was ashamed to know that she was telling the truth. Again, no acting was necessary.

"That's good because I intend to fuck you hard tonight, Lauren. You've been a very...very...naughty...girl." As he spoke, he slowly eased the rest of his thick cock all the way inside her tight, wet cunt.

Lauren gasped and cried aloud to feel the broad head pressing hard against the mouth of her womb as he bottomed out inside her. His thick shaft was all the way inside her, stretching her mercilessly, filling her to the limit and beyond.

"Does it feel good, *Solnyshko*, my cock inside you?" he whispered, for her ears alone.

"Y-yes, Master," she gasped, giving what he wanted, what she couldn't help giving when he demanded it—her submission. "You d-don't have to..." She was trying to tell him he didn't have to pull out, that she didn't want him to. Apparently Kris understood.

"No," his voice hardened a little and he began to withdraw from her body, as slowly as he had entered her. "No, I will not make love to you until you ask me to do it the right way."

"The right way?" she gasped under her breath, feeling the thickness sliding out of her wet sex with something very like regret.

"The way we make love is twofold. I refuse to do this with you unless both my fangs and my cock are buried deep inside you, Lauren," he said. "Is that what you want?"

"I...no. Not what I want," she gasped, thinking about the bond, about being tied to this irritating, fascinating man for her entire life. She didn't know him well enough, damn it!

"Very well." She felt him leave her body and then his shaft settled lower, cradled between her smoothly shaved pussy lips. She felt his hands settle on her hips and he began to rock back and forth in long, smooth strokes that she realized would look exactly like real fucking to the watching audience.

Lauren gasped and threw back her head, reveling in the hot sensation of the broad head and thick shaft rubbing against her sensitized clit. She was so swollen and wet down there she knew she was on the razor's edge of orgasm.

"Tell me that you like it, tell me that you need it — my cock inside you, Lauren," Kris demanded, grinding against her roughly. "I want to feel you come, come all over my cock," he growled.

"Oh, God...oh, Master...yes! Yes!" At last Lauren felt herself tipping over the edge of orgasm, spasming hotly as his thick cock rubbed against her swollen clit. She was dimly aware of the audience roaring its approval and the heated scratch of the couch arm against her sensitive nipples, but the feel of Kris' hot seed spurting, not into her, but onto her bare belly, eclipsed everything else.

She couldn't admit, even to herself, how empty she felt, how much she wished she'd given in and let him bury both cock and fangs in her body and make love to her for real. Let him seal the bond.

Chapter Twenty

The rest of the night was a blur. Kris raised her from her bending position and made her take a bow, of all things, and then hustled her back to her room. Lauren, completely worn out by all the emotion and by the amazingly intense orgasm, could barely react.

"Come, *Solnyshko*, let's get you cleaned up." He drew a hot bath and put her in it, bathing her as gently as he had the first night, as gently as though she were a child. He washed his seed from her belly and shampooed her hair, stoking her skin as though she was some cherished possession that might break if he wasn't careful.

"Kris," she made herself ask, though her eyes were closing in sleep, as he toweled her off and slipped her between the delightfully cool sheets. "What's going to happen now. To us, I mean?"

"There is no 'us', Lauren, or did you forget?" There was a faint trace of bitterness in his voice, though his tone was not angry. Then he sighed and his voice became more gentle. "All is well, my darling. The show was a great success and Simon will be forced to let us go. By tomorrow night you and I will be on a plane to Prague and the night after that, the Gathering will be held. Once you explain your formula they will have no choice but to allow us to go public and those of the Second Life will gain their rightful place in society."

"What's the matter?" Lauren asked him. Even half asleep she couldn't miss the sadness in his voice. "I thought that's what you wanted—why you dragged me all over Houston in the first place."

"Indeed, at one time I would have said it was my heart's desire." Kris' deep voice was still sad. She tried to pry open her eyes to see if his face matched his voice but her eyelids suddenly felt like they were dipped in lead.

"What…" She yawned. "What happens after…Gathering?" she managed to ask him.

"Then, Lauren, you will be free to go your own way and we will most likely never meet again." His voice held more than a tinge of bitterness this time.

Lauren wanted desperately to open her eyes and ask him why it had to be that way. Why could they never see each other again? Just because you'd simulated sex acts in front of an audience with someone didn't mean you couldn't still be friends, did it? Or even more than friends?

"D-don't want…" she mumbled, trying to tell him she didn't want to never see him again. But then sleep rolled over her in a crushing wave that could not be denied and she was dragged beneath the surface of unconsciousness.

* * * * *

The next day she prudently stayed in her room, only opening the door once to accept a tray of food from Sophie, who seemed too intimidated to chat. "My Master says not to talk to you," was all she said when Lauren tried to make small talk.

Before she knew it the light from the windows was fading and nighttime was upon them. She was looking out at the cool blue twilight that had covered the teeming city, she could see but not reach, when the door behind her opened and Kris stepped into the room.

"Well, all packed and ready to go, Lauren?" Tonight he was all business, as though the hot sexual encounter of the night before had never happened. Lauren felt herself blushing at the thought and then tried to put it out of her mind. If Kris was willing to act like nothing had happened then she could certainly play along.

"I'm ready, but did you tell me last night that we were going to Prague?" She crossed her arms over her chest protectively, turning to face him.

"Yes, that is where the Gathering is to be held."

"Look, I...couldn't I just tell you wh-where it is and you could let me go?" She stepped closer, smelling his clean, fresh scent and breathed low into his ear. "My computer at home. The formula you need is under the file labeled 'Grocery List'. We can go right now and get it. You can drop me off on your way to the airport, okay?"

Kris smiled a little. "A very nice try, but I need not only that of which you speak but your lovely self to explain it. You forget that many of my kind are ancient and almost none hold medical degrees."

"Kris, I understand that coming *here* was necessary, but I don't appreciate you dragging me all over the world." Lauren struggled to keep her voice low and reasonable. "I mean, why the hell do they have to do this Gathering thing all the way in Prague anyway? Why not just rent a banquet hall at the nearest Hilton or some damn thing like that?"

He frowned. "Prague is where the Council of Ten sits in judgment over all of those of the Second Life. Not many of our kind keep their headquarters in the new world, as we still refer to America. The Dark Eye is the only organization that immediately comes to mind. They are said to be located not far from your nation's capitol—they like to be near the seat of power, I suppose."

"The Dark Eye—those are the vampires who don't—"

"Want to come out. Yes." Kris nodded. "My own organization, the Brotherhood, has its headquarters in London, where we will be making a short layover on our way to Prague."

"Layover? Couldn't get round trip, huh?" Lauren made a face. If he was really going to drag her all the way to Prague, and at this point it looked inevitable, then she would have preferred to fly nonstop. In her experience, layovers in strange airports were almost always painful experiences. At least her passport was up to date.

"Unfortunately the layover is necessary as the flight is close to twelve hours long." Kris crossed to the bed and began packing a small case he had brought with the few pieces of clothing he had picked out for her during their stay at The House of Pain. Lauren was wearing a new outfit, one that Sophie had left outside her door. It was a dove gray business suit with a white silk blouse and nylons that made her feel much more comfortable than the slinky green gown Kris was currently packing.

"Why should the length of the flight have anything to do with it?" Lauren handed him the toothbrush and several other personal items that had thoughtfully been provided for her. She supposed that the clothes and all the extras were included in Simon's guest package and could only conclude that they had all been well paid for by their "show" the night before.

"The length matters because the darkness does not last forever. Dawn will be nearly breaking when we reach London. From there, I will be riding in the baggage compartment."

"In the baggage compartment?" Lauren looked at him, uncomprehending.

"In my coffin," Kris clarified. "If anyone asks, you are a recently bereaved widow. Members of my organization will be meeting you when we touch down in Prague—other concubines, not those of the Second Life, of course."

"Oh." Lauren felt a little faint. The idea of Kris traveling in a coffin…it was just so strange. Her dismay must have shown on her face because Kris drew a little closer and placed a large hand on her shoulder.

"Lauren, is there a problem?"

"No, I…" She shook her head. "It's just that I guess I got used to thinking of you as a…regular person. To think of you riding the last leg of the flight in a coffin…"

Kris drew away from her, his face growing cold. He looked paler tonight, Lauren noticed. There was a pinched, tired look around the ice blue eyes that worried her and she suddenly wondered who he had been feeding on since she had denied him herself. She was surprised to feel a small stab of jealousy at the thought of him sinking fangs into someone else, which, of course, was silly.

Kris was still regarding her icily. "No, I am not, as you say, a 'regular person' for which I make no apologies." His deep voice practically had icicles dripping off it, his tone was so frigid.

"Stop being so touchy." Lauren felt annoyed. "You act like I've made some kind of a racial slur every time I say anything about what you are. Do you really hate being a vampire that much? You have unlimited wealth and power and you apparently live forever or close to it as far as I can understand—what's so bad about that?"

"What's so bad, you say?" Kris rounded on her angrily. "Do you know what the peasants who live in my mother country do when they suspect someone who has died of being a vampire?"

Lauren shook her head, speechless.

"They dig up the body, chop off the head and take out the heart with a curved sickle. They then fry the heart in an iron pan. It is believed," Kris continued in a cool, scholarly tone, "that the heart of a true vampire will squeak like a mouse and try to jump out of the pan. Sometimes it is literally staked to the pan to prevent this. After it is cooked to death, the ashes of the heart are mixed with water and given to the vampire's 'victims' to cure them of his curse, so that they, in turn, will not become vampires when they die."

"Are you...is that really still happening today?" Lauren thought of the bizarre needle in the belly button custom Simon had spoken of and remembered his vague hints about Kris' "tragic past".

"Yes," Kris said shortly. He had turned back to his packing and would not meet her gaze. "In much of the old country we are not the figures of dark romance your American authors have made us out to be. We are hated and reviled—the Undead. Unclean abominations against God and humanity."

Lauren drew away from him, a little afraid. She had never heard him so upset before, not even the night before she he had come bursting into the bathroom demanding to know what she had said to Simon. "I-I'm sorry," she said. "I didn't realize you felt so strongly about it."

Kris' face softened a little and he sighed. "Do not concern yourself, *Solnyshko*. It is only that what I am has long been a sore spot with me. It didn't bother me so much, perhaps, before I met you. But being with you these past few days has made me remember many things—what it's like to be human for one. The time before my Second Life was so long ago now…"

Lauren wasn't sure if this was the right time to talk about it but she said softly. "Simon…sort of hinted that you had a difficult time. A tragic past, he called it."

Kris laughed humorlessly. "Ah yes, I am not surprised, Simon always has his nose in the business of others. I suppose you would like, as they say, 'the gory details' of my failed love affair?"

Lauren shrugged uneasily. "Not if you'd rather not say…"

"Well, we have no time for the long version but I shall give you the short one, no?" Kris sat on the bed, legs crossed casually, for all intents and purposes perfectly composed. Only his eyes, blazing a pale blue, betrayed his agitation. "I was born in pre-Bolshevik Russia into a very wealthy home, some time before the Revolution. In that time there was no 'mixing' between the peasants and the nobles. Do you understand?"

Lauren nodded. She sat beside him, but not too close.

"Jenica was her name—the girl I fell in love with. A beautiful girl, with hair like sunshine, much like yourself." Kris nodded at her, reaching out to finger a tendril of her hair.

"But she was only a poor shopkeeper's daughter and my father forbade our love. I was the only son, his firstborn having died along with his first wife in childbirth. He expected me to make a fine match, perhaps to wed the daughter of the nobleman to our west and unite our lands."

"So you ran away together?" Lauren guessed, thinking that it sounded like some sort of a Shakespearian tragedy.

Kris laughed again, bitterly. "No, for on my way to her house to elope I was taken and turned into what I am today. When she…when Jenica saw me, saw what I had become, she was horrified and repulsed. She shielded herself as best she could and shut the door against me. I was heartbroken. I moved to the new world—to America to try and start again." He shrugged. "So that is my tragic past. Are you satisfied?"

"Jenica?" Lauren couldn't help asking. "What happened to her?"

Kris looked away for a moment and when he turned back, his face was hard and cold again. "I heard that she died young." He rose from the bed, the subject obviously closed.

Lauren stared at him. Was this the reason he so wanted to become a legitimate part of society? His personal "stake" in the issue of artificial blood? She thought of how Jenica had rejected him after he had been changed. No wonder he hated what he was. No wonder he craved the vindication a public "coming out" of the vampires in the world would certainly result in. She shivered, she certainly wouldn't want to see it if Kris ever found his "Maker", the vampire responsible for all this pain and bitterness.

"I didn't know," she said in a low, contrite voice.

"There is much you do not know of me." Kris' face had gone back to being cold and uncommunicative. "Come now, Simon has a limousine waiting to take us to the airport."

* * * * *

The limo was the longest and blackest Lauren had ever seen. She clutched the small, black bag filled with everything she currently owned, noticing how the tinted windows seemed to suck up the light from the outside entrance of the club like small black holes instead of reflecting it.

They were at a side door, the front was packed with a mass of teeming humanity waiting to get into The House of Pain. All the humans were dressed in leather and chains, some wearing dog collars or leashes or even more outrageous accessories. Lauren had caught a quick glimpse of them as they walked out into the muggy Houston night. To her, the club goers looked like pale shadows of the vampires and concubines she had met while staying there. What would they think if they knew the real thing was here right under their noses in the back of the very club they were so eager to get into?

She turned to Simon who had accompanied them out. All the way down the long maze of stone corridors and out to the waiting limo their host had been surprisingly quiet.

"Um…" she wasn't quite sure how to put this but the good manners her Gram had bred into her were too strong to resist. "Thank you for your hospitality," she said.

Smiling gently, Simon took her hand in his and made a low, sweeping bow over it. It was the kind of gesture he must have made often at the court of Versailles and it made Lauren feel like she ought to have a long dress with sweeping skirts on so she could return it with a proper curtsey.

"You have more than earned any small pleasures or luxuries we were able to afford you, *ma chérie*," Simon murmured. Cool lips brushed her knuckles, making Lauren jump and draw away.

Scowling, Kris put himself between them. "Enough. We paid your price."

"More than paid." Simon's laughter was soft and mocking and very unpleasant. Lauren shivered, glad to have Kris between her and their host.

"After you." Kris strode forward and was holding open the door of the limo. She slipped inside, clutching her small bag and hoping that he had her precious Mac somewhere about his person. He had promised her it was in "a safe place" but she still felt anxious. She had shown Simon and company much more of her private fantasies than she had ever expected to and she didn't like the idea of him reading them after she was gone.

She slid into the coal-black interior, feeling the buttery-soft leather upholstery of the long, black seat beneath her fingertips. Kris started to enter after her but then Simon's voice called him back and his dark head disappeared back out into the night.

Lauren wondered what Simon could possibly have to say now that couldn't have been said on the long, awkward walk out of the club when he had been unusually silent. She heard a snatch of conversation from outside the long black car, something about "final destination" and "payment in full".

Then, with no warning the door of the limo slammed shut. Lauren looked at it uneasily, had they needed privacy to discuss something else? Some kind of vampire business she wasn't supposed to hear about? Looking around, she noticed that the black windows didn't let in the tiniest bit of outside illumination, apparently the entire back of the limo was light-tight. She wanted to ask the driver if he knew anything but for the first time, she noticed that the dull black shield between the passenger compartment and the driver's section was closed.

She leaned forward, meaning to knock on the partition and ask the driver to roll it down. But as her knuckles were about to connect with the dull black glass, the long car lurched forward and she was thrown on the plushy carpeted floor.

There was a sensation of acceleration and Lauren looked around wildly. What the hell? They were definitely moving but she was sure they shouldn't be. Maybe the driver had the idea that she and Kris both were in the car and was already going to the airport.

"Hey…*hey*!" She crawled forward on her knees and reached up to pound on the glass partition. "We're not all here yet, you're leaving m-my Master." The word still tasted funny in her mouth but she was chagrinned to realize how natural it felt to say it.

"Hey!" she shouted again, but there was no response from the front of the limo. Was the damn driver deaf?

Suddenly a faint hissing noise began to rise from the floorboards accompanied by a pale cloud of gas and a sickly sweetish odor. Lauren looked around wildly. Was the car on fire now? But as the cloyingly sweet scent began to penetrate her senses, another possibility occurred to her. There was no fire and it was no accident that they had taken off without Kris.

Some kind of drug...she thought, choking on the syrupy fumes and then she found herself lying on the floor somehow. Her eyelids were beginning to feel heavy and she had a very bad feeling in the pit of her stomach.

"Kris..." she croaked, and then the interior lights of the limo went out and she was plunged into absolute blackness.

Chapter Twenty-One

"What have you done with her? Y-you..." Finding no words adequate to his rage in English, he swore heavily in Russian.

Simon merely smiled at him, that lazy, cat-that-got-the-cream smirk that Kris abhorred. He longed to knock it off his host's face but no matter how enraged he was, his common sense had not left him. Time enough to challenge Simon to a duel later. For the moment, he had a limited amount of time to catch up to Lauren and get to the airport.

"Now, Kristov, you forget that I speak your native tongue quite well—it was most unkind of you to call me that."

Kris threw common sense to the wind and grabbed Simon by the lapels of his fashionable black leather jacket. "I said, *what have you done with her*?" he grated, enunciating each word in a low growl.

Simon, to give him credit, remained cool and composed. But it might have been the solid stone wall of The House of Pain behind his back filled with his followers and concubines that gave him that composure. "As to that, I have done nothing with her, *mon cher*. She is off of my property and no longer my concern or responsibility." He shrugged, managing to make the gesture look lazy and nonchalant even with his lapels caught tight in Kris' fists. "My debts are paid."

"You sold us." Kris shook him but Simon was solid and unmoving, his face unreadable. "You sold us to The Dark Eye."

"No." Simon's voice was cold and formal. "We sold only your concubine and her interesting secret. Did you really think you could keep her knowledge hidden from us within the halls of our own house? We know all about her research and your pathetic plans to use it at the Gathering." He glared at Kris, his brown gaze cold. "Did you really think you could convince the Council of Ten to bring those of the Second Life out into the open like a foul secret that needed airing?"

Kris released him with a jerk and stepped back in disgust. "What was your price, Monsieur Travain? What did the Dark Eye promise you? Their support when you tried for a seat at the Council?"

"They needed no further inducement than the prospect of your possible success, Kristov. Do you really think the human world would let us in, just like that?" He snapped his fingers in Kris' face. "Fool! We would be hunted—outcast. You of all people ought to know of the unreasoning prejudice humans feel for anything outside their narrow comprehension. Consider your own past!"

Kris felt his face grow cold. "What do you know about my past?"

Simon sneered. "More than you think, *mon cher*. But we are wasting valuable time. As close as you got to the little human doctor, I am certain she must have told you much of her research. Probably even enough to present to the Council without her. Do you not have a plane to Prague to catch?" He laughed, a low, unpleasant sound. "I wish you good luck on convincing them with no evidence to display. But who can say? Perhaps they will be feeling charitable." He smiled again, one eyebrow arched upwards.

Kris leaned forward, placing a hand on either side of Simon's head, pinning the grinning vampire to the stone wall behind him. "You are older than I, Simon, but he who made me was very strong and the time of my equinox grows near. I vow to you here and now that I will return to redress this wrong. If anything, *anything* happens to Lauren because of your treachery, I will wreak a vengeance on you the likes of which you cannot imagine."

Simon didn't move but Kris could have sworn he grew just a little paler in the nearly full moon. "Do you not have a plane to catch?" His lips barely moved as he spoke.

"Indeed." Kris punched the wall beside his host's head, leaving a sizable hole in the solid stone.

Then he turned and left.

Chapter Twenty-Two

She was shoved back into consciousness by a piercing, burning pain in her right wrist. She opened her eyes with a scream already rising to her lips but what she saw made her swallow it.

Glowing yellow eyes, slit vertically like a cat's, peered down into hers. They were set in a pale face like a long, narrow skull. The eyes never blinked as the thing went back to her wrist.

"No! Get away from me!" She tried to shout but the words came out as an ineffectual whisper. She yanked feebly at her hand, her movements still sluggish and drugged but it did no good. It reminded her of the way it felt to struggle against Kris, like fighting an immovable brick wall. But surely this...*thing* couldn't be one of Kris' type, could it? A vampire, one of the Second Life?

It looked up from her wrist, withdrawing yellowed fangs colored red with her blood. The fangs were thick and curving, almost like tusks, twice as long and deadly as any she had seen on the vampires at The House of Pain. Lauren stared at it, wide-eyed, unable to speak now that the hideous pain was fading.

"A delicate flavor—most unusual, but quite spoiled, I'm afraid, by the taste of another. He has been feeding from you often, I take it, my dear? I taste his essence in your blood." The thing's voice was thick and grating, like the hinges of an ancient door clogged with soil.

"I-I don't know who you mean." At first Lauren thought the thing that had been feeding on her had black mold growing on its skin but, when she looked closer, she could see that its pale skin was actually mottled dark and light, almost like a marble floor. It didn't look remotely human although it had a face and two arms and legs as far as she could see.

"Do not lie." The thing raised her wrist to its blackish lips, like two pieces of rotted liver, once more in a threatening gesture. "As yet I have refrained from injecting you with my essence but I will not continue to refrain if you lie to me." It licked her blood from the yellowish, sharpened tusks protruding from its cavernous mouth suggestively. Lauren saw with horror that the liquid that dripped from those curving needle tips wasn't pale blue like Kris' but a thick, black ichor.

"I..." but she couldn't go on.

"Tell me, has my sweet Nickoli fed from you often?" the thing repeated its question with deadly patience.

"I-I had the Taint. He had to cure me," she said in a low, frightened voice.

"That is more like it—the revenant I sent fulfilled its mission then." The thing straightened, dropping her wrist and rose to tower above her. It was wearing a long, black robe that swept the cold stone floor she was lying on with a low whisper. The stone was icy cold but she couldn't concentrate on anything but the horror above her.

"Nickoli should be coming for you shortly. Excellent."

"I don't think so," Lauren heard herself saying. "H-he had some kind of a meeting he had to get to." She thought of how she had told Kris where the formula for NuBlood was stored in her computer at home and wished she hadn't.

"He will come," the thing said in its low, clotted voice. "You look too much like his lost beloved to give you up. He will come."

"How do you know so much about him?" She sat up and scooted back over the hard stone floor, trying to put as much distance between herself and her captor as possible.

The thing chuckled, a burbling, underwater sound that made her stomach do a slow flip-flop of revulsion. "He will come." It looked at her more closely, bending down from an unimaginable height. "Can you not feel it through your bond to him?"

She shook her head. "I don't...we aren't..."

The thing scowled heavily, making the long, skeletal face into a horrible fright mask. "Not bonded! How is it he healed you of the Taint and never sealed the bond between you? The truth!" it demanded angrily.

"I-I didn't want him to. I-I was afraid." Her teeth were chattering, both with the cold and with fear. It seemed to exude an aura of menace that sucked all the courage right out of her. She didn't dare lie.

"Afraid!" It sounded contemptuous. "You will know true fear if he does not come for you, little human." Its face smoothed and then it smiled, which was somehow even worse than the horrible scowl. "But he will come. And either way you will be dead in the end — dead or revenant."

The words sank in slowly but when they did, she could scarcely contain her fear. To be turned into a mindless feeding machine like the old man-thing that had bitten her in the parking lot of Le Jardin... "You wouldn't...you couldn't." The words came out in a croak, eliciting another burbling laugh from the black-robed thing.

"Oh, would I not?" The yellow eyes gleamed with a terrible promise. It strode back across the room and grabbed at her wrist, sinking its thick tusks into her tender flesh again before she could jerk back. It pulled her to itself, hugging her to its cold, black chest and began to feed. This time as it fed it injected its essence, that black, oily liquid she'd seen dripping from its fangs. Lauren knew what it was doing because she could feel it invading her system, bringing with it an unimaginable horror and pain.

When Kris had injected her there had been only a brief stinging pain and then a rush of overwhelming pleasure that she could feel everywhere in her body. But this was the exact opposite — a feeling like shards of jagged ice scratching behind her eyelids and jamming into the tender vee between her legs.

A vague thought passed through her mind, Kris telling her that if another vampire was to try to feed on her when her system was so full of his own essence that it would feel like rape. Then the hideous, invasive agony blotted everything else and she was writhing and scratching at the thing's strange, marbled skin which felt as cold as the stone floor had beneath her. *In me. Oh God, in me!* her mind screamed as she tried to close her legs and mind against the dark intruder.

It dropped her at last with a final, satisfied slurp. "That is just a little taste," it promised in its thick, grating voice. It turned and swept from the room, black robes rustling, and slammed a thick wooden door behind it.

Lauren huddled back against the cold stone wall behind her, clutching her wounded wrist to her chest and wept until misery and exhaustion overtook her.

* * * * *

A little later she woke up for the second time, this time alone in the bare stone room. She stretched carefully, feeling stiff, and looked around. The only light seemed to be coming from a small, barred window in the thick wooden door. The House of Pain had been made up to look like some medieval castle but this place was an actual dungeon. She was surprised she didn't see any chains hanging from the chilly stone walls. She wondered where she was and how long she'd been there. But most of all she wondered if Kris would come for her or not.

She had trusted him in The House of Pain, trusted him to take care of her and keep her from harm. But could she trust him to come and find her instead of attending his precious Gathering? For a century he had been longing for vindication and a return to society, would he give up that chance for a woman he'd only met a week ago? She wasn't sure.

"But even if he comes, what can he do?" Her own voice in the echoing chamber was spooky and unreal. What indeed? Was that...*thing* that had been feeding on her connected to Kris in some way? Why was it so sure he could come for her?

She shivered and looked down at the place on her wrist where the thing had bitten her. Kris' fangs had never left a visible mark on her flesh but the dirty yellow tusks of the thing had left deep punctures. Her wrist was bruised as though a very inept lab tech had attempted to take a blood gas reading from her and missed. She wasn't sure how long she'd been out but she thought the punctures should have begun healing by now. There was no sign of scabbing, however, just a slow leak of blood that smeared crimson across the white silk blouse and dove gray suit jacket she still wore.

Looking closer, Lauren saw that some of the bruising was actually blackish tracks crawling up her arm. The thing's ichor — she couldn't bring herself to call it essence, as it in no way resembled the pale blue liquid Kris had injected her with to heal her — was invading her system. It was slowly infecting her the same way the Taint had done when the revenant had bitten her.

Lauren shuddered, wondering if she should try to suck the stuff out, the way you'd suck the venom out of a snake bite. But she just couldn't bear to. Couldn't bear to put her lips on the wounds on her flesh and suck out the infected blood. *The way Kris did*, her memory whispered. She remembered the way he'd held her, the pleasure he'd given her when he touched her and sucked the Taint from her system. The low, masterful tone that had made her melt, made her want to do anything he asked, to give herself to him utterly.

I was afraid, she'd told the thing when it demanded to know why she wasn't completely bonded to Kris. And now, huddled in this dank stone room with another vampire's poison crawling through her veins, she admitted to herself that it was true. She'd been afraid — but for all the wrong reasons.

She'd told herself she was frightened of him feeding on her, of being tied to such an irritating and fascinating man for eternity. But what had she really feared? What had caused her to run from him from the very beginning? Kris' words came back to her. "You dream of being dominated and yet you fear to lose control," he had said and she knew it was true. She'd been dreaming her whole adult life of a man to call Master, of one who would love and cherish her, who would dominate her sexually while still respecting her intellect.

Kris had done all those things. He had fulfilled her fantasies while still deferring to her knowledge. When she'd tried to get him to go to Prague without her, he'd insisted he needed her expertise to explain the NuBlood formula to his ruling Council. He had washed her hair as gently as her Gram had when she was a little girl and held her when she was upset. He had tolerated her anger at him when he was only doing what was necessary to save her life and had put himself between her and danger. He'd done nothing but care for her and shield her from harm and how had she repaid him?

"Rejection," Lauren whispered to herself. "I rejected him and everything he is the same way that girl did, the one that he loved before he was turned into a vampire." She remembered the cold, stiff look on his face when she'd expressed her fear and revulsion of a possible bond with him. Now she wished she had such a bond. Maybe she'd be able to know where he was or what he was doing somehow, the way the thing had implied.

Would it really be so bad to give in to her fantasies and let herself be mastered? She thought longingly of how strong Kris' arms felt when he held her close, of the demanding press of his lips against her own and the heat he started in her body when he touched her.

She looked down at her wrist again. The dark streaks had risen past her wrist and she had to pull up the sleeve of the dove gray jacket to see that they were nearly to her elbow. A burning pain followed their tracks. And what would happen when they reached her heart? Would she die? Go into some kind of delayed anaphylactic shock? Or would she become a revenant? A mindless eating machine roaming the night in search of blood like some monster in a horror movie? She didn't want to know.

Still cradling her wounded, throbbing wrist to her chest, she drifted into an uneasy sleep again, uncertain of what she would be when she woke up.

Chapter Twenty-Three

This time it was the low creak of the hinges that woke her. Lauren blinked sleep out of her eyes, her heart suddenly hammering in her chest. Was it coming back for another meal?

She looked up for the slitted yellow eyes and the strangely marbled skin but saw nothing at all in the open doorway. Only darkness, and a slight movement that might have been a shadow.

Then a large hand was covering her mouth and she was being wrapped in a set of arms like flexible iron bands. A shriek rose to her lips but someone whispered low in her ear one word.

"*Solnyshko.*"

Lauren relaxed and the hand covering her mouth was removed as he gathered her close and pressed her face into his chest.

"Kris?" she gasped at last, when most of the tears had run their course. She could feel him but not see him. She felt up and down the invisible arms and broad chest, wanting the comforting sight of him to go with the sensation.

"Forgive me." He reappeared, looking pale and drawn in the dim light spilling in through the open doorway. He sighed. "Being Unseen for such an amount of time is quite exhausting but after a while one almost forgets what is exhausting one. I was concentrating on not being visible as I looked for you." He cupped her cheek in one palm and Lauren nuzzled against it.

"I thought you'd go to the Gathering without me," she murmured, unable to meet his pale blue gaze. "Since I'd told you where the formula was."

"And leave my favorite concubine to the mercy of The Dark Eye? Never." He grinned at her tiredly and reached down to clasp her hand in his. His seeking fingers brushed over her wounded wrist and Lauren gave a little yelp of pain and drew back.

"What is it?" Kris asked in a low, concerned voice. He raised her arm, which was now almost as painful as it had been when the Taint had been in her system, and examined it anxiously. When he looked up, there was fire in his pale blue eyes. "Who has done this to you?"

Lauren closed her eyes, the horrible images she'd been trying to repress from her previous encounter with the thing that had bitten her, rushing back. "I d-don't know what it was exactly but Kris…" Her eyes flew open suddenly. "It seemed to know you somehow. It said you would come for me—you shouldn't be here!"

"Describe it," he said ignoring her confused warning.

Lauren closed her eyes again and tried to center herself. As well as she could, she described the marbled skin, the slitted yellow eyes, the curved, dirty tusks.

"Can it be?" There was doubt in Kris' voice. "Could there truly be one of the ancient ones, an old Master still among us?"

"Old Master?" She'd heard that somewhere before but she was so tired and confused she couldn't remember where or who had said it.

"One of the Second Life that did not have to pass through the First Life to get there. But the Council of Ten declared them anathema years ago—I am surprised any still exist among us." This time Kris' voice was grim. "They are very rare, some say extinct. But if one was to appear, I am not surprised that it was in the headquarters of The Dark Eye. Only here would such a monster be embraced and welcomed."

He looked at her wrist again, eyeing the dark streaks that were moving up the underside of her arm grimly. "I'll have to suck this out and soon—this is more serious even than the Taint.

If the essence of this Master reaches your heart and brain while you have no previous bond with another of the Second Life…" He broke off, shaking his head.

"What?" Lauren bit her lip. "I-it said I would die o-or turn into a revenant."

He frowned. "I should have bonded you to me when I had the chance but I knew you did not wish it."

"Kris, I—" She wanted to tell him that she'd been thinking. That she didn't feel as frightened as she had of such a commitment before, but he hushed her with a kiss.

"Do not say it, Lauren." The look on his pale face was as close to pain as she'd seen it. "This will take only a moment and then we will leave this place and go far away where I can care for you properly." He raised her wounded wrist to his lips. "I am very much afraid that this will hurt, at least until I draw his essence out of your system, my darling, but you must remain silent, do you understand?"

Lauren nodded, not trusting herself to speak. She closed her eyes tightly, not wanting to watch as his fangs extended and his mouth closed over her wrist. The pain was a sharp, bright red agony that pulsed behind her eyelids and she brought her other hand to her mouth and bit savagely hard on the heel of her palm to muffle her screams. There was a pulling sensation, as though something long and sharp, like a poisonous thorn, was being drawn out from under her skin and she heard the muffled sound of Kris sucking, trying to finish quickly so her torment would be over.

Then the pain lessened a little and she was free to think instead of just feeling. She felt sorry for him, having to take the black ichor into himself and hoped that it wouldn't hurt him in any way to ingest the stuff. The pain eased away to nothing and she sighed in relief and relaxed against him. So she was totally unprepared when the pleasure started.

A sweet, orgasmic wave of sensation rolled over her, as intensely right as the sensation she'd gotten when the thing had bitten her had been intensely painful and wrong. And along with the powerful sensation flowing through her veins was a sense of connection, of being very close to the ultimate completion. Of being close to Kris. *The bond strengthening...but it's not...quite...enough...* Her thoughts were hazy as the pleasure built and built. Sitting in his lap she could feel the thick bulge of his cock pressing against her thigh insistently. *Yes...that's what we need...*

She arched her back against him and stiffened, feeling the wonderful rush gathering inside her and wondering why she'd ever fought against it. This was perfect, this was right, this was exactly what she needed, what *they* needed. Then, suddenly, it stopped.

"Oh...why?" She opened her eyes, looking at Kris who was staring back at her, an almost hungry look on his pale face. But though he still looked pale and drawn, as though he hadn't fed for several nights, the hunger she saw in his light blue eyes was not for blood. It was for her. He licked his lips, erasing all traces of her blood and his fangs retracted reluctantly.

"Forgive me." He sighed. "I did not mean to inject you with my own essence, but only to cleanse your system of his. I know how you feel about anything that might strengthen the bond between us."

"Kris, no. I don't—"

There was a grating sound behind them that made her jump.

"Is this not a lovely picture? I told you he would come for you, little human." There was no mistaking that clotted, burbling voice. Lauren looked up in fear, and felt Kris' arms tighten around her protectively.

"Kris, this is..."

"I know who it is. Or should I say *what* it is, for such as that was never truly human." Kris rose, spilling her from his lap and put himself between her and the thing.

"How touching. And I thought you would not remember me — I took such care that you should never see my face." The thing grinned, its leering horror-mask face twisted into an expression of pure evil delight.

"I never saw your face, true. But I could not forget that voice." Kris' voice rose and he took a step forward, staring directly into the glowing, slitted yellow eyes. "It haunts my dreams and has for nearly a century." He bowed, a curt gesture that somehow managed to convey his rage more forcefully than any action of violence could.

"I greet you, my Maker."

The thing returned his gesture, its jack-o'-lantern eyes lighting up with some ancient and alien emotion Lauren couldn't define. Perhaps it was anger mixed with pride.

"Welcome home, child of my making." Then it stepped aside, revealing a horde of pale, blank faces behind it, waiting for orders. It nodded at Kris. "Take him."

Chapter Twenty-Four

Kris was taken by many hands, the minions of the Master, for such as this thing could never make a normal concubine. They were too many to fight, though he felt the power, long dormant, beginning to grow in his blood. But the night of his equinox was not yet upon him. Still he resisted.

"Your promise that she will not be harmed," he demanded, looking into the yellow eyes.

"Done, for tonight anyhow. Come, child. We have much to discuss." The broad, marbled head nodded at him.

Kris turned, assisted none too gently by the guards around him.

"No!" Lauren reached for him but Kris shook his head. Tonight he was in no shape to fight but tomorrow night might be a different story.

"I must go, Lauren. If I don't, they'll hurt you and I couldn't bear that."

"But..." Tears were slipping slowly down her flushed cheeks. She gripped his hand in one of hers.

"Take heart, *Solnyshko*. I will return for you." Kris tried to put as much confidence into his voice as he could. Still she held on, unwilling to release him.

"Trust me," Kris whispered. He squeezed her slender fingers once and then let go. He turned to face his Maker. "I am ready," he said.

* * * * *

There were almost as many passages in the headquarters of The Dark Eye as there were in The House of Pain but at last they came to a high, thin door that led into a study decorated in red and gray. Kris looked around warily. The study had high walls, lined with dark walnut bookshelves filled with ancient volumes. The scent of old leather and parchment filled the air. So his Maker was a scholar, or wished others to think he was.

"Leave us." His Maker gestured grandly and the many hands and blank faces withdrew. He sat on a high, wing-backed chair before a low fire that was burning in the grate at one end of the study and gestured for Kris to take the chair opposite him.

"What do you want with me?" Kris asked, his voice low. "If what you seek is a stay against my fight for our kind to come into the light, all I can offer you is a hundred-year reprieve. I have already missed the Gathering."

"Yes…" A low chuckle, that deep, clotted laugh that mocked him in his dreams. Kris had to grit his teeth while his Maker continued.

"So touching that you were willing to forgo your quest for a far more noble one, the search for true love. You must care deeply for the little human doctor." Yellow eyes glinted in the firelight and a log snapped, sending up a spray of red sparks.

Kris shrugged nonchalantly. "She is my concubine."

That laugh again. "That she is not. Not even properly bonded to you and yet you came for her. She is very much like Jenica, is she not? Tell me, does she hate what you are? Is that why you are not bonded?"

Kris felt the fury build in him and swallowed it down. Lauren was in the power of The Dark Eye and any unwise words on his part might result in pain or death for her. "It is you who made me as I am. I blame you for the loss of my first love — you will not take another one from me. If you like, I will give up my position with the Brotherhood of Truth. Only let her go free."

His Maker stirred, the shadows cast by the fire making his face even more hideous. "In truth, I care neither for your Brotherhood, nor your little would-be concubine. She was merely the bait to get you here, child. Or should I say *brother*?"

"What are you talking about?" Kris asked impatiently. "The only brother I ever had died long before I was born. He and my father's first wife both died in childbirth."

His Maker laughed, a harsh, cracking sound that fell on the ears like a tree struck by lightening. "So our father told you, but it was not so. His first wife was taken by a vampire, a smooth-talking French nobleman who wooed her, though she was far gone into her eight month."

Kris felt his face grow cold. "You cannot mean…"

His Maker nodded. "Yes, it was none other than Monsieur Travain, he who so recently sheltered you. You should know that the revenant biting your little would-be concubine so near The House of Pain was no accident. Simon's part in this little farce was a fulfillment of the terrible debt he owed me.

"He fathered me, in a way, as much as our own father did. Fathered me to darkness as I fathered you, my dear half-brother. Such a tangled, incestuous web, is it not?"

Kris shook his head, unwilling, unable to believe. And yet he remembered Simon saying, "My debts are paid." And the dark hints that he knew more of Kris' past than he should. But his Maker was continuing.

"My Mother died the first time she nursed me, you can imagine it was not milk I was thirsty for." He grinned, the firelight playing over the long, yellowed tusks with needle-sharp tips. "After that, our father hid me away. He gave me no name, not even his own. I was kept locked in a shed, in the darkness. He fed me on animals, lambs, goats, whatever he caught on his hunts. When I grew too strong to contain he set me free but I never wandered far from home."

"You…stayed?" Kris frowned, wondering why. He himself had left the restrictive and forbidding environment as soon as it was clear he was not welcome.

The marbled head nodded in the firelight, yellow eyes glinting. "I watched over you so many years, little brother. Watched you grow strong and straight and handsome, able to walk in the sun—all that I could never be. To say that I was jealous was an understatement but I never plotted against you until you broke our father's heart."

"Jenica..." His lips felt numb, surely this must all be the most extravagant falsehood. And yet...some of his earliest memories involved going out to hunt with his father. His father who had always shot to wound instead of kill the animals they took. And was there not a little shed, dark and always locked by the abandoned well far to the back of their property? His mother had told him he must never go back there but sometimes he'd had nightmares...dreams in which he went there anyway and found the door open and a pair of yellow eyes peering back at him when he looked in...

"Jenica." Her name was a curse on his older half-brother's lips. "Our father who loved and nurtured you, who gave you everything I could never have. Even after he forbade your marriage to that worthless little whore you would have disobeyed him."

"Jenica was no whore!" Kris rose angrily. "I loved her."

"More than your family and your obligations." The marbled head nodded, unperturbed. "But it has been a hundred years, dear little brother. Your equinox grows near, your dark birthday into this Second Life which we both share so unwillingly. And so, I devised a test."

"Lauren." Kris rounded on him. "You thought because she looks a little like Jenica I'd fall in love with her."

"And have you not?" His brother leered. "I admit when I started, I was looking for any woman who looked like your lost love. How lucky I was to find one so intimately connected to your pet cause, do you not think?"

Kris thought sickly of the anonymous phone call that had led him to Lauren's lab in the first place. The voice on the other end had been strangely muffled, almost unintelligible and yet still it had disturbed him. Now he knew why. He frowned, looking away from the hideous visage of his brother half hidden in the shadow of the wingback chair.

"Why? Why the test? To see if I still love the same kind of woman?" He stared into the fire, watching another log pop in a shower of sparks. "It wasn't her hair or beauty that drew me, brother. It was her will, her intellect, her spirit."

"Again, I am touched." The tall form rose to stand beside him and Kris regarded it from the corner of his eye. Brother. Father. Maker. Monster.

"What do you want of me? Why all the subterfuge to bring me here?" Kris demanded.

"As I told you, a test." That clotted, cracking laugh again. Firelight gleamed on yellowed tusks. "You denied your family once for love but I choose to give you another chance. Will you turn your back on the girl you have come to care for and join me here, at The Dark Eye? Your equinox grows near and your power will match my own, perhaps even exceed it. I will set you high, at my right hand. We shall rule the shadows together."

"And Lauren?" Kris turned to face him.

The marbled face contorted, then grew still. "A sacrifice to prove your loyalty. To family—to me."

"You ask a lot for such a new relation—for a brother I never knew I had." Kris kept his tone light. "What if I decline?"

"Then the human doctor's fate will be the same as Jenica's. You *do* know how she died, brother?" He grinned, a leer so full of evil it hurt to look at, and flexed long white fingers until his knuckles popped. "Ah, but her blood was sweet."

Kris felt his face grow pale. He had been unable to get details of her death, so far away in America. But to find out now that she had been murdered... "You tell me this, that you killed my one true love and that you intend to kill the only other I have come to care for in a century and you expect me to join you? What sort of a monster do you think I am?"

"The same kind I am, brother. For I made you in my own image." The tall form seemed to grow taller, to tower over him but Kris was not intimidated.

"I refuse your offer and I offer you the formal challenge of Vlatzele," he growled through gritted teeth.

The other sighed and seemed to shrink back to his former height, which was still a good head taller than Kris himself. "Very well, Vlatzele it is. Once a traitor, always a traitor. I suppose I knew it in my heart but I wished to give you a chance. So you wish to challenge me for your would-be concubine's life, eh? Even though she fears you too much to let you seal your bond with her?" He laughed mockingly.

Kris stiffened. "Even so. She is mine and I will not lose her without a fight."

His brother nodded thoughtfully. "Well, you were always a fool for love, Nickoli. But your equinox is almost upon you and your power may even exceed my own as I believe I said earlier. We must even the field somehow. Let me think on it and tomorrow night we shall see."

"Very well. For tonight take me back to Lauren," Kris demanded, but his brother/Maker only laughed.

"And have you slip out with her before we've had our fun? No, little brother. You're entirely too good at being Unseen for me to take such a risk. A separate cell, for you, I think. But you have my word she will not be harmed, not tonight at any rate. Although her arm may be quite painful by now." A black, slimy tongue darted out and licked at the yellowed tusks with relish. "Her blood was also sweet."

Kris felt a cold fury build in him such as none he had ever known. How dare this monster flaunt the pain he had caused Lauren? He could still taste the oily black essence on the back of his tongue, the poison this thing that claimed to be his brother secreted. "You will pay with your miserable life for that one taste of my beloved's blood."

"We shall see,"

He bowed to Kris and Kris returned the gesture stiffly.
"Until tomorrow night."

Chapter Twenty-Five

Lauren listened to the noises outside the door but they never brought Kris back. After a very long time the door opened and a three pale, blank-faced people dressed in long black robes like the ones she'd seen the night before entered her cell. Lauren shrank back from them, though their faces were slack and expressionless, they were very strong.

She was lifted forcefully from her spot in the corner and dragged outside through long stone corridors that were, if anything, more bleak and forbidding than those in The House of Pain. She wanted to make some kind of joke about it or ask if all vampires had the same decorator but she felt too cold and tired and demoralized to make jokes, even to herself. She thought longingly of the plush bedchamber and the elegant bathroom in The House of Pain with the big clawfoot bathtub where Kris had washed her hair. *Please, God, don't let me die needing a bath*, she thought irrelevantly.

"Where are you taking me?" she asked after what seemed like miles of stone tunnels.

"Master says you are to be made ready for the ritual tonight." The voice that answered her was bland and utterly without inflection. When Lauren looked up, she realized she didn't even know which of her three guards had spoken. They all looked so exactly the same with their lank hair and black robes and blank faces.

"Ritual? What ri—?"

"We are not to speak to you." This time all three of them spoke at once and then Lauren couldn't get another word from any of them. After a while she stopped trying.

They came to a shorter corridor that had several doors leading into different rooms. One of the strange guards opened a door and shoved her inside, closing it behind her.

"Hey, what—?"

"Master says you are to bathe and dress," came the muffled reply through the thick door.

Lauren looked around and found herself in a small windowless bathroom. There was a shower stall, a commode with a stack of towels on the back of it, and a sink. Hanging on the back of the door was a long-sleeved ruby red gown that looked like something meant for a formal ball. There were shoes to match beneath it.

Lauren fingered the slippery material of the gown and felt a jagged, half-hysterical laugh rising to her lips. She choked it back down as she thought of all the strange banquets and ceremonies and customs she'd been introduced to lately. She had never been so dressed up and ordered around in all of her life since Kris had stolen her Mac and coerced her into that ill-fated dinner at Le Jardin.

She wouldn't mind so much if it was Kris doing the ordering but these strange blank-faced guards and the monster they served...she shivered, wondering what kind of ritual this was going to be. It didn't bear thinking about, she turned her mind determinedly onto a different topic.

Kris had said they were in the headquarters of The Dark Eye so presumably they were somewhere near the vicinity of Washington, DC. She knew the area a little, having grown up in the Shenandoah Valley in Virginia where several of the small towns were bedroom communities to the Capitol.

If she and Kris could just get free of here, she could take him back to the house she'd grown up in. Her father would be in Florida this time of year but Lauren knew where he kept the spare key. There was even a windowless root cellar for Kris to stay during the day...she felt another jagged laugh coming on.

Good thing her father *was* in Florida. She could just imagine the look on his face when she brought home a vampire.

Hey, Daddy, meet Kris. He's a vampire and I've been posing as his human concubine while we lived in a Houston S&M club and preformed sex acts for the undead.

Lauren shook her head. How could she go from the mundane existence of a research scientist one week to vampire sex slave the next? It just didn't make sense. She wished her Gram was still alive, she would've understood. Lauren could almost hear her in her head. *So what if he's a vampire, honey? He's cuter than a bug's ear!*

Have to stop thinking like this. I think I'm going crazy. All the stress I've been under is cracking me up. She ran a hand through her snarled blonde hair and looked in the mirror. The face that stared back was smudged with dirt and her green eyes were completely hopeless. That wouldn't do. "Trust me," Kris had said, as they led him away and Lauren knew she had to at least try. He had come back for her—had given up his life's goal and risked his own life to save hers.

He wouldn't have come here without a plan, Lauren told herself firmly. Kris wouldn't let her down—she had to believe in that. For the second time she wished the bond between them was complete or sealed or whatever the hell it was that made it solid enough to feel each other through. He was trapped somewhere the same as her, she wished she could send him a thought or even a feeling.

Closing her eyes she reached out, wishing to feel even a little of him somewhere in this place. *I'm here,* she thought as hard as she could. *I trust you, Kris. And...I love you.* A week ago she would have thought such a thing was stupid and unscientific but now she though she felt the faintest whisper of emotion from somewhere, a tendril of love and a fierce protectiveness she hoped she wasn't imagining.

I'll take him home as soon as this is all over, Lauren promised herself.

If we can ever get out of here.

* * * * *

The shower refreshed her more than she would have thought possible. She thought about not wearing the long red dress but decided, with a sigh, that she would rather put it on herself than have Larry, Moe, and Curly put it on her.

She wriggled into it and took a look in the mirror, frowning at what she saw. She had definitely lost some weight. But she didn't think her diet plan, which included not one but two vampire kidnappings in one week, was likely to put Atkins out of business any time soon.

The long-sleeved dress fit her like a second skin, dipping low in the front to emphasize her cleavage and hugging her curves lovingly. There was a high slit up one side that showed a generous amount of thigh and a pair of red, high-heeled pumps that were going to kill her arches if she had to wear them for any amount of time. Lauren would have been more worried but with three zombie guards waiting outside the bathroom door to take her to a vampire "ritual" involving a monster, she thought she had worse things to look forward to than aching feet.

She considered trying to break the mirror and using the glass shards as a weapon or maybe just attacking her guards with one of the spike-heeled, wildly impractical, ruby pumps. Then she remembered the sheer numbers of blank faces when the monster had come to take Kris away the night before and realized it was probably useless. Besides, even if she did manage to get away from her guards, she still wasn't leaving without Kris. She was just going to have to trust that he would know what to do when the time came.

There was a pounding on the door. "It is time," a deep voice intoned.

Feeling like her heart was in her throat, Lauren turned the knob and went out.

* * * * *

She was led down more corridors until they came to a large set of double doors made of some kind of black wood bound with brass. From inside the closed doors she could hear the deep, rhythmic boom of someone striking a huge gong. On the tenth stroke, the doors suddenly parted and she was led inside.

The first things she noticed were the candles, hundreds of them burning in banks all along the walls of the huge circular room they were about to enter. It looked a little like a Catholic church, she thought. But there were no pews and no pulpit. Just a row of pale faces leading from the doorway to platform with a circle of marble pillars located in the dead center of the stone room.

Her three guards escorted her down the row of faces, some of which, she saw, appeared to be vampires instead of the zombie-like servants. She could tell the difference by the cold eyes and the gleaming white fangs. But vampires and servants were all dressed identically, in the long black robes and there must have been over a hundred of them in the room.

She felt like the bride in some bizarre wedding, being led to an altar where she didn't know what kind of groom awaited her. She strained her eyes to see what was in the middle of the stone pillars but all the light was concentrated on the perimeter of the room and the space at the center remained in shadows.

To Lauren it all felt very surreal, like a dream that was happening to someone else. She became aware of a low, throbbing hum rising from many voices and realized that the entire strange "congregation" was making the noise. It had a buzzing, hypnotic quality that made her want to close her eyes and lie down somewhere.

Just as she was wondering if the strange march down the aisle of white faces was ever going to end, she caught a glimpse into the thick shadows in the center of the ring of marble pillars. Stray flickers of candlelight glinted over curving tusks and slitted yellow eyes. Rubbery black lips stretched wide to greet her with a hideous smile.

"No… *No!*" The strange paralysis that had gripped her broke and Lauren dug in her heels and tried to resist. She writhed free of her captors and darted to one side, meaning to make it back to the large double doors. But the sea of pale faces closed ranks around her and she found herself faced with rows of black robes everywhere she turned.

"So touching." The thing on the platform in the center of the pillars was speaking. Many hands gripped her, turning her back inevitably towards the center of the room. "You act exactly as Nickoli's first love did when I met her in the woods outside her village. Like her, you are a whore, stealing the love that was rightfully meant for his family, so I ordered you dressed as such. Do you like your lovely new dress, my dear? "

Lauren shook her head numbly. "No…I-I'm not…"

"So said his beloved Jenica." The dead-liver lips were still grinning as she was forced closer and closer to the monster. "I sent her a message, you see, telling her that I was he. That it was all a terrible mistake—a silly joke gone wrong. How eagerly she came to meet me and how piteously she cried when it was my arms that enfolded her instead of his. Come." Long arms stretched out to her, the hands bony and sepulchral as he beckoned for her.

"No…" But this time it was a whisper. She felt the sense of dread that seemed to emanate from this thing as she had the night before and all her courage seemed to leave her. It was like being in a horrible nightmare she couldn't wake up from.

She found she was up the few marble steps and in the circle of pillars that rose to the vaulted roof of the strange circular room. "*Please…*" She was within the circle of the monster's arms, being held close to that black-clad chest so icy cold where no heart beat.

"Now then, my dear." It spoke in that thick, clotted voice, made all the more horrible because, pressed as she was against its chest, she could feel the vibrations and smell the rotted reek of its breath. It looked down at her with amusement dancing in the inhuman yellow eyes. "I would expect you to have more affection for the brother of your beloved, little human," it grated.

Lauren shook her head, frozen within its embrace. It reminded her of the time when she was a teenager and a huge waterbug had gotten stuck in her long hair. It had wriggled madly, getting more and more entangled in the long strands and she had felt as if she would go insane with the loathsome sensation before her Gram had finally managed to get it out.

The monster was talking again. "I know we don't look much alike. Nickoli got most of the looks in the family." Its laughter skittered across her ears like a trapped spider and she felt like she might go crazy. What was the thing saying? That it was related to Kris somehow? He had acknowledged it as his Maker, though how something like the thing that was currently pressing her against its cold chest could possibly have anything to do with someone like Kris who was everything it was not...

"Look at me, little one. I want you to know these things before the ritual begins." A long crooked finger that seemed to have too many joints tilted her chin up until she was staring into the yellow lamps that passed for its eyes.

"What?" she croaked, wanting only to get away. Wanting only to never touch it or have it touch her again.

"Tonight there will be an ancient ritual enacted before your eyes, a challenge as old as the world itself. Vlatzele, we call it— the duel to the death. And all for *you*, little human, because he will not give you up." Anger burned in the yellow eyes now and the long arms tightened around her, making her terribly aware of how easily the being holding her could crush her spine.

"Please!" Lauren gasped for air and the pressure let up a little.

"In a few moments your paramour will enter the room to fight for you. Your champion, your lover. He believes that as his equinox is upon him and his strength is at its highest peak, he may defeat me."

The glittering eyes blazed down at her, the liver-lips stretched wide in silent laughter that vibrated her bones. "But know this—he cannot defeat me tonight or any other night.

Though I am his Maker, I am also his brother and he has drunk of me only once. For a century his power has grown but it is diluted, a fraction of my own. None of my blood or essence has passed into his system since that first night I made him and I took care that he should have only the least amount of me, of my power. I injected only enough essence to hold him and gave him barely enough blood to turn him to the Second Life. He would not be what he is at all if his blood ties did not echo my own."

It grinned at her again. "And so you see, he cannot win the Vlatzele and he will die before your eyes. I wanted you to know it, indeed, I want you to warn him. Scream and cry, make, as they say, a scene. My victory will be all the sweeter for it."

Not one word in ten had penetrated her frightened brain but the gist of what the thing was saying to her made it through. He was going to let Kris come in and fight for her with the idea that he could save her when in actuality it was hopeless. A trick, a trap. And she would be the bait that lured him in. She shook her head, her lips forming a soundless "no".

"Oh yes, my dear." It grinned at her and then turned her so that her back was pressed against its chest and bellowed in that cracked voice, "Let him come in but do not yet let him pass."

The wide black doors swung open for a second time that night and Lauren could see Kris standing between them, haloed by the outside light. He was wearing his white shirt unbuttoned with the sleeves rolled up his muscular forearms and there was a grim, determined look in the pale blue eyes.

"Brother, I come!" he shouted, his deep voice echoing in the cavernous room.

"No!" Lauren found herself screaming, begging him to go back even though she knew it was exactly what the thing that held her wanted. "Kris, it's a trap!" She felt hot tears flowing down her cheeks and couldn't seem to stop them.

"You may approach on one condition." The monster raised its voice to be heard above her crying and the strange buzzing hum of the congregation.

"Name your condition for I am coming," Kris cried back. He would have pressed through the sea of pale faces but they formed a wall against him, many bodies thick and he could not pass.

"Your equinox is upon you tonight, I see, little brother." The chest behind her swelled with the words. "We must level the field. For is it not said that only the Made can unmake his Maker when the time is right?"

"You're wasting time, coward. Hiding behind old tales and superstitions. I thought better of you." In the candlelight his white shirt was like a shining star in the ocean of black robes.

Lauren could feel the long, crooked body behind her clench in rage but the monster's voice was steady when it answered.

"Do you love the little human doctor enough to endure the gantlet of pain to reach her?" it shouted. "Does your love extend so far, little brother?"

"Indeed." Kris stood taller and Lauren, who had quieted in the thing's arms, almost exhausted by fear and disgust, came alive again.

"A trap! Kris, it's a trap!" She felt like she was screaming herself hoarse but it did no good. Kris just looked at her and shook his head, as though telling her not to worry, to trust him.

The aisle was opening down the center of the pale faces again but this time it was lined with gleaming fangs. The silent zombie-like servants were stepping back and letting the vampires take their places up and down the line. Eager anticipation shone in their cold eyes. Lauren didn't know what came next and she didn't want to know. Please, God, she *so much* didn't want to know.

"I am coming!" Kris shouted again. "Your gantlet cannot stop me. Pray to your dark Master for your soul, brother, if you have one."

"We shall see," the monster snarled. "Come then, if you dare."

Kris walked forward, chest out and head held high, stepping into the aisle lined by sharp fangs and cold eyes. His own fangs were retracted, his hands held out, palm up, as though offering himself for some ancient sacrifice.

Lauren watched in horror, unable to look away as he stepped forward. She saw the first vampire in line swipe at him, leaving a ragged trail of bloody claw marks along one high cheekbone. Kris walked stoically forward, though the wound must have hurt and offered no retaliation. His eyes fixed on hers for an instant, his gaze unwavering.

A second vampire stepped forward with a low hiss and clawed at his chest, tearing a long, ragged rip in the white shirt. As Lauren watched, the edges of the rip bloomed with blood, proving the vampire had not missed its target, but still Kris walked on as though nothing had happened.

"No! Kris, go back!" she begged him with her voice and pleaded with her eyes but he walked forward, ignoring the gleaming fangs and sharp claws that blocked his way. Two more of the Second Life stepped forward. One grabbed his shirt and ripped it completely off and the other sank fangs into one of his broad shoulders. Kris shrugged them off, ignoring the strip of skin the vampire biting him took with it as it fell away. And still they came.

His pale skin was more red than white now, the blood flowing from his shoulder, arms, neck and sides. It was agony for Lauren to watch him stride stoically onward while the vampires in black robes ripped at his skin and clawed at his flesh. Yet he never showed a single sign of pain or weakness, he only kept his eyes on hers and continued.

For me…he's doing this all for me. It was hard to comprehend and yet an undeniable fact. He was halfway up the long aisle and the buzzing hum from the throats of the black-robed servants had risen in pitch to a whining drone that was maddening to listen to.

Lauren thought it was hard to tell with all the blood but some of his earlier wounds seemed to be healing. And yet, remarkable as his regenerative power was, it couldn't keep up with the wounds they kept inflicting on him. She could smell a heavy, flat, metallic scent in the air. It coated her tongue and the back of her throat and she knew it was the scent of fresh blood — Kris' blood.

A new thought came to her. How much blood did he have to spare? He'd drunk from her only a very little the night before while sucking the monster's essence from her arm and she remembered thinking in their room at The House of Pain that he looked white and drawn.

She'd forbidden him to drink from her, had told him she wasn't his "blood bank" and now he was in a fight for his life with little or no nourishment in his body. It was like asking a starving man to go two out of three rounds with the heavyweight champion of the world in a fixed fight. He was walking into a trap.

"Kris, no!" The words left her lips in a gasp as the thing behind her pulled her tight against it. Kris was nearly three quarters down the aisle now, his bare torso gleaming with blood like a sticky red bodysuit in the candlelight. *He's going to make it…he's really going to make it*, Lauren thought. But that was when the remaining vampires converged in the center of the aisle.

It was as though the scent of his blood drove them mad. Like sharks in a feeding frenzy, they fell upon him, burying him under a mound of black cloaks, the humming, droning, buzz rising to a fever pitch as they fed and fed and fed…

"*No!*" She shrieked it, feeling his pain, feeling his need, his anger, his love. Feeling everything that made him Kris.

"Well, my dear, what a shame our Nickoli could not make it through to save you. So very sa — "

Its words were cut off abruptly as there a sudden commotion along the aisle. The black backs writhed and rippled like water in a pond and Lauren saw one strong, bare arm raised above the crowd. Then there was a convulsive heave and the vampires exploded outwards, thrown back with a force that seemed impossibly strong. It was as though there was a sudden earthquake and they all happened to be standing on the fault line.

Black-cloaked figures flew in every direction and there was Kris, bloody but unbowed, striding forward again. His face was a mask of crimson, terrible to see because of the way his pale blue eyes and pearly white teeth flashed out in the middle of all that red. His fangs were out now, no longer a sacrifice—now he was an avenging angel, a wrathful god bent on vengeance.

"Brother!" he roared, wading relentlessly forward, shoving black figures out of his way like matchstick men as he came. "I come! Release my concubine!"

"She is not yours, you are not even bonded to her!" The thing behind her tightened its grip until Lauren was gasping for air and struggling feebly in its grasp. It was actually lifting her off the ground. She kicked back with the spiked heels, feeling one of them leave her foot, but the other connected with something solid.

The monster roared in surprise and pain and flung her away. Lauren flew through the air, like a rag doll thrown by a petulant toddler. Her forward motion was halted by one of the large, marble pillars and she saw slow-motion fireworks explode behind her eyelids when her head struck the solid stone.

Concussion, she thought, sliding down the slick, cold surface of the pillar's side and then everything went gray for a moment.

When she came to, Kris and his Maker were circling each other, like wrestlers looking for a good hold. The floor of the small platform was growing red and slippery with the blood that was raining down from Kris' wounds, which were too many to count.

"Cry off, little brother, you cannot win." The voice of the monster was thick with amusement.

Kris wiped blood from his eyes—his dark-chocolate hair was thick with it—and laughed. It was a low, hoarse sound but there was a grim humor in it all the same. "You forget, *brother*, this is Vlatzele—there can be no crying off. I came to kill you and this I will do." He lunged forward suddenly, getting a hold on the monstrous neck and digging in with his claws.

The monster roared, baring its yellowish tusks and retaliated by locking its own, many-jointed fingers around Kris' neck. They scrabbled for an instant, each trying to get a better grip and Lauren pulled her legs up to her chest, horrified at the battle going on not two feet in front of her. If they fell on the floor she was going to be dragged into it whether she wanted to be or not. They were just too close.

The monster lost its grip on Kris' throat, slippery with blood, and pulled back. With a wrenching movement, it managed to break Kris' hold on its own neck and staggered away, laughing hoarsely.

"Give up, Nickoli. You are too weak," it gasped thickly. "How much blood have you lost and when was the last time you fed? I know it cannot have been for at least twenty-four hours for you were separated from your little whore all last night."

"You will not speak so of my beloved." Kris' chest was heaving like a bellows but he was still upright. He staggered forward. "And I have fed enough to defeat you. I sucked your essence from her veins before you found us and Lauren's blood is sweet and pure. A drop from her is enough to sustain me for hours."

"Y-you tasted my essence?" The thing staggered backwards and for the first time, Lauren, still watching from the shadows, thought it sounded anxious, maybe even afraid.

"I would not leave her flesh so polluted by your foul venom." Kris nodded at her, never taking his eyes from the yellow-slitted ones. "Push up your sleeve, Lauren, and prove to this creature that he has left no mark upon you."

Trembling, she did as he asked, pulling up the long sleeve of the red gown to reveal an arm that was pale and smooth and unmarked, healed by Kris' own essence.

"But…" The thing slipped on the bloody floor and righted itself with panicky haste. "You said nothing of draining my essence from her arm when I told you I had bitten her the night before."

"And why should I?" Kris sneered, stepping forward and pressing the advantage. His gaze blazed furiously in the bloody mask of his face. "Surely you do not believe all the old tales, *brother*, of a Maker being unmade by his own creation. Surely you do not fear the blood that ties us together and your own strength that flows in my veins?"

"No!" The thing was pressed with its back against the pillar opposite Lauren and she could see the fear lighting its yellow eyes.

"You do fear it." There was a grim revelation in Kris' voice. "All the old tales and rumors—you believe them, don't you?"

The thing shook its head, a frantic gesture of negation but Lauren could see the truth in its jack-o'-lantern face and apparently Kris could too. He stepped back for a moment, a look of wonder passing briefly over his chiseled, bloody features. Lauren understood that something of significance had taken place, though her muddled brain refused to make sense of what.

"Seeing that you believe the rumors and legends, let us test them, shall we?" He stared at the monster and Lauren did too, wondering what the hell he was doing. There was nothing for a moment and then a large blue vein began to pulse in the middle of the monstrous visage, bisecting the horror-mask of its face in half. Kris' maker clutched briefly at his pulsing head and then he sank down the pillar into a sprawled heap.

"*No!*" It was an agonized howl but it seemed only to encourage Kris. He stared harder at the monster sprawled on the floor in front of him and Lauren watched with awe and revulsion as the pulsing vein running down the center of its face, from forehead to chin, grew from the size of a worm to the circumference of a snake. It throbbed and writhed in his pale face, looking alive, the only thing alive in those hideous, inhuman features.

"You mustn't…you *can't!*" it howled, the vein growing ever larger in its marbled skin. It was a deep purple now and so thick it looked like a baby python had found its way under his epidermis and was struggling to find its way out again.

"No, I shouldn't be able to, should I?" Kris' voice was low and preoccupied, as though he was having a rather unimportant conversation with someone he didn't particularly care for at a boring party. But his concentration never wavered. "We of the Second Life cannot, as a rule, use our powers upon each other so. But for this night only, brother, our powers are one. One hundred years ago exactly you made me in your image and tonight we are equal. I give you back the gift you bestowed on me with interest to spare."

The monster was screaming now, screaming in its cracked and clotted voice that Lauren knew she would hear in her dreams for a thousand years.

"You cannot, you dare not—we are drawn together, you and I. If you kill me you kill yourself, Nickoli! *Nickoli!*"

"So be it." Kris' voice was low and final. "I will consider it a small price to rid the world of your evil."

The vein pulsing beneath the surface of the monster's mottled skin was a monstrous thing now in its own right. It overshadowed the yellow eyes and curving tusks, pulsing like an enormous tumor filled with blood and ready to pop at any moment.

Kris looked away for a split second and caught Lauren's eyes. There might have been something resembling regret in the pale blue depths but the glance was too short to be certain.

"Move away, Lauren." His voice was low and calm. "There is going to be a mess."

Numbly, she slid backwards, aided by the slippery material of the red dress, and felt her way without looking for the step behind her. Kris looked at her once more. "Goodbye, *Solnyshko.*" Then he stepped forward and stared hard at the writhing, screaming thing at the base of the pillar.

"This, *brother*, is for Jenica and for Lauren." He made a swift, decisive gesture with his chin, staring hard at the hideous face. The pulsing, blood-filled vein at the center of the monster's forehead blew in a cold, oily geyser of blue-black blood and with a last, cracked shriek, it collapsed.

Chapter Twenty-Six

"Kris? *Kris*?" He was briefly aware of someone shaking him, of a concerned face looking down into his own. Slanted green eyes like a cat's looked into his and hair like the sunshine, which he had not seen for so long, brushed his face. He smiled up at her and tried to speak.

"*Solnyshko...*" The name died on his lips. He felt the life force rushing from him, pouring out with the black and red blood puddling on the floor. Some his and some the others—his Maker's. His brother's.

So the old tales were true, the Made can unmake his Maker under the proper circumstances. But the warnings were true as well. The ties were too strong, he had killed his Maker but the death would take him down as well.

So be it. Vengeance has its price and he was willing to pay.

The last thing he saw were the tears shining in her eyes. *Sorry*, he tried to say, but it wouldn't come out in English, only in Russian, and he knew she wouldn't understand.

"Kris..." Her voice, soft and low and desperate followed him down into the void.

And then darkness ate the world.

* * * * *

So much blood! Lauren cradled his head in her lap, trying to feel for a pulse on the red, slippery throat. She thought she felt something—weak and thready—but she couldn't be sure. *I'm a doctor*, she reminded herself sternly. *I can handle this!* But none of the patients she'd had to treat in the past had meant so much to her. Death had never been so personal before.

The bottom half of her dress was soaked both with Kris' blood and the blue-black ichor that had erupted from the monster's burst vessel but she didn't even care. She would have swum through a whole vat of the stuff if only it would help Kris.

*Blood...*the thought penetrated her brain. *Blood, of course! He needs blood – a transfusion!* No, she realized, not a transfusion. At least, not in the traditional sense of the word.

She looked around eagerly for anything sharp, anything with an edge, but she was stuck on the platform in the center of the room with no company but a corpse and Kris, who would soon be one, if she didn't do something quickly. A few of the pale-faced, black-robed servants were still wandering aimlessly, like wind-up toys that hadn't quite wound down yet, but they didn't look like they'd be any help at all.

At last she had a thought. Prying Kris' jaw open, she nearly cried with relief when she saw his fangs were still out, looking needle-sharp. There was no pale blue essence to ease the way though, the fangs were bone-dry. Slitting her eyes against the pain, she gouged her wrist over those wicked-looking points, slitting the tender bracelet of blue veins that pulsed just under the surface of her skin.

The pain was immediate and excruciating and for a moment, she thought it wasn't going to work. But then, as a slow trickle of blood filled his mouth, Kris' throat worked weakly. A moment later he swallowed convulsively. Then his lips closed around her wrist and she felt a strong pull, the suction like a reflex that cannot be denied whether conscious thought is present of not.

"Kris..." She could have cried for joy, for the flood of pleasure that suddenly washed over her when his fangs sank deep and his essence flooded her system. *If he can drink he'll be all right...* She held on to that thought, that hope as she fed him from herself.

It was only when the world started looking gray and washed-out around the edges that she realized giving Kris life might mean her own death. If she fainted from blood loss she wasn't going to be any good to either one of them. She had to get him somewhere she could care for him and give the essence he'd injected into her system time to encourage her body to manufacture more red blood cells.

With some difficulty and a lot of pain, she disengaged her wrist from his mouth. She would have to tear a strip of her gown off to bind the wound…but even as she was thinking that, the blood flow stopped and the wound sealed itself, obviously an effect of his essence in her system. Lauren reflected that if she ever got back to a halfway normal life she was going to do a complete chemical analysis on that pale blue liquid. But there was no time to think about that now. She had to get Kris somewhere safe, preferably out of this castle or dungeon or whatever the hell it was The Dark Eye called home.

She thought of the dead black, light-tight limo that had brought her here. If she could get him into a vehicle like that it might be safe to attempt to get Kris back to the house she'd grown up in, in Staunton. The Shenandoah Valley where her little hometown was located was several hours drive from the outskirts of DC. She wished she knew their exact location or even what time it was. Obviously it would be safer to transport him at night…

"Lauren?"

She started at the weak voice and looked down to see the pale blue eyes fluttering. He tried to sit up and she pressed him back down.

"Lie still, Kris, you've lost a lot of blood. In fact for a minute there I th-thought I'd lost you." She blinked back the tears that wanted to come, forcing herself to hold the emotion in check. There was no time for it now.

Kris reached up and touched her face, catching a single tear on one bloodied fingertip. "And I thought I was going. I was dying but your blood brought me back."

Lauren didn't know how to answer the second part so she answered his first statement instead. "You're not going anywhere without me," she said fiercely. "So don't even think about it."

A slow smile lit his bloody face. "I will, of course, obey the doctor's orders." He struggled to sit up again. With a sigh, she helped him.

Lauren looked him over, trying to keep her mind detached and professional, as though he was any other patient she happened to be treating. His wounds had begun healing again though some of the deeper ones looked like they would take a while to close completely.

"You look like something the cat dragged in," she informed him.

He raised one eyebrow. "Oh?"

"It's something my Gram would've said," she explained. Actually her Gram would've said he looked like the walking dead but that seemed in poor taste just then. "Listen, if you can walk I think we'd better get you out of here. Most of the vampires ran away when you killed their, uh…was that thing really your brother?" She looked over his shoulder and saw that there was nothing left of the hideous beast that had claimed to be both Kris' Maker and his brother but a puddle of black goo.

"Yes, it was my brother," Kris said shortly. He took a deep breath and let it out in a long, exhausted sigh. "Lauren, I have many wounds and I don't know how long the blood you gave me can sustain me."

Hesitantly, she offered him her wrist but he shook his head. Planting a gentle kiss on the inside of her palm, he pushed her arm away. "No, my darling. You need blood to live as well—I will not drain you dry." He heaved himself to his feet and stood swaying for a moment with one hand braced against a pillar.

"Are you sure you can walk?" Lauren stood also and looked at him anxiously.

He nodded. "For a very little way. Listen, when I was looking for you last night I found the garage where they keep their cars. If we can get there before the others of the Second Life return…"

"Exactly what I was thinking. Lead the way."

* * * * *

It was considerably more than a short way and they had to stop several times for Kris to rest. Lauren helped him as well as she could but he was seriously wounded and deeply exhausted. When he leaned against her it was almost like supporting dead weight and he was so big there wasn't much she could do.

As they walked down the corridors, she saw they were leaving a trail of blood. Lauren had been sitting in, and Kris had been lying in a puddle of the stuff, both his and the monster's, and it had soaked into his pants and the entire bottom half of her dress. Lauren anxiously reexamined Kris and determined that most of his wounds were closed now, although his skin, beneath its coating of drying maroon, still looked terribly pale.

After squishing down what felt like a mile of corridors, she wished she'd asked if they could look for a change of clothes but it was too late. She'd change when she got to her old home, she always kept a few extra things there for her biannual visits. That was, if she could get them there safely.

At last they reached a functional wooden door that led out to a huge garage. Kris opened it and Lauren whistled in appreciation.

He nodded. "Yes, whatever else The Dark Eye is, they aren't poor. In a society of the wealthy they manage to outdo us, at least here." He nodded at the fleet of limousines and dead black luxury cars just waiting for drivers. Hanging on one wall was a rack with a row of hooks with the keys to each vehicle neatly numbered.

Lauren tried to smile. "Probably save lots of money on decorating and their clothing budget. By the way, I've been meaning to ask you, do all you guys have the same decorator or what?" She indicated the long stone hallway they had just left.

"As to that..." Kris didn't finish his sentence. Instead, he collapsed in slow motion to the garage's concrete floor. Apparently his small reserve of energy had run out.

"Kris? *Kris*?" Lauren bent by him, slapping his cheeks lightly. His eyelids fluttered but all she could get from him was a low moan. Unable to think of anything else to do, she pressed her wrist against his mouth. "Drink," she commanded.

His eyelids fluttered again and he shook his head weakly, trying to push her away.

"Do it," Lauren insisted. "Just enough to get you on your feet long enough to get into one of these cars. You're too big to lift and the others might be back at any second."

"Don't want...hurt you." His words were muffled but understandable.

"You won't," Lauren said, hoping she was telling the truth. To be honest, she was more than a little lightheaded and dizzy herself. "Drink just a little. You need it more than me right now."

Unable to refuse her any longer, he bit deeply, drawing in several mouthfuls while she bit her lip against the mingled pain and pleasure. After what seemed like an eternity he released her. His eyes were a little brighter now, though not by much. With Lauren's help he managed to stagger to his feet.

"Have to go soon...I'm afraid you'll have to drive, I'm not up to it."

Lauren eyed his tall, blood-covered figure with concern. "That's an understatement if I ever heard one." Counting quickly down the long row of cars, she picked a plain black Caddy that looked low-key and, hopefully, easy to drive. A digital clock on the wall marked the time at just past three a.m. so if she hurried, she might be able to get Kris back to her house before dawn.

Lauren squished briskly over to the key rack and got the keys corresponding to the Caddy. She was going to have to be very careful to drive the speed limit. She couldn't begin to think of a good enough story to explain to a state trooper if she got stopped why she was wearing a blood-soaked dress with an unconscious and bloody man who was actually a vampire in the backseat.

She unlocked the Caddy, leaving bloody footprints on the brushed concrete floor of the garage and nodded at Kris. "Climb in the backseat and make yourself comfortable. I'll be the chauffer."

He stumbled to the side of the car and collapsed into the backseat, consciousness leaving almost as soon as his head hit the leather.

Lauren felt better when Kris was safely stowed in the Caddy, which, like the limo she'd ridden in, had a black glass barrier that could be raised or lowered at will between the front and the back. She searched around until she found a switch on the wall and opened the door, noting that it was pitch black outside, without even any exterior lights to aid her. Dimly, winding away into the darkness, she could make out a rutted dirt road. She climbed into the Caddy and slammed the door, jamming the key into the ignition.

The dashboard light said three-fifteen a.m. — it was time to get rolling.

She thought the damn dirt road was going to go on forever but at last it dead-ended into an intersection where her only choices were to go left or right. Lauren looked both ways and sighed deeply. "What the hell," she said aloud, and turned the wheel to the left onto the uneven blacktop.

After twenty minutes of driving with no road signs, she was sure she was lost somewhere in the sticks when suddenly a familiar green signboard flashed into view. *Arlington — 20 miles.* Lauren sighed with relief. Once she hit Arlington, she'd know where she was. It would be a simple matter of getting on I-64 and taking it to I-81. From I-81 it was a straight shot to Staunton.

Once her anxiety wore off, however, she began to realize how incredibly tired she was. The pain and terror and anxiety of the past twenty-four to forty-eight hours or however long she'd been held captive was catching up to her. Her emotional, mental and physical reserves were almost exhausted and she was weak from blood loss and from not eating in two days. There had been two buckets in her cell, one filled with water and one for other, necessary functions, but the servants of The Dark Eye hadn't bothered to feed her a thing.

Many times she caught her eyelids closing and twice she snapped them back open just as the car was drifting into the opposite lane. Driving through the mountainous country that led to the Shenandoah Valley, changing lanes unexpectedly was no joke. She didn't want to wake up at the bottom of a ravine.

To keep herself awake, Lauren flipped on the radio which was tuned to some kind of current-events AM station. She listened until the commentators turned into a dull drone that could no longer keep her awake. Then she punched buttons until she found an eighties station which was a little more lively.

Every once in a while she turned her head to check on Kris but he was still out cold. Only the slow, even motion of his chest let her know he was still in the land of the living, or the unliving, or whatever. She sighed.

Three hours later she finally pulled into the driveway of the secluded old brick house on Bluff Avenue in Staunton, Virginia. Cyndi Lauper was proclaiming to anyone who would listen that "Girls Just Wanna Have Fun".

"Some fun," Lauren muttered to herself. Vampire rituals, being kept in a dungeon for two days straight with no food, hordes of zombie guards and having the man she was beginning to realize she had very strong feelings for nearly die on her fighting a duel for her life. Oh yeah, it beat Disney World any day of the week.

She parked and tried to slide out of the Caddy's door which resulted in a low ripping noise. The back of the silky red dress had been glued to the leather seat with the drying blood and now the dress was ruined. Well, too bad, it looked like she'd have to find something else to wear to the next vampire ritual, not that she ever planned on attending any more of them if she could help it.

She staggered out of the car, glad that the nearest neighbors were a half-mile away on the other side of the bluff. The horizon was just beginning to get pink, she needed to hurry.

It was easier to tell herself to hurry than to actually do it, however. She tripped stupidly over the neatly placed stepping stones, feeling almost drunk with exhaustion. Fumbling under the plastic rock her dad kept behind one of the shrubs, she at last managed to extract the key and let herself into the house.

Once inside she stumbled through the living and dining room, keeping her eyes averted from the loud green plaid sofa her Dad still insisted on keeping. It was hideous to look at but she had to admit, it was wonderfully comfortable—a great place for a nap. *Just a nap, let's just lay down for a minute,* a sneaky little voice whispered inside her head but Lauren knew if she did, she'd never get Kris into the safety of the dark garage.

It took a moment of fumbling with the latch to raise the wide wooden panel of the garage door. Lauren was groggily grateful that it wasn't one of the kind that had little windows set into it. She was going to have to leave Kris in here for the day and hope he would be all right. There was no way even if she'd been healthy and alert that she could have dragged him inside and down into the root cellar where she'd originally intended to put him and he wouldn't wake up no matter how hard she tried.

At last the Caddy was parked in the garage and the door was safely down. Lauren debated leaving him locked in the car but she was afraid he wouldn't get enough air. How much air did a vampire need though? Didn't they sleep in coffins? There wasn't much air in a coffin, was there? Compromising, she cracked the window closest to his feet, making sure his head was still well hidden in the shadows of the car. That way even if a little light crept into the garage under the door, he should be okay.

She took a last look at his face, so pale under its mask of drying blood. He appeared to be breathing all right but she wished there was something else she could do for him. If he'd been a human patient she would have had him in a hospital and ordered multiple transfusions of whole blood and run a battery of tests to make sure he was stable. But with no real working knowledge of vampire physiology and biology, her hands were tied.

"We're going to make it through this together and then I'm going to do some serious research into what makes you tick, buddy," she informed the inert form in the back of the car. She became aware that she was shivering. It was much colder in Virginia than it had been in Houston. Wrapping her arms around herself, she managed to get into the house. First a hot shower and then she intended to sleep for at least twelve hours. She'd earned it.

Chapter Twenty-Seven

When she woke up the first stars of evening were twinkling through her bedroom window and Kris was sitting quietly on the side of her bed, watching her.

"What?" Lauren sat up so suddenly she felt dizzy.

"My apologies, Lauren, I didn't mean to startle you. But I wished to see you one last time before I left." The deep voice was quiet and a little sad. His pale skin was still a little damp and the chocolate brown hair was slicked back from his forehead with water. Lauren reflected that she must have been very tired not to hear the noisy hot water heater kick on while he was taking a shower. Then his words sank in.

"Leave? You can't leave now," she protested. "Look, just let me…" She looked down, realizing she had gone to sleep naked and the covers were slipping beneath her breasts. She blushed and tugged at the sheet hastily. Trying to get out of the headquarters of The Dark Eye they had been almost comradely, almost friends. Now that the crisis had passed, she felt awkward and uncertain around him again.

"Just hand me my robe." She motioned to the maple bureau that was sitting against the far wall. "Top left drawer, I'm sure I left one here."

Without comment, Kris got her the silky emerald green robe that had been a present the Christmas before last. He himself was wearing an old pair of sweatpants that he must have found in the laundry room which adjoined the garage. It was the first time Lauren had seen him in anything but a formal suit, aside from the strange duel of the night before, and she reflected that he looked nice, more casual and approachable dressed like this.

She struggled into the robe, trying to get herself covered quickly. Kris' gaze on her body still made her feel hot and nervous, though she ought to be used to it by now.

She wondered where he was going to go and what he planned to do. Also, would she ever see him again once he left? There was something so final in his eyes as he looked at her. Then her stomach rumbled embarrassingly, reminding her how long it had been since she'd had anything to eat.

Kris raised one dark eyebrow. "Hungry?"

"Let's go downstairs and I'll eat something while we talk." Lauren led the way down to the kitchen, a large room with old-fashioned, dark wood panel cabinets. It was separated by a half wall from the small breakfast nook to one side. She was about to start rummaging through the cabinets when she realized she could already smell something good. Following her nose around to the postage stamp-sized table in the breakfast nook, she found a steaming bowl of soup and a hot cup of tea already waiting.

"Kris," she said surprised. "You didn't have to."

He shrugged. "I am sorry it's not very elegant but the selection of ingredients here is somewhat limited."

"That's all right." Lauren smiled and settled herself at the table, picking up the spoon he'd thoughtfully provided. "I don't really like caviar and champagne all that much. Give me Campbell's chicken noodle any time."

"So this is the house you grew up in?" Kris sat across from her, looking around attentively.

Lauren blew on a spoonful of soup and nodded. "Yup. My father's in Florida this time of the year so I knew it would be safe to come."

"I want to thank you for saving my life," he said softly, catching her eyes with his own.

Lauren blushed and looked down at her bowl of soup. "I was worried about you the whole trip back here. I-I'm glad you're okay, Kris."

"Thank you," he said gravely.

"And — " she glanced up, unnerved to see how steadily the pale blue gaze was fixed on her. "And thank you for saving my life too. I know you didn't have to come after me. And everything you did to get to me…" She closed her eyes briefly, thinking of the horrible gantlet he'd had to go through to reach her. "But I don't understand how you ended up killing th-that monster." She didn't want to say brother, it was too strange, no matter what Kris had told her. "I thought you said vampires couldn't use their powers on each other?" She looked at him questioningly.

"Normally we cannot but these were far from normal circumstances." Kris looked thoughtful, tracing a finger along the blue and white tablecloth with one long finger as he talked. "A number of factors came together, enabling me to defeat him…"

Lauren listened while she ate her soup and drank her tea. She was fascinated by the strange, interconnected relationships and the mixture of legend and science that had enabled Kris to win the duel.

"So it had to do with that…the essence you sucked out of my arm?"

Kris nodded, "It gave me the edge of strength I needed to breach his defenses. That and the coming of my equinox, the century anniversary of my birth to the Second Life, and the complicated blood ties we shared allowed me to do what would have otherwise been impossible." He sighed. "Well, the night is still young enough to travel and I must not intrude on you any longer."

"B-but where are you going?" Lauren pushed her empty bowl and mug to one side as he rose from the table.

Kris looked at her, blue eyes stern and sad. "I promised you that when this was over I would take you home and leave you to your own devices, never to bother you again. The Gathering is already over so there is no need to detain you any further." He sighed again. "Perhaps I shall try again next century."

"You gave it up for me—your dream of becoming a legitimate member of society," Lauren said softly. She rose and came around the table to him. "I know how much it meant to you."

He shook his head. "In the past week I have learned that it means less than I thought." He turned, the pale skin of his broad back glimmering softly in the dim light of the kitchen. "I must go."

"Wait," she said desperately. "Where can you go dressed like that and what will you do?"

"You forget, Lauren, I am not without resources." He turned back to face her, a small, sardonic smile playing around the corners of his full mouth and she shivered to catch a glimpse of his fangs beneath his pale lips.

"You need to feed, to drink from someone, don't you?" She stepped forward and took his hand—it was as cold as ice.

Kris looked sad. Gently he withdrew his hand from hers. "It is a fact of my life which I cannot change." He shrugged. "I need blood to survive but I wish to get far from here before I feed. I will not taint your home with my need." He turned again but Lauren put a hand on his shoulder.

"Feed on me," she said softly. The shoulder under her hand knotted with tension.

"You do not know what you are asking." Kris didn't turn around but his deep voice was thick with some emotion she was afraid to name. "And besides, I know your feelings about anything that might increase the bond which has already grown strong between us. Last night you gave of yourself freely and for that I thank you. But if I leave you here, tonight, the bond may fade in time and you will have no other effects from it than a somewhat increased lifespan."

"I know what I'm asking." Lauren struggled to keep her voice low and steady, though it felt like a million butterflies had just taken off in her stomach.

"No," Kris turned to face her, blue eyes blazing fire and ice in a way that made her breath come short. "You do not." He gripped her shoulders suddenly and pulled her closer, nuzzling under the shelf of her jaw, planting soft kisses on the tender skin of her throat. The slow, hot motion of his mouth on her skin made her want to moan.

"I do." Lauren felt like she couldn't get enough air into her lungs, especially when she felt the sharp points of his fangs tracing delicately along the curve of her neck. "If you're...if you have to leave then I want to share this with you one more time. Please, Kris..." She looked at him pleadingly, uncertain of how he would respond.

He groaned, low in his throat and then swung her into his arms with no warning.

"What...where are you taking me?" Lauren gasped, caught completely off-guard.

"Back to your bedroom." He strode towards the stairs, carrying her as though she were as light as a feather. "I will savor this one last submission, *Solnyshko*, and keep it to treasure always."

The use of his old nickname for her made Lauren's heart feel like it was skipping every other beat. She wrapped her arms around his neck and melted against him.

"Yes, Master," she whispered, and felt a small shudder run through his large frame at her words.

Kris settled himself on his back on the bed and placed her on top of him. Lauren felt a little awkward straddling his hips. The position caused the green robe to gape apart and she fumbled nervously with it, trying to keep it closed.

"No." Kris placed both hands over hers to stop the motion. Lauren let her hands fall away as he untied her sash and spread the robe to reveal her body. "You are so beautiful, my darling." His voice was soft and deep. "Let me look at you one last time." He reached up to cup her breasts, flicking the nipples gently to attention and making Lauren gasp. "Let me touch you," he murmured.

"Oh…" Lauren felt the sigh tumble out of her as he caressed her breasts.

"How does it make you feel when I touch you like this?" Kris murmured, still pinching her nipples in the way that shot sparks of pleasure-pain to the soft vee between her legs. "Does it make you hot, my darling? Does it make you wet?"

"I…yes," she whispered, unable to lie. His hands on her, his body touching hers caused her to react helplessly as it always had. But his next request caught her off-guard.

"Show me," he said softly, still touching her, still looking deeply into her eyes.

"I…don't know what you mean."

"You do, I can tell by your eyes that you know exactly what I mean. But you wish me to elaborate I see." Kris stroked the side of her face, his hand cool against the hot blush climbing up her cheeks. "I want you to spread the sweet bare lips of your sex for me and show me how wet you are, Lauren. Do you understand now?"

"Yes…"

"Then spread yourself for me, Lauren. Do it now." His order was delivered in the same, low voice but there was a note of command in it now, the steely tone of the Master that made her shiver all over with need and desire.

Hands shaking, Lauren reached down and did as she had been told, feeling utterly naked beneath his hot blue gaze as she opened the lips of her cunt with trembling fingers and showed him the tender pink inside of her sex, so wet with desire that it glistened softly in the dim light of the bedside lamp.

"Beautiful. So very beautiful, but it is not enough. Come closer, my darling."

"I-I don't understand." Lauren gestured to indicate their current intimate position, with her straddling his hips, half naked except for the green robe.

"I mean that I want to taste you one last time. One last taste of your sweet, wet cunt." His eyes were blue fire and his hands caressed her hips.

"Oh, but I—" Lauren started to protest but before she could get the words out, Kris had pulled her forward so that she was straddling his shoulders instead of his hips. "Kris, I'll crush you!" she protested.

He laughed, a deep sound that vibrated through her, filled with amusement and affection. "Lauren, did you not see the obstacles I overcame to get to you? The gantlet filled with those soulless minions of the monster that called himself my Maker?"

Lauren nodded and bit her lip. "Yes," she said softly. "I was…oh, Kris, I was so afraid you weren't going to make it."

He smiled gently. "And yet I got through—I could not bear the thought of you in the Monster's clutches. For you are mine, *Solnyshko*, at least for tonight." He stroked her hips and sides, reaching high to caress the sensitive undersides of her breasts and his eyes looked thoughtful and sad. "Lauren," he said softly, "You saw me fight my way through a vicious horde of those of the Second Life to get to you, and yet I lived to tell the tale. Do you really think you could harm me with your beautiful body?"

"I…" Lauren shook her head. "I never thought of it like that."

"I thought not." He urged her forward, both hands planted firmly on her hips. "Let yourself down, my darling. Let me taste your sweet sex once more before I go. Trust me to support you— let me make you come as I know you need to."

"Oh, God! Kris…" Lauren moaned, feeling herself relax under the commanding words and the inexorable pressure of his hands, urging her down. She gripped the headboard of the bed tightly as she felt Kris' mouth on the bare lips of her sex, kissing softly at first, and then more urgently.

She threw back her head and cried aloud as he sucked her tender clit, swollen with desire, between his lips, and began to circle it relentlessly with his tongue. She was gasping something, moaning his name over and over again, helpless to stop as he urged her even lower.

At last she could feel the sweet pressure of his tongue driving into her. Driving deeper and deeper into her tight, wet passage as though he was searching for her heart with every thrust. The feel of his tongue fucking up into her open cunt was almost too much for Lauren to bear. She cried and writhed, grinding herself shamelessly against his mouth, feeling utterly wanton, utterly right in giving herself to him this way.

She felt herself reaching the edge, coming closer and closer to the ultimate peak as he pressed his tongue inside her. He was going to make her come, one last time as he had promised, and then he would leave. *But I don't want him to leave!* The thought was almost drowned in the intense sensation as Kris' tongue inside her finally pushed her over the edge into the most intense orgasm she'd ever experienced.

"Kris…" She was nearly sobbing with pleasure and emotion as he pulled her down gently to straddle his hips again.

"Was it good, my darling?" His piercing gaze was softer now, tender—almost wistful.

"Wonderful. Oh, Kris…"

"I am so glad. Come, share your sweet taste with me." He pulled her forward and claimed her lips in a long, hot kiss that stole her breath. Lauren moaned into his mouth as he fed her the salty-sweet flavor of her sex, thrusting his tongue into her— between her lips as he had into her sex. Long before she was ready for the kiss to end, Kris pulled back.

"You are so beautiful, my darling, and you taste so sweet. It is a flavor I will never forget."

"Kris…" She traced one hesitant finger across his broad, bare chest.

"Yes, *Solnyshko*?" He raised one eyebrow at her, obviously seeing her question.

"I want…" Lauren felt unaccountably shy, but she was determined to get her request out. "I want to taste you too," she said at last, the words coming out in an embarrassed rush. "I want…" She finished the sentence with a gesture instead of words, her fingers wandering down the inside of his thigh to cup his cock boldly.

"Ah, how can I deny such a sweet request?" Kris' waterfall blue gaze staring into hers. "If you truly wish to do this, then I would cherish the memory always."

"I do." Before she could lose her nerve, Lauren found herself kneeling beside him, working the sweatpants he was wearing down and off. His cock sprang free, already hard from the pleasure he had taken in eating her. She touched him hesitantly, then, when he moaned encouragement, she took the heated shaft completely into her hand. He was as soft as rose petals and as hard as steel all at once. Experimentally, she rubbed the heated shaft against her cheek, feeling its silky warmth and inhaling Kris' heady male musk. And yet, she needed more.

Kris almost gasped as Lauren took the crown of his cock on a sensual journey, mapping out the familiar terrain of her face. Cheeks, chin, forehead, even the eyelids…*especially* the eyelids. She wanted to feel that silky delicious heat against her skin before she tasted it. She savored the rose-petal texture of Kris' shaft, rubbed it with her cheek, tickled it with a flutter of lashes until he groaned deeply, reminding her that there was a man attached to the cock she was torturing so sweetly.

"Lauren, please…" The look in his blue eyes was heated now, almost desperate. Lauren smiled at him languidly, finding that she enjoyed turning the tables on her "Master" for a change. A single pearly drop of moisture had made its way to slit in the center of the broad head of Kris' cock and she wanted to taste it. Slowly, she lowered her head and kissed the single drop away with open lips, letting just the tip of Kris' cock make contact with her teasing, wet mouth.

"*Solnyshko!*" The muscles in Kris' thighs were as tight and hard as iron with the terrible anticipation and Lauren knew she was taking things too far but she couldn't seem to stop.

Lowering her head again, she took a leisurely, teasing lick over the pulsing crown of Kris' cock, savoring the musky salty flavor, before dipping suddenly to take him deep inside.

"Oh, darling!" Kris' breathing was ragged and gasping as she began to work him in earnest. She didn't have a great deal of experience with this kind of thing but she tried to gauge Kris' reactions to her mouth on his cock, and do what felt good to him. Despite her inexperience, Lauren was surprised at how much she was enjoying this—the heated slide of Kris' thick shaft along her tongue and the roof of her mouth, his hands caressing her hair, urging her gently to take him deeper. And most of all, the deep groans this act of love was drawing from the man beneath her.

She wanted to take him all the way. Wanted to feel his salty spray bursting across her tongue, wanted to remember his flavor forever. But Kris had other ideas.

"No, my darling. No, *Solnyshko*," he murmured, pulling her gently away from his throbbing cock.

Lauren came away slowly, looking up at him with lust-clouded eyes. He had been close—she knew it. She had felt his thick cock pulsing against her tongue, almost ready to erupt. And yet he was stopping her—why?

"We must not do this—we must stop." The look in Kris' eyes was one of deep pain, almost misery. Lauren felt she would do anything in the world to take away the sorrow she saw in his blue gaze.

"Why not?" she asked softly. She moved to straddle his hips again, feeling the tantalizing hardness of his throbbing cock brush the soft wetness of her swollen cunt. "Why can't we, Kris?"

Kris didn't answer. Instead, he reached out with one gentle finger and caressed the aching bud of her clitoris, making her gasp and jerk her hips involuntarily. "Does it feel good, *Solnyshko*? When I touch you like this? Will you miss my hands on your body when I am gone?" His voice was soft and a little sad now as he continued to stroke her.

"I...don't want you to go," Lauren whispered. Her whole body was trembling now, with need, with love.

"I don't want to go either, which is precisely why we must not do these things." Kris withdrew his hand with a sigh and shook his head.

"I don't understand." Lauren looked at him, eyes pleading.

Kris sighed again. "I told you once that I should have bonded you to me while I had the chance. If I feed on you tonight I may not be able to stop myself." Putting both hands on her hips he pressed her against him and she gasped to feel the length of his cock rubbing like warm silk along her wet, open sex.

"I-I'm not as afraid of that as I was." Lauren tilted her head back, offering him the white skin of her throat blatantly. "Master," she breathed.

"Do you mean it?" Kris looked at her fiercely, demanding that she make eye contact. "Because once I start I may be unable to stop. I want you, Lauren. Need you, need to make you mine entirely. Do not tease me if you aren't serious." His fingers dug into her hips now and she could feel the hard press of his cock throbbing impatiently against her. Impatient for her, for her body — for her submission and surrender.

"I mean it," she whispered softly. "I know we haven't known each other long but I guess it's been long enough because...well, because I love you." She looked down, unable to meet his eyes but Kris raised her chin with one finger.

"No, my darling, look at me when you say that. You see what I am, you know my curse and the limitations of my life. Can you really still mean those words when I tell you that sealing the bond between us will mean an eternity with me?"

"Yes." She looked him in the eye as he had asked, and saw the emotion blazing in the depths of that river of blue fire. "Yes, that is exactly what I want." She cleared her throat nervously.

"You told me that you wouldn't make love to me until I asked you to go all the way—to bond with me. Well...I'm asking. Please, Kris. I want you to, want you in me..."

There was no need to ask a second time. With a low groan, he pulled her closer, burying his face in her neck. At the same time, Lauren felt the head of his cock, broad and thick, nudging against the entrance to her body.

She opened herself for him willingly, gasping as the head of his shaft breached her sex at the same time that his fangs pierced the skin of her neck. Kris gripped her hip with one hand and held the back of her head with the other, holding her steady and baring her throat for his conquest.

There was the momentary sharp pain of his fangs being deeply driven into her and then the familiar sweet pleasure swept through her and she felt her body opening to receive his shaft inside her.

"Oh, God!" The words were torn out of her as she felt the head of his cock finally sink into her to the hilt and the steady suction at her neck and he both drew from her and filled her at the same time. It was as though her body was one big electric circuit that could only be completed by his. By the sharp pain of his fangs and the thick thrust of his cock at the same time.

Lauren moaned as he moved inside her, spreading her legs wider, trying to be as open as she could for the motion of his shaft as he thrust into her. God, he was so thick, so deep inside her. She felt opened, owned, cherished, as he pulled her closer, sucking at her neck and fucking into her deeply.

The motion of his cock inside her and the essence he was injecting into her system was too much. She felt herself edging towards a second orgasm but this was no soft and gentle crest that she was riding. It was a tidal wave of sensation and she knew that when it came it might drown her beneath the weight of overwhelming pleasure.

All is well, Solnyshko. *I will be with you, you will not drown*...the voice whispering in her mind was unmistakably

Kris' and she realized that this must be an effect of their bonding. She clutched at him almost desperately, her fingernails digging into the broad shoulders and her head thrown back in the ultimate submission as she felt him thrust deeply into her cunt one last time and hold rock-solid and steady as he pulsed into her, filling her to the limit with his seed. Coming inside her while he drank from her, claiming her body and mind and soul.

"God, Kris! Love you...love you so much!" Lauren realized she was repeating the words over and over and yet she couldn't seem to help herself — didn't want to help herself.

I love you too, Solnyshko. *Always and forever, my darling. We shall never be parted again.* Kris' words echoed in her head, filling her with a certainty and joy that Lauren couldn't express.

* * * * *

"Oh, Kris, that was so..." There were no words to describe it so she just snuggled closer, loving the way their bodies fit together under the covers. The night outside her window was deep and velvety and the sound of his heart was steady and reassuring in her ear.

"Mmm, my sentiments exactly." His laughter rumbled up from the broad chest, vibrating against her cheek.

"It's hard to believe I've only known you a week," she murmured. "It seems like so much longer."

"We've been through a lot since I stole into your laboratory and took your little computer, haven't we?" He smiled down at her, the expression lighting his whole face.

"To think when I first took it I thought it held the answer to my greatest ambition. And yet, it held something far more important."

"Which was?" Lauren smiled at him, waiting.

"The key to your heart, my darling. A concubine I could love as no other, one who masters my heart as I master her body. Your body." He cupped her bare breast in one large hand and pinched her nipple lightly, making her moan low in her throat.

"Wh-whatever happened to my Mac, anyway?" she asked a bit breathlessly.

Kris grinned at her. "In a safe place, my concubine." He tapped the side of his head with the hand not cupping her breast. "And of course, I remember in vivid detail each and every one of your little fantasies. We'll act them all out one by one, you have my word."

Lauren tweaked his nipple and grinned when he jumped. "We're going to have to talk about this whole concubine thing. I don't mind being submissive in the bedroom but there's a limit to what I'm willing to put up with outside of it."

"Is that so?" Kris tilted her chin and gave her a soft kiss that made her catch her breath. "Then we will speak of your 'limits' later, *Solnyshko*. For we haven't left the bedroom yet."

The hand cupping her breast began to stroke down the curve of her body, tracing a path to the sensitive vee between her legs as Kris kissed her again. His voice was low and tempting in her ear as he spoke. "Now, speaking of fantasies, there is one that you wrote that I particularly like. I believe it is called *Slow and Dirty…*"

About the author:

Evangeline Anderson is a registered MRI tech who would rather be writing. She is thirty-something and lives in Florida with a husband, three cats and a college-age sister but no kids because enough is enough already. She had been writing erotic stories for her own gratification for a number of years before it occurred to her to try to get paid for it. To her delight, she found it was actually possible to get money for having a dirty mind and she has been writing steadily ever since.

Evangeline welcomes mail from readers. You can write to her c/o Ellora's Cave Publishing at 1056 Home Avenue, Akron OH 44310-3502.

Why an electronic book?

We live in the Information Age—an exciting time in the history of human civilization in which technology rules supreme and continues to progress in leaps and bounds every minute of every hour of every day. For a multitude of reasons, more and more avid literary fans are opting to purchase e-books instead of paperbacks. The question to those not yet initiated to the world of electronic reading is simply: *why?*

1. *Price.* An electronic title at Ellora's Cave Publishing and Cerridwen Press runs anywhere from 40-75% less than the cover price of the <u>exact same title</u> in paperback format. Why? Cold mathematics. It is less expensive to publish an e-book than it is to publish a paperback, so the savings are passed along to the consumer.

2. *Space.* Running out of room to house your paperback books? That is one worry you will never have with electronic novels. For a low one-time cost, you can purchase a handheld computer designed specifically for e-reading purposes. Many e-readers are larger than the average handheld, giving you plenty of screen room. Better yet, hundreds of titles can be stored within your new library—a single microchip. (Please note that Ellora's Cave and Cerridwen Press does not endorse any specific brands. You can check our website at www.ellorascave.com or

www.cerridwenpress.com for customer recommendations we make available to new consumers.)

3. *Mobility.* Because your new library now consists of only a microchip, your entire cache of books can be taken with you wherever you go.

4. *Personal preferences are accounted for.* Are the words you are currently reading too small? Too large? Too...**ANNOYING**? Paperback books cannot be modified according to personal preferences, but e-books can.

5. *Instant gratification.* Is it the middle of the night and all the bookstores are closed? Are you tired of waiting days—sometimes weeks—for online and offline bookstores to ship the novels you bought? Ellora's Cave Publishing sells instantaneous downloads 24 hours a day, 7 days a week, 365 days a year. Our e-book delivery system is 100% automated, meaning your order is filled as soon as you pay for it.

Those are a few of the top reasons why electronic novels are displacing paperbacks for many an avid reader. As always, Ellora's Cave and Cerridwen Press welcomes your questions and comments. We invite you to email us at service@ellorascave.com, service@cerridwenpress.com or write to us directly at: 1056 Home Ave. Akron OH 44310-3502.

Discover for yourself why readers can't get enough of the multiple award-winning publisher Ellora's Cave. Whether you prefer e-books or paperbacks, be sure to visit EC on the web at www.ellorascave.com for an erotic reading experience that will leave you breathless.

www.ellorascave.com